THE BONES OF LOUVERTURE

THE BONES OF LOUVERTURE

WILLIAM G. HERBERT

Deep Run Books

ISBN 979-8-9856593-0-6 (Hardcover)
ISBN 979-8-9856593-1-3 (Paperback)
ISBN 979-8-9856593-2-0 (E-book)

First Printing, 2022

Deep Run Books
6632 Telegraph Rd., Ste. 325, Bloomfield Hills, MI 48301
https://deeprunbooks.com

Cover art image of Baron Samedi by Desquiciados S.C

This book is dedicated to the memory of
Steven Gordon Herbert

I leave you to your rest, dear son.
A rest God has ordained.
Yet tasks for me remain undone
Ere heat of noon has waned.

Norman W. Scott
for William G. Herbert

Each chapter in the story that follows begins with the image of a Haitian Vodou Veve. These Veves are usually representations of Haitian spirits known as loas (in Haitian Kreyòl, loa is lwa and voodoo is vodou). Vodouisants (practitioners of Haitian vodou) believe loa to number in the hundreds. A few are prominent, many others are less known, and some even come and go over time. Several prominent loa and their Veves are profiled in the backmatter section: **A Brief Description of Selected, Well-Kown Loa.**

A Place near the Front (2016) tells the story of the author's Trinidadian immigrant father, how he came to the US, and how, as a young officer in an all-Black US infantry division, he gained his citizenship on the battlefields of World War One France. In President Woodrow Wilson's "War to end all Wars," he fought for the rights of Europeans that he, himself, could not fully enjoy in America.

CONTENTS

CONTENTS

"A compelling story about the lives and unique culture of the Haitians whose forefathers fought for and won their freedom from the French almost two hundred years earlier. It tells of the internal and external forces of power and greed that have always attempted to undermine Haitian dreams of nationhood."

Review by The BAR (Brothers Also Read), a Detroit-based literary organization of Black men dedicated to promoting the intellectual growth of its members, mentoring young readers, and transforming conversations in the community into actions that produce positive social change.

One

Voodoo Wars

As late afternoon sunset fades into twilight, low-hanging storm clouds swirl over Jérémie. Below lightning-flecked, rumbling skies, mobs of shirtless young men crowd *Rue Alexandre Pétion*. Marching to a throbbing drumbeat, they chant the anti-Duvalier rallying cry: *Dechoukaj! Dechoukaj! Dechoukaj!* (Uproot! Uproot! Uproot!) Their *Brigade de Vigilance* roams the sweltering streets on a mission of retribution. They dole out swift and brutal punishment to anyone or anything associated with the troubled nation's recently ousted dictator. The angry marchers are one of many vigilante groups that have come together in the days of terror following the overthrow of president-for-life Jean-Claude *Baby-Doc* Duvalier. In the week since the dictator's hasty exit to an exile in France, the beautiful *City of Poets* has become a war zone. The nightly marching and violence contrast jarringly with the usually tranquil setting in which colorful bougainvillea and other exotic flora are once again verdant after generations of deforestation by early French colonists eager to clear land for plantations.

The brigade continues its march to a block of one-story, aqua and salmon-colored houses. They stop at one known to be occupied by two elderly voodoo (*vodou* in Haitian Kreyòl) priestesses. As the crude structure is surrounded, three men burst out of a rear door. One wears a dress over his shirt and trousers. They attempt to escape across an open field to a tree-filled, hilly area behind the house. But they are caught, surrounded, and felled in a frenzied barrage of skull-cracking, limb-rending machete blows. The three had been hired to guard the two *mambos*. When they saw the size of the huge mob, they attempted to make a break and were immediately cut down.

Several of the attackers rush through the open rear door and find the two old *mambos* and a teenaged *hounci*, a voodoo priest in training. The three huddle in a small room cluttered with dolls, pictures of gods, *mystères, loa,* and other voodoo objects. They are brought out to face the mob at the front of the house. The two old women, both clad in simple, ankle-length black dresses, are stoic. They refuse to answer questions or show any signs of fear. They appear to be in a trance-like state. But the petrified boy, likely a family member, stares wide-eyed and trembling at the still-bloody weapons of his captors. One of the mob leaders, a tall, muscular young man who the others call Sonny, steps forward to address the *mambos*. Hanging from a cord around his neck is a charm in the image of *Belie Belcan*, the *loa* that protects people from demons and evil. *Belie* is a prominent figure in the very same pantheon of spirits against which Sonny and the brigades now rampage.

"You two have caused pain and suffering in this town for many years. When you could have helped people and made their lives more bearable, you chose instead to frighten and torture them."

Sonny positions the two sorcerers so that they stand back-to-back. He then motions to a member of the crowd who comes forward with a length of rope and a container of gasoline. "You will now get a taste of the misery you have visited upon so many others."

But before punishment can proceed, a young teenager steps between Sonny and the old women. Barely old enough to march, let alone carry a weapon, he had followed a step or two behind Sonny throughout the evening, always under the big man's protective gaze.

"Why should we burn these two and let them die without ever help-ing those they cheated for so long?" the boy asks. "They charged lots of money for their fake healing and sorcery. Instead of killing them, let's make them return the blood money. It could help many people around here who don't get enough to eat. Maybe it is worth sparing their lives if they agree to return the money and stop their sorcery."

Since Sonny does not rebuke the boy for his precocious outburst, neither does anyone else, and the mob's fury begins to dissipate. After a few moments of animated discussion between the marchers, the boy's suggestion is accepted. Sonny then gives the two *mambos* forty-eight hours to come up with payment or once again face the wrath of the crowd. If they comply, they will be allowed to dismantle their *houmfort* and return, unharmed, to the Catholic Church.

Having lost the opportunity to punish, the group stands mute as the old women agree and reenter the house with their young pupil. The mob's remaining passion dies when the purplish clouds that had threat-ened all afternoon finally release an almost torrential downpour.

The smaller crowd that returns two days later is disappointed with the size of the payment offered by the *mambos*. Several want to take the money and kill them anyway. But the two old women, now more talkative, argue that their voodoo practice is nowhere near as profitable as many believe. They claim most of the fees they receive are spent on supplies needed to make potions, medicines, poultices, and on the ani-mals, birds, and other creatures used in their ceremonies and sacrifices. Sonny convinces the crowd to spare the women and their student as all three have agreed to end their voodoo practice.

━━━━◆━━━━

Sonny always knew Jacques was smart. But the way the boy rescued the *mambos* was a strange mix of humanity and street savvy he would never have anticipated from someone so young. Standing up to a vengeful mob without cringing before their hair-trigger, murderous impulses is the kind of toughness Sonny might have expected from a seasoned street warrior, but not from a kid weighing barely sixty kilos soaking wet.

It had now been almost four years since the summer of 1982 when he first took the boy under his wing. Sonny had only recently begun working the fishing boats but often lived from hand to mouth on odd jobs at the waterfront. Only seventeen years old but full-grown and sturdy, he usually slept on the beach. In bad weather, he would find cover in empty buildings and stairwells—wherever it was dry and not too crowded with others in the same unfortunate circumstances. During a heavy rainfall one night, he took shelter in an old wooden fishing boat that had been dry-docked for repairs at the waterfront. Halfway through the night, he awoke to the sounds of someone slipping onto the ship. Armed with a marlinspike, he confronted the intruder and was surprised to face a shivering twelve-year-old who hadn't eaten a full meal in days. Sonny took in the young Jacques Maurice that night and had been looking out for him ever since. In the following months and years, the two became proxies for the brothers, sisters, and other family members missing from each other's lives.

The boy had never known his father. In 1981, when his mother moved to Port-au-Prince to find work, she distributed him and his two brothers among her own siblings. The sister that young Jacques was left with never liked him and treated him as if he was an indentured servant. A few weeks after he was dropped off, he slipped away. For the next six months, he ran with a street gang of outcasts and orphans who stole and begged for their sustenance. When some of the older boys began picking on him and stealing his belongings, the undersized Jacques abandoned the group. He took his chances alone on the street until he fell in with Sonny.

Using his brigade-leader connections, Sonny enrolled Jacques in a local free public school that served its students free lunch, the only hot meal most of them would eat each day. These public schools were shunned by the more well-to-do who didn't want their children mixing with street riffraff. Middle-class people who enrolled their children in public schools faced ostracism by family members and others of their social strata. Parents with the means and desire to educate their children sent them to expensive private schools usually run by the church.

Accumulating knowledge kept Jacques's mind off the problems he faced as a child of the streets. He dreamed that someday he might be a teacher, a respected scholar who dispensed knowledge and wisdom to eager students. Bright and curious, he learned that he did not have to be physically strong to impose his will. He found he could exert his own kind of power and influence over any of his peers, and sometimes even over Sonny.

After saving the *mambos*, Jacques began talking to Sonny about why so many people in Jérémie were poor and struggling. He didn't remember much about the Duvaliers and didn't understand why most Haitians so despised them. With the dictators gone, he wondered whether conditions might improve so that there wouldn't be so many poor people living on the streets. Perhaps there could now be a president who looked after Haitians and helped them to a better life.

Uneducated and not well-informed, Sonny couldn't answer many of Jacques's questions. It was difficult for him to engage the boy in conversations about politics or social justice. An orphan himself, he had not even completed as much schooling as Jacques. He had survived in the streets mainly because of his size and strength. From what he saw and heard, elections would soon be coming. He and everyone he knew were hopeful they could choose a leader who would not talk in riddles about the greatness of the country while stealing from it and living in luxury. He tried to explain to Jacques how everyone felt that if they could get rid of the evildoers and takers who lived well at the expense of others, they could elect a president who would finally lead the country into an era of peace and prosperity for all.

———— ◆ ————

Six months after the February 1986 ouster of *Baby-Doc*, most of the visible remnants of the Duvalier era have disappeared. Gone are the

Duvalier street names and the presidential family images displayed in public street art. But the righteous zeal and pent-up passion of aggrieved citizens have descended into a frenzy of cruelty and greed. *Dechoukaj* is now focused on reclaiming the ill-gotten gains of the few remaining voodoo practitioners and members of Duvalier's secret police, the dreaded *Tonton Macoutes*, who do not enjoy the protection of Haiti's new ruling class, the military. Undisciplined brigades are now usually high on the weed and rum that ease their consciences, liberate their ruthless behavior, and unleash their impulses to inflict pain. Their endless violence and cruelty now seem no different than the brutality of their former oppressors.

On a humid June evening, Sonny and his brigade are once again on a mission of retribution and reclamation. Tonight they stand before a stately old plantation home that had been built by a French planter before the revolution. Isolated from any other nearby structures, it had long been owned by the late Madame Saintfleur. The well-known *mambo* had counted among her list of clients many of Jérémie's wealthiest and most influential citizens. Not wanting their reliance on voodoo known, this group valued the confidentiality afforded them by Mme Saintfleur. Her son, a voodoo priest, continued to serve many of the same clients after his mother's death, living quietly with his family in the elegant residence.

Brandishing burning torches and weapons, brigade marchers shout at the shuttered mansion. They demand that the occupants present themselves. When no one responds, they stone the home. Led by Sonny, a few begin hacking at the shutters with their machetes. As windows are forced open, gunshots ring out from an unlit room at the front of the house. One of the vigilantes is hit and blown backward off his feet, blood spurting from a gaping wound in his neck. Sonny and the others at the windows retreat to the cover of a grove of trees surrounding the mansion. Sonny is surprised by the unexpected gunfire and the sight of his fallen comrade lying in a pool of blood on the brick walkway. He screams obscenities at the mansion when he realizes he too is bleeding from a bullet wound that has taken off part of his ear. His usually cool and thoughtful leadership blurred by a week-long high, he orders the mob to toss torches through the hacked-open windows.

Its curtains and rugs immediately ablaze like so much dry kindling, the old all-wood home is quickly engulfed in flames so intense that a wave of heat is even felt by the marchers behind the wall of trees. As parts of the burning house begin to fall, shrieks are heard from upstairs. The front door bursts open, and a young teenage girl runs out of the house dragging two small children. Scrambling to escape the flames, she screams that several family members are trapped inside. Before Sonny or any of the others can even think about a rescue, a fiery explosion brings down the rest of the house. It collapses in a massive shower of burning embers and debris.

Two hours later, with no house to loot, the brigade has dispersed. As they leave, several grumble about Sonny's poor judgment and quick temper. Only he and Jacques remain with the distraught girl. The youngster still clutches her baby sisters. She stares in shock at the mound of hot ashes and smoldering timbers that was her home just a few hours ago.

"Why did they burn it?" she asks over and over, mistakenly thinking she is talking to locals from the nearby village who had come to help.

"My mother, aunt, uncle, and my little brother were trapped inside. Why did they have to burn them?" she demands, sobbing between each word.

Jacques, the same age as the distressed teenager, sits down near her. "The people who did this were angry and frustrated. They thought there was evil inside the house, and it made them crazy."

"Where is your father? Was he in the house?" Sonny finally asks, his head wrapped in his own bloody shirt, his face twisted into a grimace.

Rocking and crying, her face buried in the hair of the two children she held, the girl at first says nothing.

Finally gathering herself, she answers, "My father is in Port-au-Prince. A week ago, he told us he would have to go away for a while. He brought my aunt and uncle to stay with us, and said he would return as soon as he could. He left a shotgun, a pistol, and some bullets he bought from a soldier in Port-au-Prince. He told my uncle he might have to use them if mobs tried to break into the house.

He should have been back by now. Maybe some kind of trouble has come to him also," she adds, the awful words bringing her again to tears. "Oh my God, what has happened to my family? What will we do?"

"Do you have any other family around here?" Jacques asks. "Sonny and I will help you reach them."

"No, there's just us three now … and my father," the girl sobs. "Everyone else was in the house."

"We will try to find you and your sisters somewhere safe to stay until your father comes back. For now, you are welcome in our place. Right, Sonny?"

The big man nods.

⸺•◆•⸺

Juliette and her sisters stay with Sonny and Jacques for the few days it takes to arrange their lodging with one of the teachers at Jacques's school who rents rooms in her home. After they are settled, Sonny and Jacques visit them every few days. They usually bring fresh fish from the harbor market.

In the months after the house burning incident, Sonny cuts back on his brigade marching and begins working more hours at the waterfront. But at times, he stays high for days on end, settling his nerves with non-stop weed smoking. With the meager wages from working the boats and repairing fish nets at the harbor, he barely comes up with the few gourdes rent Mme Picard charges for the room he shares with Jacques in the tiny shack at the rear of her farmhouse. He now hustles every odd job he can find to also pay the modest boarding fee for Juliette and her sisters. The three girls are still unaware that he and Jacques were part of the mob that had upended their lives. Because Sonny often isn't able to come up with the agreed-upon rent, the girls have to make up the difference by working as servants in the schoolteacher's home.

By the end of the summer, the ongoing brutality of *Dechoukaj* has taken its toll on Sonny and his brigade. The heady first few months of liberation from the repression of the Duvalier years have ended. But the grim reality has also set in that conditions in Haiti are as bad as ever. Voodoo wars and revenge marching against perceived enemies of the people have vented anger and inflicted pain but have not improved the lives of anyone. In fact, the gulf between the haves and the have-nots has grown wider. Duvalier and his *Ton Ton Macoutes* are gone, replaced by the army. Except for the privileged elites and wealthy mulattos who live in luxury in the hills above Port-au-Prince, life remains a struggle for most Haitians. Any of the middle-class of the Duvalier era that hasn't clawed its way into the ranks of the elite has either already left the country or is trying to get out. For everyone else, nothing has changed but the names of the powerful few who plunder the country at the expense of the poor.

Gangsta' Man

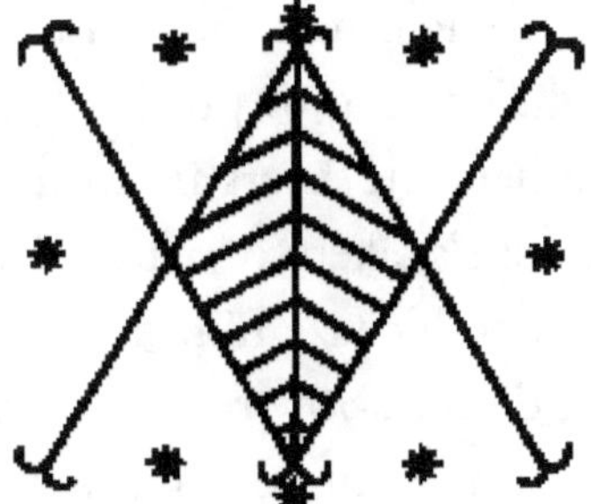

"Sonny! Hey Sonny! Wake up, man," Jacques pleads as he throws open the windows of their bedroom to let in the fresh air that might revive Sonny from his almost day-long, weed-induced stupor. Jacques slept in the same room the night before. But he had been up and out for hours, long before the midday heat and bright sun had turned their cramped sleeping quarters into an inferno. When he returned from work and stepped back into the stifling bedroom, he was nauseated by the smell of dirty clothes, stale weed, and the garlic-charged vapors of Sonny's snoring.

"You need to get out of that bed and shake the funk off yourself. This whole place stinks of weed, and so do you. It ain't healthy, man,"

Jacques continues as he stands at the foot of Sonny's bed, staring at the huge, coarse feet protruding from the sheet the big man had pulled over his head. Although Sonny usually wore shoes or sandals these days, his ashy, calloused heels and thick, discolored toenails were evidence of many years of walking barefoot on Jérémie's unpaved streets and gravel roads.

"And we need to talk about Juliette. She's having big problems over at the LeBlancs."

"What's the matter with her?" Sonny responds, squinting through bloodshot, swollen eyes.

"It's bad enough that the schoolteacher treats her like dirt, ordering her about at all times of the day and night," Jacques answers. "But now her husband has become a problem. His real estate office is next door to where they live, so he's in and out of the house all day. Whenever Mme LeBlanc is not home, he's trying to put his hands on Juliette, and it doesn't matter whether her little sisters are around.

"To cover herself up, she's taken to wearing baggy clothes that aren't always so clean. But it doesn't faze him. I saw her this morning, and she looked terrible. If I didn't know better, I'd think she dressed from some dirty clothes she found right here in this room. She's still in a bad way over what happened to her family, and now she's got to deal with LeBlanc. It looks like she's ready to pick up and run."

"Where the hell does she think she's going with those kids and no money?" Sonny replies, slowly coming to life.

"I don't know, but she's dead serious."

"I'll talk to LeBlanc later," Sonny responds.

"Later won't get it, Sonny. You need to talk to him right now, with this in your hand," Jacques answers, gesturing toward the unsheathed machete leaning on the wall near Sonny's bed. The massive weapon glistens under the oil Sonny applies to keep its razor-sharp blade blemish-free and its handle supple and easy to grip.

"It was us that got her into this mess. The least we can do is to keep any more harm from coming to her. That fat bastard LeBlanc needs to be worried that the next time he puts his hands where they don't belong may be the last time he gets to put them anywhere!"

"Yeah? And what's that going to get us?" Sonny answers, now fully awake. "Sure, I could rough him up and maybe scare the hell out of him for a minute. But this guy's got a lot of friends in high places who could cause us a lot of trouble. He'd have us out of here in a hurry and would fix it so we couldn't find a job or a room anywhere near Jérémie."

"He could do that to a brigade leader?"

"Hell yes, he could! Anyway, *Dechoukaj* isn't the answer to every-thing. Sure, we've taken down some bad guys and settled a few scores. But LeBlanc is too well-connected to be terrorized by any brigade. And even if I killed him and told his wife about him, do you think she'd listen me? This guy keeps her in a beautiful house, a nice car, and plenty of expensive jewelry. That's all she cares about. She doesn't want anything to happen to her meal ticket."

"Well, if that's the real deal," Jacques fires back, "then *Dechoukaj* isn't the answer to anything! It's a total failure!" The boy continues, "You can't go after a child molester? And if you recover blood money from any of these greedy voodoo hustlers, you're supposed to give it right back to the same neighborhood fools who paid for the phony healing in the first place? What kind of sense does any of that make? Maybe if you held onto some of that money, we wouldn't have to live like this."

"Listen, Jacques," Sonny pushes back, "*Dechoukaj* may not have been the answer to all that's wrong in Haiti, but it damn sure wasn't a business. At least I didn't see it that way. I wasn't busting all those heads and burning all those houses just to put some blood money in our pockets. We were trying to strike a blow for good, so we could elect a leader who would help us all live better lives."

"It sure doesn't seem to be working out that way," Jacques grumbles. "Everything is so messed up. In school, they keep telling us that elections are just around the corner. They've been saying that for months, but we're still living in this shithole. We burned down Juliette's house and killed most of her family, and now she's got to put up with LeBlanc. Where's the justice and the good in all that?"

"Well, maybe that's where smart kids like you can make a difference," Sonny says. "Your generation can be the next wave of Haitian leaders that pick up where the last generation failed. That'll be better than trying to steal *Dechoukaj* blood money."

——◆——

Although Sonny and most of the other brigade leaders had become heavy pot smokers, Jacques never took up the habit. The smell of burning weed sickened him. Sonny enjoyed getting high and escaping into a guilt-free zone that imposed no emotional consequences for continued brigade violence. But Jacques didn't like the feeling of lost control that accompanied his occasional smoking. For Sonny, weed made the unpleasant more palatable. Jacques, however, could not abide the loss of sharpness and alertness he experienced when using. He was so small that even with Sonny's ever-present protection, he wanted to be in full control of his faculties to keep from being trampled in the violence of *Dechoukaj*. But as much as he rejected the foul-smelling drug for his personal use, he was fascinated by the business of weed and how this locally grown herb could generate wealth, and in the midst of poverty, create new classes of winners and losers, powerful and powerless, takers and the taken.

Jacques begins to observe Sonny's purchases. Because the big man enjoys status in the neighborhood, his supplier doesn't mind that Jacques often tags along on buys. Sometimes he even slips the youngster a few gourdes to run an errand or make a delivery. But when Jacques shows up alone one day at the *Pump de Gas Total* station where Sonny usually meets his dealer, eyebrows raise.

"What you doin' here all by yourself, youngblood?" Milton Nazzaire asks Jacques.

"You got Sonny's ok to be hanging out here? He's one of my best customers. I don't want to cross that *Gro Nèg* and have him turn on me and hunt me down with that crazy-ass machete army of his."

"All I want is a little information," Jacques answers as the two stand in front of the now-quiet gas station that doubles as a popular evening hangout for many of the younger street crowd. Despite its four gleaming new gas pumps, the station's rickety wood building, old calendars, and manual cash register make it look like a relic of the 1940s. Its main attraction, parked in front of the station, is a decades-old, bullet-ridden limousine, a remnant of a generations-past presidential coup that somehow found its way to Jérémie. The old antique, a customer favorite, embodies the station's edgy, gangster atmosphere.

"Information? What in the hell you talkin' 'bout?" demands Nazzaire, head of a small posse of dealers that conduct business at the popular fuel stop. Jacques had timed his arrival so that he could talk to Nazzaire before the busy time after sundown when cars crowded the station, their drivers buying gas, beer and wine, junk food, CDs, and whatever weed and other contraband the hustlers were pushing.

"Anything you want to ask me, you better clear it first with Sonny," the combative dealer continues. "Until you do, I don't even want to see you around here unless you're with him, understand? And if you come back here without his approval, I might just have to whip your little black ass. And then I'll tell Sonny what you've been up to so he can whip it some more," cracks Nazzaire, a once-promising middleweight prizefighter who had to quit boxing when he lost an eye in a drunk driving accident. Although it was many years ago that he traded his gloves for dealing, he always seemed ready for a fight.

"And if you need information, ask one of your schoolteachers. I'm not in the information business."

"C'mon, Milton, don't do me like that. How come it's all right to talk to you when you want me to drop off a package, but you got a problem now that I want to ask you a question? Anyway, I already talked to Sonny," Jacques lied. It was true he had told Sonny he was coming to the neighborhood. But he'd said he wanted to study with one of his classmates. He hadn't mentioned anything about talking to Nazzaire or any other dealer. Confident that he will be able to smooth things out with Sonny, Jacques continues his bluff.

"What's the best price I can get for ten one-gram bags of your good weed?—I'm talking about your best stuff, not that mess you sometimes give Sonny with all the seeds and stems."

"Ten bags? What the hell is up with that? And good stuff too, I beg your pardon?" Nazzaire spits back at Jacques in a ridiculing tone. "Sonny's always around here bragging about how much you hate this shit and how you're the righteous young brigade crusader who's busy stamping out evil and saving lives. And now you want a ten-bag stash? Ain't that just about a bitch?" Nazzaire continues, breaking into a sneering laugh as he quotes Jacques a ridiculously high price to end the conversation.

"And where you would you get the money to buy ten bags anyway?"

"I thought maybe you could front it for me," Jacques responds. You know Sonny and I ain't going nowhere, so I'm good for it. And I've got some people real eager for a steady supply."

"Is that so? And who might they be?"

"None of them are customers of yours. In fact, they're not even from this area," Jacques parries, knowing better than to give Nazzaire any more information than necessary.

"They sure in the hell better not be. You don't think I'm stupid enough to sell you weed at a discount so that you can turn around and sell it to my potential customers at a higher price. If there's a markup to be made anywhere in this neighborhood, it's going into my pocket, not yours."

"Let me think about this," Nazzaire growls. "Check with me tomorrow. But Sonny's got to be cool with it. And if I agree to front you, you better understand that I expect to be paid in full before you even think of forming your lips to ask for a new supply. And don't ever make me have to come looking for you for payment. If I do, it won't be pretty, Sonny or no Sonny."

"Don't worry about it, Milton. I've thought it all through, and there won't be any problems."

To the small group of hustlers standing within earshot, Nazzaire turns and, in a loud whisper, wisecracks: "Looks like we got us a brand new wannabe, gangsta' man!"

—◆—

Dispensing with the usual small talk, Jacques pleads his case as soon as he sees Sonny that evening.

"Sonny, I need to run a little something by you. Some of the guys at the Brother Paulin school are smoking weed. They're paying a lot for their supply—much more than you pay Nazzaire for your stuff. Their buys must be passing through a bunch of middlemen and getting a lot of markup. If I can get a reasonable deal from Nazzaire, I can sell to these guys at a price that saves them some money and puts a little something in our pockets. You ok with me setting this up?"

In response to Sonny's scowl, Jacques adds, "It's not like I'm starting anybody on any bad habits. These guys are already using, and they're going to continue, with my help or without it. I just want to fill their need in a way that has some benefit for everybody, especially us. It's all about supply and demand."

"Listen, Jacques," Sonny begins after a long, hard stare. "It's always been my hope that you would become an agent of change who educates himself and then passes some of that passion for learning to other Haitians. I've always believed you could be one of those who lift people out of ignorance and voodoo superstition and into a better life. It bothers me that someone with your talents is willing to settle for the same kind of thuggery that plagues our community."

"I never thought you'd even consider making a living by taking advantage of the weakness of others. But if that's where you're at, I've got a few questions for you. First, do you really think you're going to be able to buy from Nazzaire and undercut the dealers already working the Brother Paulin neighborhood?"

With a scornful stare, the big man continues: "And do you actually think you can parachute in from nowhere and become an instant success just because you've got a handful of customers and some bullshit kind of new salesmanship?

When Jacques offers no response, Sonny presses on. "Things don't work quite like that in the real world. You're crazy if you think you can barge in here and begin freelancing. Every sale you make will be cutting into someone else's business. That school you want to work is part of someone's turf. As soon as you sell your first joint, he will be looking to bring you down. "Now let's talk about Milton. Do you think he's freelancing at *Pump de Gas?*

Sonny answers his own question. "Hell no! Monsieur DuFrane, the old man we sometimes see at the station, calls all the shots. Nothing goes down in that neighborhood without his knowledge and stamp of approval, whether it's weed sales at the gas station, the operation of the station itself, or anything else in that part of town. He's got juice with the police. And he's got the cover to deal with anyone who tries to cut in on his action. It's going to be the same way in the neighborhood you're looking at. Somebody's already got the inside track. So you'd better think twice about jumping into the drug business. You have no idea of what you're getting into and whose toes you'll be stepping on."

Jacques wasn't buying it. He didn't express any outward disagreement with Sonny and didn't even answer him. But isn't that what *Dechoukaj* was supposed to be all about, he wondered? Didn't it stand for shaking off the shackles of the old ways and starting fresh? Of all people, shouldn't Sonny know that? Anyway, he was sure that nothing was being sold currently at Brother Paulin. If he started selling there, he was sure he wouldn't be getting in anyone's way.

After several weeks of badgering Sonny, arguing that his proposed drug activity would not replace but only help him reach his educational goals, Jacques gets the big man's reluctant approval. He immediately shows his natural talent for the weed business and is soon selling pot to his high school customers as fast as he can get it. In addition to being a quick study who never gets high on his own supply, he has an innate hustler's cunning. Although most of the boys in his own class would like to buy some of his weed, none of them have the funds to do so. His public schoolmates are poor and lucky just to be able to get to school every day. The students at Brother Paulin, however, particularly the seniors, always have pocket money. They prefer buying from him since his prices are lower than their other sources in Port-au-Prince.

Jacques finds a niche with these college-bound boys who are sons of Jérémie's better-off families. Not quite equal to the wealthy Pétion-Ville elites, they are still the cream of Jérémie society, such as it is, and Jacques has a way with them. Since he can't impress people with the strength and rugged good looks of a Sonny or the menacing toughness of a dealer like Nazzaire, he calls on other attributes to bond with his customers. He uses his gift of gab, his intellectual demeanor, and an innate sense of style to present himself as a gentleman and connoisseur of the finer points of cannabis usage. He researches and accumulates knowledge on his product and assumes an air of expertise as to the various strains of weed, their best sources, and techniques for deriving the greatest pleasure from their consumption. He even begins referring to himself as Jérémie's *Sommelier of Weed*. It is an image the well-off like since when they buy from him, they don't quite feel they are committing a crime.

When his customers pass him money, he never counts it in front of them. Instead, he pockets the funds as if he has received a gift from someone with whom he shares a bond of trust. Of course, there is no real friendship in any of the transactions. But the charade makes for a relaxed situation that customers appreciate. They are far more comfortable dealing with him than with threatening thugs like Nazzaire from whom they buy only as a last resort.

By the end of his second month, Jacques has two dozen customers at Brother Paulin. His sales are profitable enough that he no longer has to ask Nazzaire to front him. He even enjoys volume discounts for his weekly quarter to half pound purchases. If things continue this way, in a few weeks, he will be able to start putting a little money in Sonny's hand.

Everything goes well with his Brother Paulin sales until midway through his fourth month. Three strangers stop him as he approaches the school one afternoon. They demand he turn over the entire contents of his pockets—his cash, wallet, and any drugs he is carrying. When he is slow to respond, one of the men hits him in the face, bloodying his nose and knocking him to the ground. All three begin kicking him until he produces everything he has, including the stash he just purchased from Nazzaire. His attackers then pull him to his feet and demand the names of all his student customers. When Jacques answers that he doesn't use real names in his transactions, either his own or those of his customers, one of the men snaps open a switchblade and inserts the point into one of Jacques's nostrils as the other two hold him in place.

Its cold steel point piercing the skin and causing a small trickle of blood, the knife blade feels like a machete stuffed into Jacques's nose. As he pushes it even further, the knife-wielder continues: "You'd damn well better start remembering some names real fast if you don't want your nose split in half and this shank up into your eye." Jacques blurts out all the names he can remember and then makes up a few more until his attackers seem satisfied.

"We're going to let you go now, the man with the knife announces as he withdraws the blade and wipes it on Jacques's shirt. But if you decide you want to come back around here selling again, we get half of everything you take in."

———◆———

"Some people just won't believe fat meat is greasy," Sonny comments later that day as he looks down at Jacques lying in bed, his nose still swollen from the knife prick. "For all your brains, I guess you're one of those people," he adds with a frown.

"You've been playing on very dangerous turf, my friend. You're lucky you made it home in one piece. Trying to do a weed deal by yourself with no experience could have gotten you killed. Maybe next time you'll listen to me when I give you some advice. You'd better stay home for a few days. By the end of the week, I should be able to find out who it was that got after you."

A few days later, Sonny revisits the Brother Paulin situation with Jacques. A serious and taciturn man usually of few words, Sonny gets straight to the point. "You already know I don't like the idea of you in the drug business. I don't see how it fits into your educational goals. But if this is what you want to do with your life, I won't stand in your way. I only hope you don't end up regretting any of this. I'm not always going to be there to get you out of hot water.

"Now the person who has to clear it for you to do business in the Brother Paulin neighborhood is Julien DuFrane. He's the same guy who controls Milton Nazzaire's turf. I spoke to him yesterday, and he'll be ok with you working the school, but his cut will be ten percent of the take. That's pretty much the standard.

"DuFrane doesn't know anything about the guys who shook you down. Since they have nothing to do with him and they're not selling, he guesses they're just some petty thieves who stumbled onto you and made you as an easy mark. He says he'll have some of his men track them down. But he thinks it would make a good statement if we deal with them ourselves."

The following Saturday, Sonny and Jacques are visited at Mme Picard's by four *Brigade de Vigilance* companions who had been with Sonny on many campaigns in past months. As he collects his machete, Sonny tells Jacques they are going back to the neighborhood where the attack occurred. He had come up with some information on the assailants and where they likely could be found. Jacques is surprised to see a pistol tucked into Sonny's waistband, the first time he had ever seen the big man armed with anything other than his machete.

"Going after these drug boys and gang members is a little different from terrorizing old *houngans* and *mambos* or *TonTon Macoutes* in hiding," Sonny comments. "Most of these kids are packing, and I've heard that some of them are starting to get their hands on automatic weapons. It's a whole new day. We've got to meet fire with fire and hope our firepower matches theirs.

"Since we've only got three pieces between us tonight, we'll also have to use machetes and the element of surprise. The guys who jumped you probably figured they scared the shit out of you, and that if you ever show up around there again, you'll be happy to give them whatever they demand. They don't know you now have DuFrane's approval to operate in the neighborhood and that he's looking for them also."

An hour later, they stand before *La Renaissance*, a small greasy-spoon bar and eatery near the Brother Paulin school where neighborhood bad boys, gang members, and their girlfriends are known to hang out. The ramshackle one-story structure looks like it has been pieced together from thousands of bits of tin and corrugated metal, every piece of scrap metal that could be found in Jérémie. It is the seediest building in an otherwise well-kept section of town. As they enter the noisy and crowded club where rap music blasts from a boom box near the cash register, Jacques recognizes one of his attackers. When he sees Jacques, the man rises from a table at the rear of the room and makes his way to the back exit. Jacques signals Sonny, who bolts across the room and collars the man before he can reach the door. Sonny's four companions stand at the front of the room, their weapons now drawn, silently daring any of the fifty or so patrons to interfere.

Sonny points at Jacques and addresses his captive. "A few days ago, you and your friends stole from this man and cut him." With the point of his machete pressed against the throat of the cornered man, Sonny continues: "He has business in this area and will be back in the neighborhood from time to time. My friends and I expect you to treat him with respect. And Monsieur DuFrane will expect the same. But in case that doesn't register with you, I'm putting you all on notice that if anything should happen to this young man, the least little skirmish or accident, we will come back here for you and your friends, and you don't want to even think about what we'll do. Do you understand?"

Before Sonny finishes his comments, Jacques confronts the man who still stands stiffly with Sonny's blade at his neck, the point threatening to break the skin. Jacques reaches into his pocket, pulls out, and flicks open a large switchblade knife. He inserts the blade into one of the petrified man's nostrils and begins talking in measured and deliberate tones.

"The Bible talks about an eye for an eye. Do you know that passage?" he asks the profusely sweating man who says nothing and doesn't move a muscle but cranes his neck to relieve the pressure of the blade against his nose.

"Well, I believe in those words," Jacques continues in a slow and menacing growl, the only sound that can be heard in the now silent but still packed club.

"And I also believe in a nose for a nose!" Jacques roars as he yanks the blade up and outward from the man's face, slicing open his nose in an instant gush of blood.

"Next time I have to deal with you or any of your punk-ass partners, you'll lose a lot more than your noses," Jacques adds. He, Sonny, and the others then leave *La Renaissance* and pile back into their Toyota SUV for the short ride back to Mme Picard's.

"Damn, Jacques, where the hell did all that come from?" Sonny asks as they drive off from the club. "I knew we were going to have to punish somebody to send a message to the gang and the neighborhood. I hadn't decided how to do it. Your way will work, I just didn't know you had it in you to go off like that."

Until that day, Jacques hadn't known it either.

———◆———

To offer the best prices and attract customers without sacrificing profitability, Jacques begins to think about growing his own supply. He pesters Nazzaire about visiting one of the farms from which he gets his product. He is surprised to find that the dealer, himself, has never seen any of them and doesn't even know their location. He learns that growers are super-secretive about their farms. They fear that anyone who knows their actual location will be tempted to kill the owner and take over the farm. Because several farms have changed hands that very way, growers only allow special visitors on their property. The few visitors that make it are usually transported blindfolded and under armed guard.

As he contemplates the pros and cons of moving into growing, Jacques has an unexpected stroke of good fortune that expands his fledgling business in a way he could never have dreamed possible. Jean Sams, the father of one of his Brother Paulin student customers and a respected Jérémie physician, had discovered his son's weed stash and demanded a meeting with Jacques. To keep the peace with influential movers and shakers, Jacques was ready to promise he would never again sell drugs to the doctor's son or anyone else at the school. But inspired by his son's description of Jacques as a gentleman and connoisseur of weed, the father has something else in mind. Sizing up Jacques in the privacy of his medical office, the doctor is impressed by his visitor's articulate conversation, tasteful dress and grooming, and even his shined shoes. He surprises Jacques stating: "Look, I know my son has smoked some, just as I did when I was his age, and I'm all right with it if that's as far as it goes. Even though he'll be in college in a few months, he and his friends are too young to mess with anything else. But among a more mature crowd here in Haiti, there could be a demand for a recreational drug that has not yet been used in these parts. You might be the man to bring it to market."

"Have you ever heard of MDMA?" Sams asks.

"I read about it somewhere recently," Jacques responds in a bluff, not wanting to admit ignorance. "It piqued my interest, and I want to know more."

"MDMA is a recreational drug, better known by its street name, *Molly*," Sams continues. "It became trendy in the States a few years ago but never made it to the Caribbean. There could be a big demand for it here in Haiti.

"The *Molly* capsules I buy in New York for around ten dollars a pop provide a four-hour high unlike anything else I've ever experienced, and I've tried a lot. It doesn't have the devastating long-term effects of heroin or cocaine. And you don't have to smell like an ashtray full of weed to get high. *Molly* has sparked a whole bunch of dance floor romances in New York, and it could do the same here in Haiti.

Rising from his desk and stepping toward the sofa on which Jacques was seated, Sams continued: "As a medical doctor, I'm able to carry small quantities under the guise of medical research. But I don't want to try to bring in too much and risk losing my license to practice medicine. However, a talented import/export businessman could do some excellent sales here if he can work out the means to get the product into the country.

"Maybe that's where you come in," Sams adds. "But I don't want to get you into anything over your head. Even though you have the demeanor of a businessman, you don't look much older than my son."

"He and I are the same age," Jacques responds. "But don't let that bother you. Having a youthful appearance is a benefit in this business. If I get caught up in a drug bust, authorities are more likely to slap my hands and issue a warning than dish out jail time as they would for someone older."

"All right," the doctor continues, "If you're interested, I can put you in touch with a guy who brings *Molly* into the States from Canada. If you can figure a way to get it into Haiti and keep me supplied at a reasonable price, I'll become one of your customers. And I can steer you toward a few others."

Pausing to stare intently at Jacques, the doctor adds: "There's only one commitment I need from you."

"What might that be?" Jacques asks, bracing himself for some kind of a shakedown or silent partner proposal, hopefully, nothing so outrageous as to be a deal-breaker.

"Stay the hell away from my son and his schoolmates. I know that if you refuse to sell to him, he's smart enough to find another source. I just don't want it to be so damn easy. I don't want him buying from fellow students."

Ignoring the hypocrisy of the stoner doctor who thinks he can play the self-righteous protective parent and hide his own habit from a pothead son, Jacques quickly takes stock of the situation. The doctor's demand is a tough one since Jacques's only customers at the moment are the Brother Paulin schoolboys. But he decides it is worth the temporary inconvenience of giving them up so that he can break into a new and sophisticated drug market, one in which, at least for the moment, there is no known competition in Haiti.

Jacques doesn't want this MDMA opportunity to slip through his fingers. He can always pick up a new set of pot smokers later on. Even though he'd had only a moment to contemplate the venture and had no idea whether he would be able to acquire drugs in the States at a price that would earn him a profit here at home, Jacques follows his hustler's intuition. He accepts the doctor's condition on the spot. Sams immediately calls his New York contact and tells him that Jacques Maurice, a trusted associate, will be calling him soon to set up an importing arrangement.

Jacques had saved up enough to help Sonny get them out of their current hovel-like living space and had already been looking for new quarters. He favored remaining in Jérémie so as not to interfere with his recently begun studies at the local *Collège Saint-Louis*. But he decides that better use of his relocation fund will be a quick trip to New York and an initial buy if a reasonable price can be agreed upon. Following a brief telephone conversation with his contact using coded transaction terms provided by the doctor, Jacques arranges his first buying trip to the States. He is encouraged that his contact agrees to a wholesale price. Now on good terms with M. DuFrane, to whom he regularly pays ten percent of all his sales, Jacques calls on his new godfather to help him get a passport and visa.

Three weeks later, on a pleasant fall evening, Jacques stands in the will-call ticket line of New York's *Blue Note* jazz club. His contact had requested a meeting at the popular Greenwich Village nightspot and had left a ticket for him. Jacques had arrived earlier that same day. After dropping off his bag at the Harlem apartment of the Haitian family with whom one of his Brother Paulin customers had arranged for him to spend the weekend, he takes his first-ever subway ride downtown to the trendy club. He marvels at the sights and sounds of a city the likes of which he could never have imagined.

"I'm meeting Carlos Marquez here this evening," Jacques announces to the door attendant when he reaches the front of the line on the busy street outside the West Village club. "I believe he's left a ticket for me. My name is Jacques Maurice."

Jacques is escorted to an empty table for six near the bandstand. The room is already crowded with a lively audience that listens to prerecorded jazz and orders food and drinks as it waits for the show to begin. The headline act tonight is the Modern Jazz Quartet, a legendary and world-famous jazz group that Jacques has never heard of.

Moments later, a stylishly suited young man and an attractive young Black couple are brought to the table. "You must be Jacques," the new arrival announces as he extends a well-manicured hand tattooed with a small cross at the intersection of the thumb and index finger. "I'm Carlos, and these are my friends Jewell and Booker. As he talks, another young couple is led to the table and introduced by Carlos, also with first names only. Although the couples hadn't known each other before their arrival, everyone quickly eases into the festive mood of the evening, partying as if they had been friends for years. Using a smooth and sophisticated New York jargon, Carlos quickly makes his guests comfortable with each other. He deftly works into his conversation remarks about how Jewell and Booker are killing it as Wall Street investment bankers, and how Guillermo, husband of the other couple, is one of the city's top ear, nose and throat doctors.

After ordering drinks and appetizer trays, Carlos politely excuses himself and asks Jacques to join him for a moment at the nearby bar. Jacques does so, and when carded by the bartender, presents the fake ID he had earlier purchased in Haiti that showed his age as nineteen.

"Here are the supplies you ordered," Carlos says as he hands Jacques a brown business envelope. "You can check out the contents over there if you wish," he adds, pointing to a small secluded lounge area.

"Everything is ok with me," Jacques responds after glancing into the envelope and seeing several plastic sheets, each enclosing rows of individually packaged capsules. He is confident Carlos won't risk his relationship with the Jean Sams network by shorting him or giving him inferior goods.

"Of course you have the COD, as we agreed," Carlos adds.

Jacques hands Carlos a smaller envelope containing forty-four fifty dollar bills. It was all the money in the world he was able to beg or borrow. Carlos doesn't count the money. Instead, breaking into a broad smile as he places the envelope into the inside breast pocket of his jacket, he announces, "Now let's go party and enjoy some great music!"

It is indeed an odd place to conduct business, Jacques thinks as they return to their table, the artists for the evening making their way onto the bandstand of the stylishly intimate club. But it also makes sense. Amid a crowd of partying jazz aficionados, there is little likelihood of violence or a stickup. And no one will expect illegal transactions in a place like this. As Jacques sees it, Carlos's gregarious, easygoing but precise method of doing business is a lot like his own. But in the rarefied atmosphere and culture of downtown Manhattan, Carlos's sophistication and cool is at another level. Jacques likes what he sees and is determined to raise his own game accordingly, at least to the extent possible in Haiti.

The most harrowing part of Jacques's trip is getting his goods into Haiti. When he arrives at Port-au-Prince Airport and passes through the customs area, he requests help filling out his declaration forms. A customs agent escorts him to an assistance area and helps him with the paperwork. Declaring nothing, Jacques signs the documents, picks up his overnight bag and a small attaché case resembling the one that contains his MDMA capsules, and proceeds to the inspection area to have his bags checked. The inspection goes routinely, and no contraband is found. As arranged in advance, the customs agent who assists Jacques at the help desk also switches the attaché case containing the drugs with a similar case that contains only a few typewritten papers. The agent meets Jacques later in the parking lot to return the bag containing the drugs.

The bag switch had been arranged through a friend who worked at the airport and knew the agent would help bring in the contraband for a fee. The switch cost Jacques $250. It was a price he was glad he paid when he saw another arriving passenger detained by agents who found pouches of white powder taped to his body.

Now armed with two products, weed and the all-new-to-Haiti *Molly*, Jacques becomes the busiest dealer in Jérémie and one of the hottest in Port-au-Prince. He isn't a heavyweight heroin or cocaine dealer, but he is doing fine with the products he has. Channeling the Carlos approach he so admired in his New York visit, Jacques avoids cheesy and dangerous gas station sales. Instead, he focuses on supplying his customers through appointments at business offices, social functions, and for those he knows well, home visits. With his Haitian godfather giving cover and Sonny providing a very visible and muscular level of security, Jacques is where he wants to be. He is making good money and enjoying his bimonthly trips to New York to replenish his *Molly* supplies. He and Sonny have rented a comfortable home north of Jérémie, where they can enjoy their privacy and entertain guests, and he is able to pursue his studies at *Collège Saint-Louis*.

Bone Rattling

"My Haitian brethren, you noble sons and daughters of the *Pearl of the Antilles*, it is our time!" exhorts the hopeful presidential candidate. The animated office seeker speaks from a colorful, flag-draped rostrum in an open field near Jérémie's busy waterfront marketplace. His deep voice booms over the public address system as patriotic recorded music plays in the background. Under the cloudless blue sky of a bright sunny morning with the tranquil waters of the Caribbean glistening in the distance, a lively crowd revels in the prospect of real elections. It will be the first most have ever seen. The compelling scene could grace a Haitian tourism poster.

Sonny and the rest of the crowd hang on the speaker's passionate words. They cheer after almost every one of his sentences. No longer leading *Dechoukaj* marches, the big man is now interested in politics. He has pestered Jacques into accompanying him to the rally.

"We have survived twenty-nine years and two generations of dictators," the speaker continues. "Yet we still stand strong as ever. At times, things were even worse before the Duvaliers, but we survived. French slave masters couldn't break us or stop our march to freedom one hundred and eighty-three years ago. And the Duvaliers couldn't break us today. Never in the history of the world had people of color risen to break the bonds of slavery and gone on to create a free republic until we did it. We have that great legacy to uphold, and it is our time to step up once again.

"Even our powerful and intrusive friends to the north, the mighty United States, never did as much! They may have escaped the bonds of European tyranny when they broke away from the British Empire. But shamefully, they kept Blacks in bondage. More than one hundred years after emancipation, their former slaves still do not enjoy full freedom.

"So it is with love and pride that I say: Up, you mighty people! Up, you descendants of those who fought and died to gain independence. You children of our great freedom-fighting leaders, it is our time, and we must make that time count!"

The campaigner brings Sonny and the rest of the audience to a fever pitch with his eloquent rhetoric. But Jacques sneers. He grouses to a small group around him that the speaker has not said what he will do to improve the lives of average Haitians who are no longer in chains but are still enslaved by illiteracy, poverty, and poor health. A few other hecklers join Jacques, but the speaker presses on to cheers. He waxes poetic about the country's inspirational origins. He also invokes the images of its revered revolutionary triumvirate: Toussaint Louverture, Jean-Jacques Dessalines, and Henri Christophe. The three were comrades-in-arms in the 1791 slave revolution and the nation's first three presidents. The candidate describes how they did away with their former *blanc* masters and then tore the white out of the French tricolor flag. He goes on to posture himself as a reincarnation of the esteemed former leaders. He suggests that his election will help restore the nation's past glory.

The hour-long speech ends with enthusiastic applause from an audience eager for political change. But Jacques and a few others continue to grumble. How could anyone know, they ask, whether this candidate, a Jérémie veterinarian, really desires to serve and uplift the country. Or is he one of the many Duvalier-era political hacks who have reignited their political ambitions? Is he one of those who now wish to enjoy the spoils of government service from the top of the political food chain?

Despite a smattering of booing, the speaker had maintained control. He had the bigger platform and the louder microphone. But in rattling the bones of the long-dead founding heroes, he had not spoken of the price they paid for their leadership and bravery. He neglected to mention that all three died in miserable conditions. He did not tell that Louverture's life ended in a French prison two years before final victory and independence in 1804. Or that Dessalines was assassinated two years after independence and that Christophe died by his own hand in 1820 when he was sure that he too faced assassination. Perhaps the hopeful office seeker did not know his history. Or maybe he did not recognize how Haiti's reoccurring cycle of coups, presidential murders, and political power struggles likely foretold the turmoil that would continue to plague the troubled nation. He did not seem to recognize the cruel irony of how a country with such a glorious beginning had become an ugly caricature of the heroic lives of the men who had brought it to life.

⬦

While campaigners throughout Haiti are making questionable commitments, the real power brokers meet behind closed doors. In secret sessions, they map out the future of the troubled nation. On the day of the animal doctor's address at the Jérémie waterfront market, one such meeting takes place at the army headquarters building in Port-au-Prince.

"Gentlemen, our work is cut out for us," announces General Henri Millevoix, the top-ranking officer in the Haitian army. The general addresses twenty senior army officers. They are finishing brunch on the shaded terrace outside his spacious office at the *Fad'H (Forces Armées d'Haiti)* headquarters compound.

"It is now eighteen months that the country has been without a president. While it is good to be rid of Duvalier, the ship of a state cannot stay afloat without a leader at the helm," he continues.

It is an unusually hot day, and the general is not comfortable. He sweats so profusely in the sweltering midday heat that his pomaded comb-over has begun to separate itself from his bald pate. He labors to regulate his speech and moderate his tone, as he usually speaks in a loud and strident voice. It is his way of masking a lifelong stammer. His shouting works well enough when he addresses large groups of soldiers. But it is out of place in more intimate settings. Engaging in a relaxed conversation during a meal is hard work for the bullnecked soldier.

"To maintain the status quo with the US and not jeopardize our aid package, we must show progress toward an election. And we must put a president in office within the next twelve months. That's not going to be easy with the dozen or so people now campaigning. Few of them look at all presidential, and some are dangerous radicals, if not communists. They could cause real problems if elected.

"We've also got to put an end to this *Dechoukaj* madness. Understandably, the public had to let off steam after two generations and almost three decades of Duvaliers. If they believe it was their voices and demonstrations, not the army, that forced Jean-Claude out of office, that's ok. It was all right for them to raise a little hell about their achievement. But the retribution, marching, and demonstrations have gone way too far."

In his speeches and dealings with the public, Millevoix always takes pains to give the impression that Jean-Claude's departure had nothing to do with any kind of a military takeover. But many Haitians believe a coup is exactly what happened. In the fall of 1985, a wave of public demonstrations against food shortages and perceived government abuses had culminated in the tragic Gonaïves incident in which the president's security force shot and killed four school children who were participating in a protest demonstration. Overnight, the children became national martyrs. Under the cover of the resulting explosion of angry street violence, the army forced Duvalier to flee the country.

"If the people felt they had to exterminate a few Macoutes and voodoo priests in their post-Duvalier purges, all well and good," Millevoix continues. Their victims should have had the common sense to lay low until these so-called *Voodoo Wars* blew over. But what started as a grassroots crusade for government reform has now morphed into outright lawlessness and thuggery. Our country is on the edge of anarchy. To the rest of the world, the image of Haitians has gone from righteous crusaders against dictatorship to lawless human rights abusers. The situation is a sure way to put our US aid package back into jeopardy. It is long past the time to restore order.

"Finally," adds the general, patting his uncooperative hair, "we have a drug situation that has gotten completely out of control. Say what you want about them, but when the *Ton Ton Macoutes* were around, the drug problem was never this bad. We're going to have to clean up this mess one way or another!"

Millevoix didn't mention to his brunch guests a developing opportunity to partner with Colombian drug lord Pablo Escobar, head of the notorious *Medellín* Cartel. He would later discuss the opportunity privately with trusted aides. The partnership would establish Haiti as a primary conduit for the movement of cocaine from Colombia to the US. To the military and the public, the general would maintain his image as the tough but genial anti-drug crusading soldier. But through his inner circle, he would work with the Cartel to activate a big-money cocaine flow.

Millevoix's electoral calendar is published a few days after his staff meeting but is not well received. An energized but deluded public once again takes to the streets. Citizens believe they can force the army to back down the same way they thought they had run Duvalier out of office. But this time, Millevoix declares martial law. Aggressive army detachments begin round-the-clock street patrols in search of unlawfully assembled crowds. They attack such gatherings with indiscriminate gunfire, leaving many dead or dying in the streets.

———•◆•———

As the government and the presidential election process spiral out of control, the military begins harassing candidates it does not favor. At first, the harassment involves only heckling at campaign events. But as election day approaches, it becomes more aggressive and violent.

Two weeks before the election, a popular presidential candidate stands before an enthusiastic audience at his *Restore Justice* campaign rally. A former judge, the candidate had been forced into US exile in the final days of the Duvalier era. He addresses the crowd in front of the burned-out legislative building. With his judicial robes neatly folded across his arm, he bemoans the lawlessness of an out-of-control military. Days earlier, the army had set fire to the legislative hall in broad daylight with hundreds of citizens watching.

Sonny and a reluctant Jacques sit in the first row. Also in the audience are many members of Sonny's old brigade. Called back together by the big man, they appreciate the candidate's message of reform. They also support his call to purge the government of Duvalierists and former Macoutes. Most of all, they embrace his bold new ideas. They share his outrage that almost two centuries after its hopeful beginning, Haiti is still dependent on aid packages, handouts, and scraps from the table of its new *blanc* master, the US. Sonny appreciates the campaigner's promise to improve the education system, create new jobs, and groom a new generation of scientists, innovators, and critical thinkers.

Sonny's men are all farmers and fishermen. Most can no longer earn a decent living working Haiti's overfished waters and depleted farmlands. The old brigade companions embrace the candidate's promise to attack Haiti's environmental crisis, the deforestation caused by a continuing, almost stone-age reliance on wood as a main energy source and charcoal as a principal export. They are inspired by his promises to take a machete to the corruption and political wheeling and dealing that enriches Haiti's wealthy elite at the expense of its poor.

Most of all, they appreciate the hopeful office-seeker's practical talk. Instead of spouting empty hyperbole and rattling the bones of past leaders, he speaks in the language of the working man. He calls out the phony flag-waving of other candidates. He dismisses their craven pandering with the words of the old adage: *Patriotism is the last refuge of a scoundrel.*

Halfway through the former judge's speech, two young men, first thought to be enthusiastic supporters, approach the smiling candidate. When Sonny and several of his brigadiers stand to block the men, the candidate waves the brigadiers off. But upon reaching the speaker, the two calmly pull out pistols and shoot him in the face, killing him on the spot.

With the military detachment that was present during the early part of the speech nowhere to be found, Sonny and his men spring into action. One of the assassins is immediately shot, but in the wild melee that follows, the other escapes. Moments later, the soldiers reappear and disperse the angry crowd but do not search for or apprehend the missing assailant. Later that day, the gunman is tracked to a small dwelling near the outskirts of the village. Sonny and his group surround the tiny house, but are stalemated when they learn that the attacker has taken the residents as hostages. Through shuttered windows, the gunman warns that he will start killing his prisoners if anyone attempts to storm the house.

The standoff continues for hours until the army finally shows up. They convince the assassin to surrender and avoid the bloody end he will meet if the brigade gets their hands on him.

Their candidate dead, Sonny and his dispirited group head for home. Sonny is not sure whether the post-Duvalier political world into which he has ventured is any less cruel and brutal than the *Dechoukaj* he left behind.

As the date of the election nears, the army increases its violence. It harasses candidates it deems undesirable and the audiences that assemble to hear them speak. The public is terrorized by frequent army patrols and indiscriminate shooting of innocent citizens. Few venture out onto the streets, even in their own neighborhoods. No matter what the public perceived its role to have been in Jean-Claude's downfall, they know the army is now in charge.

The night before the election, there is excitement on every street corner and in every market, church, and restaurant. In every town and village, Haitians discuss prospects for long-awaited presidential voting. But shortly after sunset, army trucks begin to cruise the streets of Jérémie and other cities. They announce through bullhorns that all public thoroughfares are to be immediately cleared. The entire nation is placed into a state of martial law. The surprise announcement means that a curfew will be in effect throughout election day. Citizens are given only minutes to clear the streets.

It takes the trucks one hour to make the rounds through all neighborhoods. When they return, the streets are empty and quiet. A few scattered crowds have gathered to protest the army's heavy-handed attempt to keep people away from the polls. As the trucks retrace their routes, the bullhorns are silent. Teams of soldiers now stand in the back of the vehicles with automatic weapons loaded and cocked. When they encounter crowds, without warning they fire point-blank at protesters. They kill scores in neighborhood after neighborhood.

The following morning as polls open, martial law remains in effect. Peering through their windows out onto the empty streets, citizens are distraught to see of the bodies of their friends, neighbors, and family members strewn about the streets, decomposing in the stifling heat. The election is a charade in which most voters stay away from the polls. Busloads of Millevoix accomplices are shuttled from one polling place to another, repeatedly casting votes. As expected, Leslie Manigat, the general's hand-picked candidate, is declared the winner. He is sworn in as president on February 7, 1988, two years to the day after Jean-Claude was removed from office.

The Manigat presidency is on a bumpy ride from the beginning. US aid had been cut off months before his installation in response to the reckless army brutality and terrorism leading up to the election. The treasury was almost empty. Manigat concludes that the only way he can stabilize the economy is to crack down on the widespread corruption that bleeds the country dry. To reestablish aid, he immediately informs the US of his intentions to clean up the government. He goes to work on his reforms, but his program puts him in conflict with Millevoix and the army. In a sudden coup not quite five months into the new presidential term, Millevoix removes the president from office. Manigat and his family are sent into exile in the Dominican Republic.

After hasty meetings among the military leadership, the general assumes the presidency. But he is angry and vengeful at having been humiliated by a puppet president. Stressed out from years of political in-fighting, and often under the influence of alcohol, Millevoix frequently appears on television drunk, unhinged, and in battle dress. Wearing a steel helmet and sometimes waving an Uzi, he rants about the need for strong leadership under the firm and steady hand of the military.

The public once again protests. But Millevoix unleashes reconstituted *Ton Ton Macoutes* on any church that speaks out against him. Raging Macoutes break into churches and attack parishioners with pistols, machetes, and clubs. Macoute leaders follow their raids with brazen television statements boasting of their responsibility for the attacks. They promise further violence against anyone who speaks out against the president or his policies.

General Millevoix knows he will not enjoy a long term in office, as a mood of unrest is palpable throughout Haiti. Somewhere not far from where he now sits, a group of ambitious young officers, betrayal on their minds, might already be planning the next coup.

The general has always believed that all Haitians have a bit of Macoute in them. Expecting the worst from all those around him, he prepares for each day as if it might be his last. So that when the fateful day finally comes, he will not have to leave office empty-handed, he gives his inner circle the go ahead to meet with Carlos Escobar and start the Colombian drug flow.

Four

The Colombian Connection

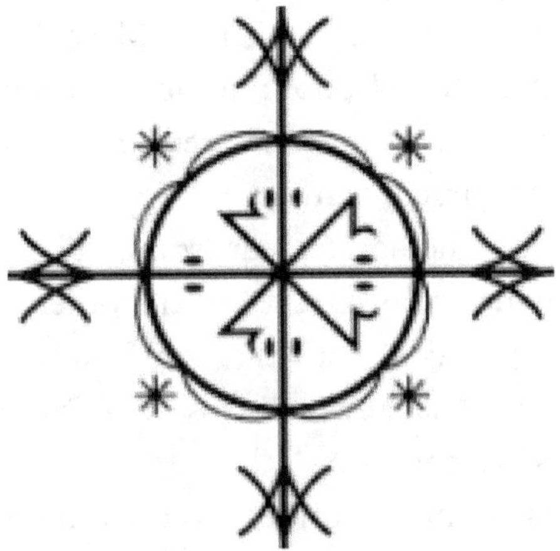

Where the hell is Milton Nazzaire? For several days, Jacques has been looking for the pugnacious dealer in his usual spot in front of *Pump de Gas*. But neither he nor any of the other neighborhood pushers are anywhere to be found. Jacques's weed supply is gone, and several customers are anxious to make purchases. He asks Fritz Leconte, the station's proprietor, if he has seen or heard from Milton or any of the others.

"The army picked them all up four days ago," Leconte tells Jacques. "Loaded them into a truck, hauled them off, and that's the last anyone has seen of them. I hear they were taken to a holding pen at the *Fad' H* headquarters for interrogation."

Leconte usually preferred not even to acknowledge the presence of the dealers that held court in front of his business. He feared trouble with authorities who might demand a cut of the drugs if they thought he was involved in the selling. But he welcomed the crowds that congregated every night. People who might have come only to buy weed ended up hanging out for hours. They socialized, bought food or gas, and listened to loud rap music from the steady flow of cars passing through the busy station. Without the dealers' presence these last few days, there had been a significant falloff in business.

Later that evening, Sonny tells Jacques about a stranger from Port-au-Prince who had inquired about them at Mme Picard's house earlier in the day. The visitor left a telephone number. He requested they call to arrange a meeting to discuss 'urgent matters.' But he left no explanation as to the nature of the urgent matters.

Jacques wondered whether the request might have something to do with the disappearance of Nazzaire and the other dealers. Could the abductors have been tied in with the army's anti-drug squad? If so, maybe they'd squeezed Nazzaire to disclose his customers, and Jacques's and Sonny's names had come up.

No one answers Sonny's return call to the number left by the mysterious visitor. He and Jacques have the rest of the evening to stew over how they had come into the crosshairs of whoever was looking for them. Jacques is unsettled by the unexpected scrutiny. But he takes comfort in knowing that the Nazzaire crowd is not aware of his *Molly* dealing. They couldn't have disclosed it to anyone. But even though he isn't cutting into anyone else's action, somebody in the army hierarchy might have heard of his new venture and wanted in on it.

The next morning, Sonny again tries to return the call. This time he reaches an investigator who claims to be working for the *Haitian Development Alliance.* The investigator explains that the Alliance is an independent non-government organization looking into the Haitian drug trade. He tells Sonny that it will be in his and Jacques's best interests to come to Alliance offices and answer a few questions. If they cooperate, the investigator informs him, there is no cause for worry. He assures Sonny the interviews will not take long.

After several hours of driving through the lush green countryside between Jérémie and Port-au-Prince, Jacques and Sonny stand at the entrance of a shuttered two-story structure across the street from *Fad' H* offices. Both had passed the building many times. But with no signage or markings, neither had ever paid much attention to the nondescript structure. When Sonny presses the doorbell, a gruff voice responds through a speaker above the heavy security door.

"Who are you, and what is the purpose of your visit?"

After identifying themselves, the two are buzzed in. Following a short wait in a small room that had no chairs, an inner security door opens. They are invited further into the building by a tall, bone-thin guard. The man's somber, almost scowling face and dark blue jumpsuit mark him as some kind of a militiaman. They are escorted to a starkly furnished office and introduced to a similarly dressed and unsmiling Andre Hercule.

They sit opposite Hercule at a bare conference table with the guard standing ramrod stiff at the door. Regardless of what they have been told about an 'independent' alliance, Sonny and Jacques know they are in the midst of an army-sanctioned operation. Their hosts are likely *Ton Ton Macoutes*, recalled into action by whomever the Alliance represented.

"As you were advised by telephone yesterday, our agency is looking into the issue of drug use in Haiti," Hercule begins. His voice is deep and nasal and his facial expression austere. They conjure up the macabre image of *Baron Samedi*, the Haitian *Spirit of the Dead*, a potent and fearsome *loa*. As keeper of the dead, the baron can grant people eternal relief from the burdens of the mortal coil or force them to continue living. The Baron's image is often invoked by Haitian men of authority, like Hercule. With his unblinking eyes darting between Sonny and Jacques and his shaved head motionless, the chillingly cordial investigator sizes up his guests like a cobra poised to strike.

"I won't waste time questioning you two about your drug activities and how you get your contraband. Milton Nazzaire has shared the details of your contacts with him at the gas station. We're aware of the volume and frequency of your purchases.

"Monsieur Maurice, we also know about your successful entry into the MDMA market two years ago. We're impressed with your innovative approach for getting your product into the country." Hercule continues to address a now-rattled but still outwardly calm Jacques. "With your comrade here watching your back and Julien DuFrane providing cover, you appear to be well on your way to becoming a major player in the Haitian drug trade."

"And you, sir," Hercule says, turning to Sonny, "have made quite a name for yourself. First, with your *Dechoukaj* leadership and now as security man for young Maurice here.

"Now we're not interested in persecuting either of you for your prior activities. And we don't intend to shake you down for a piece of whatever it is you've been doing. So you can calm down and get that off your minds. In fact, we may be able to work together to better manage the drug situation for the benefit of all parties." Hercule pauses to allow his visitors to take in the unexpected suggestion of a cooperative relationship.

"Just as Prohibition never worked in the States," he continues, "trying to eliminate drug use in Haiti is something that can't be done. It's too easy to grow marijuana here. And we're too close to South American suppliers to keep cocaine out of the country."

"What we need is a structure, a protocol if you will, whereby the public can indulge in its guilty pleasures without reflecting badly on the country or being victimized by thugs. Milton Nazzaire and people like him who engage in violent turf warfare endanger the public. And they give us an international black eye. Do you follow me so far?"

Jacques and Sonny still don't know what to make of the unexpected conversation. Even though they were not prepared for an invitation to join in any kind of partnership, they nod in affirmation.

"Before I proceed, however, I need to know whether you gentlemen are prepared to end your *Dechoukaj* connections. It will be necessary for you to do so before we even consider working with you."

Jacques tries to answer before Sonny derails the meeting by slipping into his community activist persona. But Sonny cuts him off.

"For my entire life, all I ever knew was Duvalier rule. For as long as I can remember, there were the chosen few living a great life, the president and his 'royal' family, the military brass, the wealthy elites, and even some in the middle class. But for everyone else, life was pure hell.

"How could the common man not be angry, having to raise his family in a shack with a dirt floor and tin roof, feeding them on a salary of centimes, provided he could even find work? And if he dared raise his voice in protest, he faced disappearance at the hands of the *Ton Ton Macoute*.

"What kind of life was it for his children never to see real doctors and instead be preyed upon by voodoo charlatans? So when we had an opportunity to strike back and help bring down Baby Doc in 1986, we did, and I'm happy for every blow we struck. But now we've got to move on. Our retribution and payback haven't put food on our tables or money in our pockets. More than two years have passed and most Haitians are still dirt poor.

Jacques is relieved that Sonny hadn't moralized and declined the opportunity to work with the Alliance. Jacques says only: "Sonny looked after me when I couldn't look after myself. I got into *Dechoukaj* to support him. If he's ready to cut ties with the brigades, so am I."

"All right, now that we've got that straight," Hercule says, "let me tell you about our plan and how you fit into it. But before I continue, I must ask both of you to stand and unbutton your shirts so that we can make sure you're not wired. On a few occasions, we've had people come in here and try to record our conversations."

Hercule motions to the guard who first steps toward Sonny and then Jacques to glance inside their shirts and pat down their pant legs. Finding nothing, he returns to the door, and Hercule continues.

"First, because we don't want ignorant thugs like Nazzaire creating problems, we've taken them completely out of circulation. We expect the drug trade to continue. But we want it conducted by people who will take care of their business without making a spectacle of the country. And we want to see some of the gains of their enterprise serve the greater good through appropriate channels.

"I would like to report to Alliance leaders that you gentlemen are willing to conduct your business without the excessive street violence that has become so commonplace in Haiti. I would also like to tell them that you are willing to allocate a reasonable portion of your earnings to the proper causes. If I can do so, I am confident you will be allowed to continue your enterprise.

"Even better, you will be allowed to operate in a designated region without harassment from the government or other competing enterprises. And with our help, you may even be able to expand your range of offerings. We have friends in certain South American countries who are anxious to provide additional products, such as cocaine."

Hercule pauses, his eyes continuing to dart between his visitors. He then asks: "Is this the type of enterprise that interests you? Is this an environment in which you could operate?"

Jacques is now comfortable that Sonny will not contradict him. He answers, emphatically: "Yes, we are definitely interested in proceeding. Of course, we must know more about what you have in mind. We don't want to get tied up in an unprofitable venture."

The two visitors are now sure their suspicion of an army-backed operation is on point. The alliance business, philanthropy double-talk, and concern about public safety is most likely a cover for a Macoute-run project to get rid of the warring gangs and their godfathers. The way will then be clear for an efficient drug distribution operation that could cut the army leadership in for a piece of the action.

Their take is correct. The old gangs weren't sharing with the politicians. And they were causing too much trouble with their street violence. Millevoix was fed up. He wanted to organize a reliable group of drug partners that could provide a steady revenue stream without adding to the problems that were drawing international attention to the troubled nation. But he and his inner circle didn't just want a piece of the existing pie. They wanted a partnership with a South American cartel that could create an even bigger pie with larger shares for all.

Sonny understood the army's desire to get in on the drug gravy train. But he wondered how it expected to divide Haiti into neat drug markets. How did it expect to convince a bunch of ambitious hustlers to play by rules and operate within assigned territories? It was the very nature of drug dealers to always expand their turf and eliminate competition.

"Now I'm sure you're wondering what kind of a market there could be for cocaine in an impoverished nation like Haiti," Hercule continues. "Many people here can hardly afford food. Even weed is out of the question for them. It's obvious that the opportunity to sell cocaine here is pretty much nonexistent. But we're not trying to import Colombian cocaine into Haiti. We want to pass it through Haiti to the real target market—the US.

"That, gentlemen, is the idea in a nutshell. I can't tell you much more at this time. But if you are interested in proceeding, sometime within the next few weeks, we will be organizing a visit to South America. During that trip, we can discuss the project in more detail with the *Medellín* people, our contacts in Colombia. We will call you soon to arrange trip details and fill you in further on the project."

⸻ ◆ ⸻

As soon as he gets to school the following morning, Jacques begins his research on Colombia and the *Medellín* Cartel. He gathers books and newspaper clippings and devours them with the same excitement he experiences in all his studies. For Jacques, the joy of research is two-fold. First, there is the pleasure of accumulating knowledge in a mind that always hungers to learn and know more. But equally important is the prestige and status within his academic circle that come from his reputation as a talented young scholar. He tackles every new challenge with the same intellectual curiosity and desire to excel as he did when he branded himself as the *Sommelier of Cannabis*.

To understand the environment in which he will operate, Jacques begins by reviewing news coverage of current-day Colombia. He then reads about the country's past and how it evolved into what it is today. He goes back to the death of Simon Bolivar in 1830 and learns about the *War of a Thousand Days* that claimed more than one hundred thousand lives in 1899. He also reads about the 1950 murder of a promising young political leader that sparked an explosion of unrest in several cities and caused the deaths of an additional two hundred thousand people. He learns how the rioting, random destruction, drunken looting, and fighting among private and public armies over many generations has become a core component of Colombian culture. The persistent and brutal unrest even has its own name, *La Violencia*. A beautiful country that breeds outlaws, Colombia's tradition of violence makes Haiti's own history of *Dechoukaj* and political turmoil seem almost tame by comparison.

The *Medellín* had turned Colombia into a narco-state in which the Cartel was above the law and untouchable. To Jacques, nothing more embodies the unholy relationship between the Colombian government and the Cartel than the concept of *Plata o Plomo* (silver or lead). With the enormous profits from its lucrative cocaine empire, the *Medellín* can offer large bribes to officials throughout Colombia's government and judicial systems. But it takes things a step further, punishing or killing those who dare to refuse a bribe. One either accepts the Cartel's *Plata* (its silver), or its *Plomo* (its lead). Pablo Escobar and the Cartel forever own those who take the bribes. Through this system of bribery and intimidation, Escobar controls the entire Colombian government.

A few days later, over dinner, Jacques tells Sonny what he has learned about the *Medellín*. He spares no details about the culture of violence and the extraordinary wealth that has been created.

Sonny responds with what seems to Jacques an odd question. "Do you think the army people know what they're getting into, hooking up with the Cartel?"

"Of course," Jacques answers. "They're sending us in to get the operation started, aren't they?"

"I don't think they really have a clue," Sonny responds, his words slow and carefully measured. "These Columbians are pros. They've succeeded because they're smarter, tougher, and more ruthless than their own government. But our military is so blinded by greed, it can't see what's involved in throwing in with Escobar.

"For all its problems and incompetence, at least the Haitian government still runs this country. But from what you're telling me, that's no longer the reality in Columbia. Corruption and violence have broken the government down so far that it couldn't clean house and regain control even if it wanted to."

"What does voodoo have to do with it?" Jacques quickly answers, glaring at Sonny.

"I know the prospect of big paydays has got you turned around, too," Sonny responds, a hint of distain in the stare he directs at Jacques. "But our culture has too many horror stories about what happens when people fall under the control of powerful, outside forces. It's hard to believe that any Haitian could be blind to the risks.

"Do you remember Hector, the guy who mysteriously disappeared at sea the first time I ever went out on a fishing boat? None of the crew ever talked much about it, because they didn't want to embarrass his wife and family. The word was that Hector used to mess with other men, and sometimes little boys. He kept it a pretty good secret and never let anybody see him making his moves. But he couldn't keep the secret from himself, or from the *loa* that got a hold of him," Sonny continued as he touched the image of Belie that hung from the chain around his neck.

"I believe to my core that when Hector refused to change his ways, he gave up his soul. His *loa* took over and began riding him hard, driving him to drink and act out in crazy ways. One day when we were setting out nets, Hector started running around the deck in circles, prancing as if he was a galloping horse. His eyes bulged out of his head, and he growled and foamed at the mouth. He suddenly rushed to the side of the boat and jumped into the ocean, his feet still horse-trotting as he sunk. We all tried to stop him, but he was too strong, and his *loa* was too determined to destroy him.

"Even though Hector was a good swimmer, he didn't try to save himself. He didn't want to. He let himself disappear into the depths, never to be seen again. Even though I've never been much into voodoo, the memory of that event has stuck with me, always reminding me of the problems with losing control. Everybody in Haiti probably knows of a similar story. I'm surprised these army guys can't see the danger of getting into bed with the Columbians."

The notion that the *Medellín* might be a modern-day *loa* that could drive Haiti to its ruin seems bizarre to Jacques. But since Sonny isn't trying to block the deal, Jacques doesn't argue with him.

The ambitious young dealer doesn't give much thought to Sonny's worries about the Colombian opportunity. Just as he has no patience with ignorant peasants who lose both their money and health trusting voodoo charlatans, he will have no concern or sympathy for the greedy generals if, or when, they are mounted and ridden to destruction by their drug-dealing partners. He knows no *loa* is going to destroy him. He is thankful for the opportunity the reckless military men have created for him. And he is determined to achieve his goals even if the army and the rest of Haiti are dragged to hell in the process.

⸺ ◆ ⸺

Three weeks to the day after the meeting at Alliance headquarters, Jacques, Sonny, and a dozen other hopeful drug entrepreneurs stand with Andre Hercule and his assistant on the tarmac of a private runway at Port-au-Prince Airport. A recently landed Gulfstream II taxis toward them. As the big jet's twin engines whine to a stop, two men emerge from the plane and descend the steps exposed as the passenger door unfolds to the ground. One of the men, smiling broadly, his thick black hair pinned into a ponytail, approaches Hercule.

"Que mas, Caballero?" (What's happening, my man?) he says to Hercule. The austere militiaman and his sullen sidekick put forth their best imitation of smiles as they return the greeting and exchange handshakes with the new arrivals. Having traveled to the airport from Alliance headquarters in a government bus, Hercule and his party bypassed customs. Their overnight baggage is quickly loaded onto the Gulfstream. Moments later, they are seated in a stylish cabin that looks more like an exclusive men's club than an aircraft interior. It has comfortable, widely spaced easy chairs, a bar, and two large TV screens. There is more than enough room for the entire group. From a small galley, a breakfast of smoked salmon, eggs, and toast is served with coffee and champagne. As they eat, Hercule introduces his guests to each other and the hosts. When the big jet reaches cruising altitude for the two-and-a-half-hour trip to Bógota, Diego Hoyos addresses the group. After relaying a welcoming message from Carlos Escobar, he reviews the trip itinerary. It will include a quick driving tour of Bógota, a visit to a *Medellín* cocaine processing plant and dinner with *El Doctor*, himself, at one of his country estates. The group will spend the night at the mansion and return to Haiti in the morning.

As the travelers enjoy their breakfasts, Hoyos explains the challenge they face in this venture. He assures them it will not be difficult to get cocaine out of Colombia and into Haiti. Their big hurdle will be moving it to the US.

The *Medellín* was already supplying eighty percent of the cocaine entering the US. But, it needed new channels to circumvent ever-tightening drug interdiction programs that began in the States in the 1970s with Richard Nixon's *War on Drugs* campaign. To create these new channels, Hoyos explains, the Cartel will need the skills and creativity of the men on board. The Alliance had assembled these men because of the innovative smuggling techniques they had devised in the past.

As Hoyos talks, an attractive and scantily attired female flight attendant sets out several bowls of white powdered cocaine. The guests dig in, a few using miniature spoons carried in pocket cases, and one, a Superfly-styled neck amulet spoon. Most, however, use straws to snort from trays distributed throughout the cabin.

Everyone comments on the quality and potency of the unexpected treat. Although not a regular user, Sonny enjoys a few lines of the coke with the rest of the travelers. Jacques, however, claims a recent flare-up of asthma as his reason for declining to partake. It is one of the many excuses he has perfected for avoiding drug use without appearing to be a stiff or a killjoy.

It is ironic that Jacques feigns illness to cover his reluctance to use drugs. Despite his small size and the thin frame on which he is already developing a protruding midsection, he enjoys good health and is usually illness-free. But unfortunately, his robust health is not reflected in his physical appearance. His only distinctly masculine trait is a mellow, baritone voice that grows deeper and richer as he ages. Together with his mental agility, impressive vocabulary, and dramatic enunciation, Jacques uses his distinctive voice to impress everyone in his expanding orbit of influence.

As his guests get high, Hoyos goes on to describe the network of airstrips and harbors set up along Haiti's porous coastal perimeter. The strategic placement of these assets allows small planes and powerful offshore speedboats to bring large drug shipments to Haiti. This avoids detection by local authorities and US vessels that patrol the waters around Haiti. Hoyos reiterates that the primary challenge will be to get drugs from Haiti to the States. He pledges all the necessary resources to help those assembled in the Gulfstream to move their product.

Sonny and Jacques enjoy the tour of a vibrant and developed Bogotá and the visit to a sprawling and efficiently run plant. At the facility, they observe the meticulous end to end processing of locally grown coca leaves into a 'coca base,' which is cooked into the final powdered cocaine product. But the highlight of the day is the visit to *Hacienda Los Nápoles.* The magnificent seventy-four-hundred-acre country estate just east of *Medellín* is one of several owned by the Cartel leader. It features an airport, a heliport, several swimming pools, and man-made lakes. The mansion, which can sleep one hundred guests at a time, is packed with pool tables, pinball machines, party rooms, and every imaginable toy and extravagance. And it isn't even Escobar's primary residence.

Escobar joins the group for dinner and surprises them with his straightforward manner and affability. Nobody knew what to expect from someone, who though not yet forty, was said to be one of the world's ten richest men, his Cartel pulling in earnings of more than twenty billion dollars per year. Far from the classic, menacing image of a criminal heavy, the pudgy Escobar wears shoulder-length hair and a stringy mustache, and sported jeans, a baggy pull-over shirt, and white Nike gym shoes. But the grim-faced bodyguards that hover everywhere and searched the group one last time before Escobar ambled into the dining room reminded the guests that their host was no ordinary thug.

The word on Escobar is that his drug of choice is weed, not cocaine. When he greets his guests, he appears to be high but in control. He laughs and talks with them about his passion, soccer, and even offers to join them in the morning for play on one of the estate's soccer fields. But before the evening ends, he covers a small bit of business. He assures his visitors that within one month, Diego Hoyos will begin shipping orders to Haiti for distribution in the US. He commits to a first delivery by January, 1990 and reiterates Hoyos's offer for any help necessary to initiate and maintain the flow of the product. He also promises consulting assistance and training to bring Haitian wholesalers up to speed on the most effective and useful large-scale smuggling techniques. Escobar explains that the Haitian project is important to him and that he intends to provide all required backing. Sonny and Jacques are pleased by Pablo's commitment of unlimited support as much as they are chilled by the brutal concept of *Plata o Plomo*.

Five

Fort Greene

The tension could be cut with a knife in the empty warehouse a few streets from the Alliance headquarters. Twenty prospective drug mules sit around a long table in a dimly lit room. The nervous candidates are all poor local villagers anxious for a payday. Like real mules, they will soon be used as beasts of burden to transport cocaine to America. But unlike the four-legged variety that bear their burdens on their backs, these unfortunate creatures, known in the street as 'swallowers,' will carry their deadly cargo hidden in their bellies.

The only light in the cavernous, shuttered room comes from a low-hanging fixture suspended above the oil-cloth-covered table. With all but one of its bulbs missing, the battered chandelier casts eerie shadows and barely lights the faces of those seated around the table. Thirteen young women and seven even younger men sit in silence staring at the paper plates in front of them. Each plate contains fifteen grape-sized objects wrapped in plastic and sealed with wax. The group cannot see Phillipe Estrada, who addresses them from the shadows near the table. With him are Jacques, Sonny, and the four brigade marchers who had assisted in the *La Renaissance* raid a few weeks earlier. The *Medellín* has sent Estrada to help set up the initial smuggling runs. The use of drug mules is one of several techniques that will be used to kick off the Haitian pass-through operation. Over time, the young cocaine entrepreneurs will develop their own preferred smuggling approaches.

"I want everyone to relax," Phillipe begins in his Spanish-accented English. "We've already talked to each of you, so there should be no confusion about why you're here. Tonight we will practice for our first delivery to Miami this coming Saturday. Those who make it through today's session will be invited to come back on Saturday. Ten of those will be selected to make the trip to Miami. They will return the same evening and rejoin their families with the quickest 14,000 gourdes they will ever earn. The rest of you will get your turns on future trips.

"In your plates are grapes covered in plastic and wax, nothing that can harm you. What we will do tonight is easy. First, you will swallow each of the grapes whole, with no chewing. Then we will relax and wait six hours without going to the bathroom. If you feel the urge to move your bowels, swallow a few of the guava seeds we will provide you. They will bind you up temporarily. At the proper time, we will take you to the bathroom to relieve yourselves, not in the toilet, but in pans we will provide. The grapes you swallowed should come out in your stool with the plastic covers intact. You will wash and return them to us as soon as you come out of the bathroom. That's all there is to it. There should be no problems if you follow my instructions."

To calm a few who appear uneasy, Estrada continues: "Our stomachs can easily hold fifteen grapes. People have been known to swallow one hundred objects this size. But ingesting that much at one time could be painful and dangerous. We wouldn't want to hurt you or damage the cargo, so we'll limit your intake to fifteen."

"You will again swallow fifteen capsules Saturday morning before traveling to the airport. But on Saturday, the capsules will contain the drug product we are moving, so everyone must be alert. Later in the day, after we clear customs in Miami and leave the airport, you will eliminate, wash the pellets and return them intact to get your money. It's that simple."

"Is everyone in?" Estrada asks.

There is a flurry of nervous chatter among the prospects. Most of them know each other as they all have children at the same public school, the main reason they were chosen. Estrada had recommended that the identities of the courier's children and other family members be known. To protect their loved ones, the mules will be motivated to perform their duties properly and not steal any of the product or disclose the scheme.

Everyone answers affirmatively except for two who are unwilling to swallow the capsules. They are escorted out of the building and warned not to mention the events of the afternoon to anyone.

One woman who gags as she tries to swallow is given 300 gourdes and excused. One of the men who thinks he might have bitten into one of the capsules is allowed to continue but closely watched. If a cocaine pellet is damaged and ruptured, it could result in a severe overdose, not to mention the loss of the product.

After many nervous and noisy minutes of near gagging as the group ingests their quotas, the room quiets for the six-hour wait. The couriers will have to retain their capsules for approximately the same length of time in Miami before they can be eliminated, cleaned, and turned over to Jacques and Sonny. There is nervous talk among the group, and a few swallow handfuls of guava seeds. At the end of the waiting period, Jacques and Phillipe begin escorting the candidates to the warehouse's two bathrooms. They wait at the doors as the couriers eliminate and wash their capsules. Two candidates return ruptured capsules, and one is unable to pass anything even after taking a laxative. These three are dismissed after being given 1,200 gourdes apiece and warned not to discuss their experiences with anyone. The one who is unable to eliminate is assured that the pellets will eventually come out in her stool. But it might take a few hours longer than would be acceptable for Saturday's mission. The remaining fourteen candidates all pass their capsules intact. Even though everyone doesn't thoroughly clean their capsules, Jacques and Sonny carefully inspect each one to ensure that the contents, grapes today but expensive cocaine next Saturday, are intact.

The group is instructed to report back to the same warehouse with their passports at 4:30 a.m. sharp the following Saturday, February 3, 1990. Ten will be selected to ingest fifteen capsules each and be transported to the Port-au-Prince Airport by van. During the flight and while clearing customs, no one is to use or even go into a bathroom for any reason. After clearing customs, the couriers will meet up with their assigned handler, who will have arrived on an earlier flight. Under the handler's watchful eyes, the capsules will be recovered at a Miami health clinic secured by the Alliance. The contents of all capsules will be checked and validated before any courier is allowed to return to Haiti.

Things proceed as planned. Jacques, Phillipe, and Eric, one of Sonny's old brigade marchers, take a Friday flight and spend the night in Miami. The early arrival ensures that someone will be waiting for the couriers the moment they clear customs. Jacques doesn't want to risk the possibility that someone might wander off, use the toilet, or possibly be abducted. Sonny and Allain, another brigade man, fly in on Saturday on the same flight as the couriers. Although no one had reported any history of air sickness, all were issued Dramamine capsules along with their guava seeds. The couriers are all seated separately. They are instructed not to talk to each other or their handlers, all of whom use code names. If trouble goes down with any of the couriers, Jacques doesn't want the rest of the group or their handlers caught up in the problem.

By 11:45, the 7:30 a.m. American Airlines Flight 514 from Port-au-Prince to Miami has landed, and all ten couriers have made it through customs. They are loaded into a rental van for the twenty-minute drive to the *Little Haiti Health Clinic*. Since the busy facility closes at noon on Saturdays, there will be no prying staff or clients in the way during the nerve-racking pellet recovery process. Only the watchman is on duty outside the building.

As an extra precaution against the possibility that a courier might try to turn in a bogus capsule containing some fake substance in order to keep and later sell the real cocaine, Sonny had devised a color-coding scheme. The capsules had been covered in several different colors of plastic wrap before final encasing in wax. Although the contents of all capsules were precisely the same, each courier was issued a different combination of color wrappings. Any attempt to game or substitute capsules would immediately be apparent.

No irregularities are detected. After the unpleasant job of cleaning the capsules, inspecting their contents, and combining the entire kilo of cocaine, the couriers are paid. They are immediately sent back to Miami Airport along with two of their handlers. They are in Haiti later that afternoon.

With the difficult job of getting the shipment into the States behind them, Jacques and Sonny now concentrate on moving the product to the wholesale buyer. He is located in Fort Greene, a gentrifying, but still heavily Hispanic section of Brooklyn, New York. The toughest part of that task will be operating under the radar of the still-in-force *War on Drugs* program. The program had been amped-up after the election of Ronald Reagan to the U.S presidency a few years earlier. The troublesome campaign was resulting in increasing numbers of drug busts, drug-related convictions, and longer jail terms for those apprehended in urban centers.

The *Medellín* had already flooded the Miami area with cocaine and was moving its distribution northward along the US East Coast. As

New York has not yet been saturated, it will be Jacques's main point of sales.

To avoid further air travel that will risk the discovery of the cargo by drug-sniffing airport dogs, he rents a car for the eighteen-hour drive. Automobile travel will save the costs of three airplane tickets to New York. With the high quality of his product, Jacques is confident the kilo will pull in the eighteen thousand dollar wholesale price he has discussed with his New York customer. But he will have to control costs to end up with the one-third net profit he is after.

On the long drive, Phillipe shares his view of the US drug trafficking scene. He describes how US narcotics agents attack the trade from two perspectives, importing and distribution. The importing component gets the product into the US. The distribution aspect transfers the product to US wholesale buyers. These middlemen break down the shipment, cut the product and move it down the drug chain to lower-level dealers.

US NARCs address the first challenge with close surveillance of all products and merchandise shipped or flown to the States from known drug exporting nations. DEA agents impound random samples of imported products to check for contraband. They disassemble and, if necessary, destroy the samples in search of smuggled drugs. Distribution is monitored by maintaining an awareness of street demand and by surveillance of key individual distributors who are known to have the necessary resources and network to handle large drug transactions.

Phillipe explains that NARC surveillance of a suspected drug deal can be a long, complicated process involving numerous drug interdiction resources. Many things can go wrong in the investigation of an impending sale. The parties could be spooked and the transaction called off if NARCs move on the suspected players too soon without knowing for sure whether drugs are about to be exchanged for cash. But by waiting too long, wiretaps and search warrants can expire or deals can be consummated undetected. The NARCs have many powerful weapons and resources. But they all have their limitations, especially when pitted against shrewd, careful, and patient narcotics pros.

———•◆•———

Arriving in New York after a grueling all-night drive, Jacques calls his contact, known only as 'Jesse.' He is instructed to drive into Brooklyn and park in any public parking lot near Fort Greene Park. He is then to walk to *Junior's*, a restaurant at the corner of Flatbush and DeKalb Avenues. He is to be there in two hours. Jesse will be wearing a straw hat and sunglasses with reflective lenses. Jacques is to carry a *New York Times* under his left arm and a cigar in his right hand. Jesse will be seated at the counter.

At 1:00 p.m. sharp, Jacques enters Junior's. He immediately spots Jessie, who is much younger than he expects, perhaps not much older than himself. Despite all the appetizing food on display at the Brooklyn landmark, Jesse sips only black coffee. Jacques introduces himself as Sonny and Phillipe take seats at a nearby table. Wasting no time, Jesse instructs Jacques to take a cab to the southwest corner of Bryant Park at Fortieth Street and Sixth Avenue in Manhattan. With approximately a forty minute drive in current traffic, he should arrive no later than 2:00 p.m. He is to walk east through the park, looking to rejoin his host, who will be seated at a park table with a wicker picnic basket open before him. If no tables are available, he will sit on a blanket in the grassy area. Jacques is told not to stop at Jesse's spot but to continue through the park. He is to enter the New York Public Library building through the Forty-Second Street entrance and immediately leave via the Fifth Avenue main entrance. He is to proceed south on Fifth Avenue to Fortieth, then west to reenter the park on the Fortieth Street side. If Jesse has spotted no tail on Jacques, he will be waiting at the table, helping himself to a sandwich and a container of soup from his picnic basket.

Jacques arrives on schedule and walks through the park toward the library. As requested, the kilo is stored in his backpack in a plastic food container wrapped in a red cloth table napkin. With Sonny and Phillipe some thirty yards behind him, Jacques passes Jesse, who has found a table and set out his picnic supplies. For appearances, he has also set up a chessboard with pieces ready for play. After walking through the building and back into the park, Jacques finds Jesse still at his table. He joins him with Sonny and Phillipe watching from the marble stairway to the library courtyard. Jacques thinks he recognizes, at a nearby table, a man he earlier saw watching them at Junior's. He relaxes when Jesse informs him that the man is one of his own security team.

Jesse removes a small spoonful size sample from Jacques's food container. Wrapped in a red napkin, the plastic case looks as though it might contain a tasty soufflé. When he deposits the spoonful of coke into the liquid of a freshly opened ampoule of the test kit he had brought in his picnic basket, the liquid turns a deep purple. The color is a measure of the purity of the product, the darker the color, the purer the coke. Knowing that this quality will allow him to cut and dilute his new supply even more than planned, Jesse relaxes and allows himself a small smile.

In exchange for the coke-filled food container, Jesse hands Jacques what looks like a deli-wrapped submarine sandwich. In it are eighteen one-thousand-dollar packets of bank-wrapped, crisp one-hundred-dollar bills. Jacques flips through the packets without even removing them from the sandwich wrapping. Since Jesse had been recommended by the *Medellín* people, Jacques is comfortable that the cash is not counterfeit. To pass bad money would violate a Cartel rule and result in severe consequences—at best, no further deals, but more likely, bloodshed.

The transaction now complete, Jacques and Jesse eat their food and wrap up their picnic, Jesse explaining that despite the elaborate routine, a bigger purchase would have required even more safeguards. On this transaction, Jesse explains, one of the best things Jacques has going for himself is that, relatively speaking, his is not a major deal. His single kilo is somewhere near the dividing line between small-potato 'gram' dealing and the multi-kilo transactions on which US NARCs concentrated. There just aren't enough narcotics agents to follow up on every small deal.

Jacques knows that if he moves to larger deals, as he plans to, the pool of potential buyers will grow smaller and smaller. And those who can afford large buys may already be on some NARCs' radar. He will have to figure out how to avoid becoming collateral damage in the busts of deep-pocket wholesale buyers who draw too much attention. Some prospective buyers might be so dangerous that, on occasion, he may have to walk away from a deal, absorb the losses, and live for another day.

At the same time, he will have to find safe and cost-effective ways of moving drugs on a large scale. Mules aren't the answer. For his first one-kilo deal, the cost of the mules and their handlers cut deeply into his profits. And after the one-third of the wholesale price that went to the Alliance through Hercule, he barely ended up with the one-third profit on which he had set his sights. But it isn't only the economics of using mules that is problematic. Worrying about a cocaine pellet rupturing in the stomach of a courier and causing a fatal overdose, or fretting over whether a courier might unexpectedly shit out a pellet or vomit one up during a flight and somehow point the finger at him is something he does not want to experience again anytime soon.

When he returns to Haiti, Jacques learns that the four other fledgling smuggling operations hatched after the Colombian trip had not fared so well. His Fort Greene operation was the only one that earned money and didn't result in a bust. The other ventures had been led by four ambitious young weed dealers, who, like himself, aspired to bigger things. One involved hiding cocaine in statuettes and art objects. The coke was discovered when US customs agents in Atlanta opened a case of figurines and found cocaine spilling from two small statues that either had been poorly constructed or not correctly packaged to prevent travel damage. In two other ventures, the smugglers were able to get their shipments past customs and into the US. But they were still apprehended by narcotics agents, one in Philadelphia and one in Washington, DC, at the moment the product was passed to buyers. In both cases, the deals took place in locales where supplies had been running very low at the street dealer levels. Local NARCs, knowing that shipments would soon be arriving, had been closely watching several known high-level buyers through whose hands new shipments would likely pass. The two Haitian smugglers were picked up when they tried to close deals with these 'radioactive' buyers. The fourth entrepreneur, following a *Medellín* recommendation, tried a complicated scheme in which cocaine powder was mixed with water and soaked into men's sportswear that was then pressed, packaged, and flown into New Orleans, ostensibly destined for wholesale sales to local department stores. But after the goods cleared customs, the drugs were not properly recovered. The local dry cleaning plant that had agreed to re-soak the garments and extract the cocaine discarded the cocaine solution before the powder was retrieved.

The bottom line was that, of the five initiatives to move Colombian coke through Haiti into the U.S, only two were able to avoid interception. Of those two, only Jacques got the product into the hands of the customer. His stature enhanced in the eyes of the Alliance, he was now expected to assume the lead role in Colombian pass-through operations.

He quickly set about identifying more effective smuggling approaches. Tops on his list is the trusty bag-switching scheme that continues to work so well for his MDMA importing. Using his growing network, it isn't long before he identifies a US agent in Miami willing to participate in the same routine he uses to bring *Molly* into Haiti. But the cost will be much higher, two thousand dollars per kilo moved, still a bargain since he knows local wholesale buyers are willing to pay more than twenty thousand dollars per kilo for the quality of the product he can provide. Avoiding the strain and cost involved in sweating out a mule transport operation makes the bag-switch option a no-brainer.

Since his main market has been designated as the New York metro area, Jacques's ultimate goal is to set up a switch operation at New York's LaGuardia Airport. If he can do so, he won't have to fly his goods into Miami and then move them again further north to New York. But establishing the Miami bag-switch operation is a good start. The rest will come in time. He knows he just needs to be patient.

ViVi Michel

Jacques suspects the black Renault is following him. Shortly after leaving school, he noticed the small sedan maintaining its position two or three cars behind his Toyota as he made his way north through Jérémie on his half-hour drive home. After improvising a few quick turns and still spotting the Renault in his rearview mirror, he knows he has a tail. With no unusual markings, there is nothing to distinguish this very common car from the many others like it on the road. The vehicle stays far enough behind so that Jacques can't identify anything about its occupants other than that there are two of them.

Not wanting to lead unwanted visitors to his home, Jacques heads for the busy waterfront district. With his knowledge of the area from years of hanging around Sonny's job, he is sure he can lose the tail. Although it had been many months since Sonny last worked at the market, Jacques still remembers the neighborhood well.

He parks his SUV behind the patchwork of sheds and open stalls known as the *Seafront Market*. He makes his way through the old building where Sonny used to repair fishing nets. He passes the maze of vendor stalls that reek of fish and brine and heads back out onto the teeming street. He stops under a street peddler's umbrella to observe the traffic. A half-hour later, with no sign of the Renault, he hails a tap-tap for the rest of his trip home. He leaves the Toyota in case his followers had spotted him parking and were waiting to resume the tail when he returned to the car. He will come back later with Sonny to pick it up.

It is a hot and jarring ride home in the beat-up taxi, its long-gone suspension bottoming out at every slight road imperfection. Jacques puzzles over why someone might be following him. Sonny has been accompanying him on all his business meetings and travels these past few months. The only time he is alone is when he attends his twice-weekly university classes. Is it a coincidence that he is followed on one of the few occasions when Sonny isn't with him? Could someone be staking him out and looking to catch him alone? Is he being scoped out for a hit or an abduction?

That night as he and Sonny return to the waterfront to pick up his car, they replay the day's events. They conclude that the tail probably has nothing to do with the Alliance, the army, the police, or anyone else in Haitian government circles. To Sonny, it has the earmarks of a rival sizing up the competition. To know for sure, Jacques wants to draw another tail and lead his followers into a trap.

Sonny worries that the surveillance has already yielded enough information that the very next interaction might be a real hit. As Jacques has now been heading a thriving and growing drug enterprise for three years, Sonny believes the wise move is to increase security immediately. He doesn't want the young dealer to ever again be without protection.

Even at home, he would have to be under guard, and the house would have to be made more secure.

Jacques disagrees. To project an image of strength, he wants to instill fear in his enemies as he believed he had done in his nose-slicing, payback attack at *La Renaissance*. As he sees it, it is worth the risk to offer himself as bait if he can find out who is tracking him. Thus, two days later, following his normal routine, he leaves home alone for *Collège Saint-Louis,* taking his usual route.

Although his pickup truck is parked in its usual spot in the driveway that morning, Sonny is not at home. He sits in a large van parked along the route that Jacques will take to school. With him in the unmarked vehicle are Eric and Allain, the two former brigade members still working with him and Jacques. After Jacques drives past the van, Sonny lets a few other vehicles pass. He then pulls out into the stream of traffic working its way south into Jérémie. He follows Jacques to school but notices no other cars in pursuit. On the return trip home a few hours later, he again spots no tail. He is ready to call off the long-shot entrapment effort and move into full twenty-four-hour security. But Jacques wants to continue to bait the trap. He has a hunch his pursuers will soon reappear.

Sonny and his crew follow Jacques on the next few round trips to school. During the many hours of driving and waiting for Jacques's pursuers to reappear, Sonny reflects on his evolving relationship with the younger man. It is clear that the power dynamic between them has changed. Sonny had always tried to raise the boy like the father neither of them had ever known. But now the protégé had become his own man. The big man was ok with that. It had always been his goal to empower the youngster to take charge of his life and make the bold decisions necessary for success. He had always hoped that success would come in the field of education and that Jacques would use his god-given smarts to teach and uplift others. If it was necessary for Jacques to risk selling weed to escape the streets, it was a gamble worth taking. He even accepted a subordinate role in the younger man's fast-growing drug operation. These were the compromises and sacrifices that had to be made to help a son succeed, even a son not of blood.

After three more uneventful roundtrips to school with Sonny and his men following discreetly, the Renault is once again spotted on Jacques's tail. According to a prearranged plan, Jacques alters his route. He detours through the congested streets of one of the city's roughest neighborhoods. When the Renault comes to a stop at a busy inter-section a few cars behind Jacques's Toyota, Sonny's van pulls up behind it. Sonny and Eric jump out and rush to the Renault. With handguns drawn, they yank the startled driver and passenger out of the car. They drag them past several gawking pedestrians and into the middle row of the van.

Allain sits in the third row with his pistol pointed at the two young captives. Sonny returns to the driver's seat, while Eric takes the wheel of the Renault. When the traffic clears, Eric pulls off with the van follow-ing. The two vehicles follow Jacques's SUV into Port-au-Prince. They stop at the warehouse Jacques and Sonny use to prepare and package drug shipments.

Once inside, Jacques confronts the two captives seated at the table of the dimly lit room, their hands now tied behind their backs. Sonny, Eric, and Allain watch from the shadows.

"I want two pieces of information from you two. As soon as I get it, you can go home. If I don't get it, I promise you will suffer. Who sent you to follow me, and why?"

The two men, both appearing to be in their early twenties and dressed in jeans, gym shoes and, logo T-shirts, sit grim-faced and stoic. Neither responds.

Without another word, Jacques slowly approaches one of the men. He cocks his pistol and places the muzzle to the temple of his tight-lipped prisoner. He pauses for a moment then fires a thundering gunshot that sprawls his victim to the floor and splatters blood, bone shards, and pieces of flesh onto the other shocked captive who screams and bolts for the door.

Unfazed by the spectacle of the dead man lying facedown at his feet, Jacques once again cocks his pistol. He steps in front of the other captive who has been brought back to the table and is restrained in his chair by Eric and Allain. Glaring scornfully, Jacques addresses the violently trembling man. "I'll ask you one more time, who sent you, and why?"

Before Jacques has a chance to put the pistol to his head, the terrified prisoner yells: "Antoine Joseph! He wanted us to watch your comings and goings. He plans to set up a hit using a professional assassin."

Jacques recognizes the name. Joseph had been on the Colombian trip and headed up one of the five groups that moved cocaine from the initial *Medellín* shipment. From what Jacques had seen on the Colombian visit and heard about the man's later pronouncements, Joseph had been trying to frame himself as the cream of the up-and-coming crop of Haitian smugglers. He was resentful and angry that his first serious international smuggling mission had failed. He blamed the failure on the Colombian scheme that involved hiding coke inside statues and figurines. He argued to anyone who would listen that he should never have been required to use such a foolish approach. He believed he would have been successful had he been allowed to devise a plan of his own. A revenge hit seemed to Jacques like something the cocky Joseph would now try to pull off to redeem himself. Knocking off the only successful operator in the recent operation might help him regain some of the respect he had lost.

In a move straight out of the Carlos Escobar playbook of ruthless and cold-blooded intimidation, Jacques orders his captive to drag the lifeless body of his much larger comrade out of the warehouse and load it onto the rear seat of the Renault. It is a difficult struggle and Jacques refuses to allow anyone to provide help. But the blood-covered survivor finally gets the body into the vehicle.

Jacques wants Joseph to understand that not only has his surveillance failed but that his own safety shield has been penetrated. He orders the prisoner to drive the Renault to Antoine Joseph's home and deliver the corpse to Joseph, personally.

Jacques knows that Joseph will not take well the delivery of the body to his doorstep. He will likely punish the returning emissary for his weakness and failure. To make sure the driver doesn't attempt to ditch the vehicle and run off to avoid facing an irate, humiliated, and vengeful boss, Jacques and his crew follow the Renault. He bluffs his dispirited victim, claiming he already knows where Joseph lives. He warns the driver that if he does not proceed directly to Joseph's home, the car will be stopped, and he will be executed on the spot.

Twenty minutes later, Jacques watches the Renault pull into the driveway of a small home on *Rue D Martineau*. The front door opens; three men step out and approach the vehicle. His mission of retribution and disrespect complete, Jacques signals Sonny to drive off.

Sonny reminds Jacques that although he has won this round, the war is far from over. Joseph is now a wounded and angry adversary. He will forever be looking for an opportunity to knock Jacques off his perch. The more success the young dealer enjoys, Sonny counsels, the more he will become a target for the envious Joseph and others like him.

With the refinement of his bag-switching technique, Jacques is now moving weekly shipments of cocaine into the US through both New York and Miami. He has three couriers transporting a total of more than twenty-five kilos each week through New York's JFK Airport. An additional courier moves eight kilos per week through Miami International. Since all his wholesale customers are now in the New York metro area, Jacques is even considering dropping the Miami connection. Doing so will avoid the inconvenience of moving drugs from Miami to New York.

While the bag-switching routine is the model of simplicity and efficiency, Jacques knows that there is always the risk the operation could be discovered. A bust will result in the apprehension of both the courier and the cooperating customs agent, as well as the confiscation of the product. He has been using the scheme now for almost two years with no trouble but doesn't want to push his luck. Since the DEA is always getting smarter, he will have to keep adjusting his routine to stay a step ahead of them.

In recent months he has rarely carried product himself, although from time to time, he flies on the same flight as his couriers. Instead, he focuses his monthly trips on meeting prospective customers and negotiating new deals. When he meets new clients, he often uses aliases. He has also begun exploring new smuggling techniques. His goal is to diversify and expand his operation and hedge against the possible loss of his bag-switching routine. He has recently worked out a process for embedding cocaine-filled containers into the shipments of asphalt from Trinidad that work their way through the Caribbean to their ultimate destination in the States.

With the benefit of his various smuggling schemes, receipts are pouring in. They come in not only as cash but in the form of jewelry, art, and even automobiles. Acquiring expensive vehicles helps Jacques launder the large sums of money he moves out of the US.

At Sonny's urging, Jacques begins looking for new living quarters that will provide improved security and closer proximity to the Haitian political and cultural center of gravity. An upgrade will allow Jacques to showcase the lifestyle and symbols of wealth expected of a man of his growing stature. With the completion of his latest *Collège Saint-Louis* degree, there is little to tie him and Sonny to Jérémie. They begin searching for property near the capital.

After several months of prospecting, they settle on a large gated mansion in the *ViVi Michel* hilltop enclave outside Port-au-Prince. They modify the property to incorporate bulletproof glass windows, electrified perimeter detection equipment, and a helicopter landing pad. The mansion already had waterfront access and no natural or man-made barriers that would interfere with the use of satellite communication.

Six months after buying the property and completing extensive modifications, Jacques moves into the compound in the Spring of 1992. He calls it 'The Ranch.' It incorporates comfortable quarters for Sonny, who is usually on hand to supervise round-the-clock security and counsel with Jacques. But the big man holds on to their modest Jérémie house. He uses it as a getaway for those few moments of privacy he might wish to enjoy when his presence is not required at the Ranch.

Several weeks pass before Jacques and Sonny acclimate themselves to the mansion's size and luxurious accommodations. Jacques can hardly believe his eyes when they come upon a climate-controlled wine cellar that the realtor who sold them the villa had overlooked.

"Damn, Sonny, can you believe this place? It wasn't but a couple of years ago that our whole living space, including the bathroom, could have fit into this wine cellar with room left over."

"Yeah," Sonny answers, "we've come a long way since that sauna at Mme Picard's we used to call a bedroom. I wouldn't be surprised if there aren't a few more hidden spaces around here, maybe even a secret room or passageway we may have missed."

Jacques becomes fascinated with the whirlpool bathtubs in several of the bathrooms, one of them big enough to accommodate three people. He begins having the cook serve him snacks while he bathes and watches television. Sonny's favorite area is a large screened porch that looks out over a backyard arboretum of flowering plants and trees. He often enjoys a cigar and brandy while relaxing in one of the porch's comfortable rattan easy chairs. He loves the vivid colors of the tranquil setting and is fascinated by the old-fashioned screen door. Pulled closed by a spring, it slams with a sound that reminds him of the porch door on the very first house he remembered living in as a child.

At the urging of his godfather, Julien DuFrane, Jacques hosts an elaborate reception a few weeks after he moves into his new home. The event provides an opportunity to introduce himself to the movers and shakers of Haitian political and business circles. Sparing no expense, he entertains his guests with the finest champagnes and spirits and an elegant buffet meal prepared by several of the most sought-after chefs on the island. He consults his New York *Molly* contact, Carlos Marquez, to incorporate an element of New York sophistication into his soiree. Through Carlos, he brings in a popular Afro-Cuban jazz ensemble that is a regular at New York's *Blue Note*. The group shares the entertainment duties with a local Haitian band. One performs in the banquet room, the other on a large, shaded outdoor terrace.

More than two hundred guests are invited to the lavish party. Jacques had previously known no more than a dozen of the invitees, as M. DuFrane has created the guest list. But Jacques has no trouble engaging his company. He impresses them with cultured and enlightened conversation. His behavior defies the expected image of a brash young entrepreneur with questionable income and an unknown pedigree. He has specifically invited a small group of administrators and faculty from the *Université d'Etat d'Haiti*. He charms the university president with an animated discussion of his commitment to higher education and his desire to provide financial assistance to the university. The previous June, Jacques had earned a BA in Psychology at the *Collège Saint-Louis* and the flattered administrator promises to support his application for admission to the forensic psychology PhD program.

The gregarious Jacques warms up to his duties as host. He sharpens his charm offensive and enjoys his role as an important new addition to Haiti's power elite. But he is caught off guard by the attention showed him by many of his female guests. Having grown up a poor undersized street kid who had been shunned even by his own family, he is unprepared for the situation. Because of his awkward and unfulfilled past, he had developed a feigned posture of disinterest in the opposite sex. Tonight, for the first time in his life, Jacques enjoys the fawning attention of both single and married women. He knows their interest is shallow and based on his newfound wealth. But he still enjoys the proximity of the beautifully costumed and perfumed guests eager to gain his favor. Several of them not-so-discretely provide contact information and let him know of their availability and interest in furthering a relationship. To avoid sending premature signals of commitment, Jacques stays on the move, mingling with new groups throughout the evening. But there is no doubt he is excited by his new popularity with the ladies.

In the coming months, Jacques revels in his new stud status. He enjoys an endless stream of female company at home and on his trips to the States. But he begins spending most of his time with one woman. Catheline Dabrezil is a gorgeous and ambitious Haitian who had moved to Miami but is back in Port-au-Prince, working as an on-air personality for a local television broadcaster. Mesmerized by her beauty and charisma, Jacques loves spending time and being seen with the statuesque beauty who stands a full head taller than him. The newly self-aware young striver feels as if he has bested all other suitors and won the exclusive favor of a goddess. But his sense of empowerment extends far beyond his achievement with Catheline. Still, despite the cockiness, shrewdness and self-confidence that has propelled him in the disparate worlds of drug-dealing and academia, Jacques is amazed at how far he has come since his days on the streets. In little more than a decade he has become a wealthy entrepreneur and is pursuing an advanced university degree. After a whirlwind courtship punctuated by spontaneous vacation trips and extravagant shopping excursions to New York and Paris, he and Catheline prepare for a lavish June, 1993 wedding at the Ranch.

Seven

Hofstra

"So how you doing, Big Money? You got enough room under your mattress for all the loot you're pulling in?" Sonny teases Jacques over breakfast at the Ranch, the first opportunity for relaxed conversation they've had in several weeks. In the four years since Jacques moved into the mansion, he and Sonny have been together most days. But as Jacques is now completing preparations for his PhD defense, he and Sonny havn't had much time to talk other than which was necessary for business.

"No complaints," Jacques responds. "A little too busy at times, but too much business is the kind of problem I like. With the three new customers we just picked up in New York, last month is turning out to be our biggest month ever.

"Millevoix and his people are real happy to see their paydays increasing, so everything is tight with them. But one guy who's not so pleased with our good fortune is our old friend, Antoine Joseph. He's still trying to clean up his reputation after the deal that blew up on him back when we did our first Fort Greene transaction. He's been trying to work his way back into the army's good graces and was pissed when they needled him about how well we're doing. I wish I could have been there to see it."

"You got every right to be proud," Sonny replies. "But what else is going on in your world? How's Catheline?"

Jacques takes a deep breath and sighs as his shoulders slump. "Things aren't going all that well at home. Catheline is always upset about something, these days. Everything was fine our first couple of years together. But in the six months since the twins were born, things have gone downhill."

"And the teaching?" Sonny persists as Jacques falls silent.

"Still working the gig at Hofstra. I'll be teaching a couple of advanced psychology classes next semester."

The ease with which Jacques always shared the successes, struggles, and even the gossip of his narcotics hustle told Sonny how important that world had become to him. The energy and enthusiasm he invested in his work made it clear how much he enjoyed inhabiting and navigating the narcotics scene. Conversely, his reluctance to discuss his marriage and teaching plans and his inability to convey even the least sense of fulfillment in either area confirmed that all was not right in these parts of his life.

Sonny could see for himself the problems in Jacques's marriage. At times, the younger man seemed to enjoy being married to Catheline. But he also found it difficult to sever ties with the following of girlfriends he had cultivated in his bachelor months at the mansion. His extramarital involvements increased when Catheline gave birth to their children. The attention she previously showered on him now had to be shared with the babies.

Catheline tried to ignore Jacques's womanizing, hoping it was a stage through which he would pass. But when she finally confronted him about his frequent late nights out and all-night meetings, he took offense. He was insulted that she would attempt to question his male prerogative. As the confrontations increased, Jacques shed his cultured and gentlemanly demeanor. He began pushing back at what he perceived as carping and nagging. The situation deteriorated so far that in one particularly nasty confrontation in front of their children not quite two years into their marriage, Jacques hit Catheline in the face and blacked her eye. Things were never the same after that. Although they went through the motions, the life had gone out of their marriage. Catheline felt all alone but didn't yet know what to do about it.

———— •◆• ————

As little as Jacques talked to Sonny about his marriage, he shared even less about his academic life. Sonny hadn't even known that Jacques was teaching until he got a call from him a year ago asking to be picked up at Hofstra University in Hempstead, a Long Island suburb of New York City. That day in the fall of 1995 was the first time Sonny heard the name: Fernand Pierre-Paul. As he picked Jacques up, he overheard a student address him as Dr. Pierre-Paul. Jacques had been teaching at Hofstra for the previous two semesters.

At the time, Sonny had been accompanying Jacques to New York to provide security during his drug transactions. But, after deliveries, Jacques might disappear for a day or two without telling Sonny of his whereabouts. In some cases, Sonny would return to Haiti alone and not see Jacques until many days later. It was an odd situation considering Sonny's responsibility to provide round-the-clock security to the ambitious drug lord.

The big man was baffled by Jacques's reticence to discuss a university teaching experience that would make most people proud. A few days after his hurried first visit, Sonny had returned to Hofstra, uninvited and unannounced. Hoping to observe the young academic imparting knowledge to a classroom of eager students, Sonny was disappointed to find that Jacques was not lecturing or conducting office hours that day. After a brief stroll around the sprawling suburban campus, he walked to Jacques's apartment.

"Since I was in the neighborhood, I thought I'd stop by for quick visit," Sonny wisecracked when the normally outgoing and talkative Jacques answered the door, stone-faced and almost sullen.

Jacques was a different person. He was clean-shaven, wore eyeglasses, and had on a dress shirt with a necktie pulled down. A reserved, serious demeanor had replaced his cocky drug dealer swagger. Sonny could hardly believe his eyes.

"Well, this is sure a surprise," Jacques remarked dryly as he invited Sonny into the small apartment and introduced him to Lilly Rodride, a Hofstra colleague on whose PhD degree committee he sat. Lilly was seated at his kitchen table in her stocking feet, sipping coffee. Jacques's unsolicited explanation that Lilly had stopped by to drop off some work papers seemed uncharacteristically awkward. It somehow didn't ring true. Back in Haiti, Jacques flaunted an endless string of girlfriends as a perk of his drug lord status. What was it about his academic life that could make him seem so uptight and reserved, Sonny wondered. Was it all part of an assumed scholarly identity? Or was it something else?

———◆———

Sonny notices how hard Jacques works to keep his drug lord and college professor lives separate. His passport always matches the role he is in, as does his grooming and attire. But on occasion, he can't avoid commingling his roles, especially now that Sonny is involved in his dual life. As his business continues to grow, there are instances when he is in New York in his academic identity, but will slip away with Sonny to tend to some narcotics business.

Whenever Sonny is temporarily drawn into Jacques teaching environment, he uses the opportunity to learn all he can about the Pierre-Paul alter ego. On occasion, he will even sit in on Fernand's psychology class lectures. While he doesn't understand the underlying science, he is always impressed by the fascinating topics and Jacques's ability to breathe excitement into the subject matter.

When it becomes clear to him that Lilly Rodride is Pierre-Paul's constant companion and more than just a fellow instructor, Sonny tries to find out what could he can about her. But he does his digging unobtrusively, as he knows Jacques would be offended by the probing. He even attends one of her standing-room-only lectures which were attracting students from all fields of study and even visitors from other universities.

As much as he is impressed with Fernand's academic performance, Sonny is even more amazed by Lilly's. The attractive young Martinican, still in her midtwenties, is a computer scientist working on a breakthrough new technology that is causing a stir in the computer world. In the narrow, male-dominated society in which he had grown up, he'd never seen anything like the trail she was blazing. Sonny can't understand how this amazing young academic fits into Jacques's complicated life.

Eight

Inspiration

"Suppose you could read a document and see past the words on paper to understand what the author really meant to say and whether or not her message is truthful," asks the young teaching assistant. Lilly Rodride's audience is a group of Hofstra computer science students at a Fall, 1999 artificial intelligence symposium. They have come to hear about her doctoral dissertation research and possibly join her research team. Sonny has seen the meeting notice, found his way to her class and stands at the back of the packed room.

"Wouldn't it be useful to be able to read a document and then form a picture—a profile if you will—of the author? If the document is a proposal, wouldn't it be valuable to know whether its commitments can be believed? Or if the document is a sales brochure, that its claims are legitimate?"

Without pausing for an answer to her rhetorical question, she continues. "My research is aimed at creating tools that can provide these kinds of insights. I am developing computer-based processes that read documents and profile authors as to a variety of factors: age, gender, demographics, and, most importantly, personality. At the core of my work are new 'machine learning' methods. They enable computers to analyze large quantities of information, perform calculations, and make decisions without being explicitly programmed to do so. By evaluating the patterns and trends of the information it receives, the computer learns what information is essential and how to analyze that information to answer relevant questions.

"In the emerging global information environment, author profiling will have wide application. It will be useful in domains ranging from sales and marketing to forensics, security, and law enforcement. If deployed in the world of commerce, consumers might be more prepared to make informed purchasing decisions. And businesses might be better able to determine what buyers really think of their products. In law enforcement, criminal or terrorist suspects could be identified by their writing. And the process would work regardless of the size and volume of documents that might have to be analyzed. Author profiling could also have a major impact in many other areas of public interest."

Out of the roomful of mostly third and fourth-year computer science students assembled in Davison Hall, Lilly will pick five to work on her team. Having taught several basic level CS courses for the past three years, Lilly already knows most of the students in the room. She has a good idea of those with whom she might like to work. The purpose of today's meeting is to determine the level of student interest in her research.

The group begins asking questions, some out of curiosity about her topic, others because they want to be heard and noticed. In their rush to impress, some raise issues that are trite or not on point.

"So this is a computerized version of handwriting analysis?" one student inquires.

"Not quite," Lilly responds patiently. "Handwriting analysis examines the way a writer forms characters in a handwritten document. Certain writing characteristics point to corresponding personality attributes. But for my profiling, I don't care about handwriting. In fact, the source documents for my research can be handwritten, typewritten, pages from a book, or even taped conversations. I'm more concerned about the author's choice of words and the patterns in which they are used."

Some of the more interesting questions involve the ethics of the project and its impact on society, as privacy issues have recently become a hot topic of debate in the public square. There have been recent concerns about the intrusion of business and government into the private lives of citizens. A 1988 federal law had outlawed polygraphs and other lie detector tests for employment screening. Opining that her research has 'Orwellian overtones,' one student suggests that Lilly's work could destroy the concept of privacy as it is known today.

"Of course, technology can be used to both harm and help society," Lilly responds, now warming to the more interesting and thought-provoking discussion. "But as I see it, we shouldn't throttle our creativity because some new ideas might be used in a way that is harmful or not initially envisioned. If we did, we never would have seen such innovations as dynamite, gunpowder, or airplanes, just to name a few. Because those inventions were used as weapons of war does not mean they serve no useful purpose to society. The dropping of atomic bombs on civilians in World War II can be viewed as a high crime against humanity. But it does not diminish the importance of nuclear power and air travel to modern society. And as to Orwell, 1984 has already come and gone. For all our scientific progress, most of the abuses Orwell wrote about never came to pass."

The day following her presentation, Lilly selects her team. Four of them are fresh-faced undergrad kids, all with high grade point averages. The fifth, Gilbert Hunt, is older, having served a tour of duty in Afghanistan with the US Army. The rookie Nassau County cop is twenty-seven years old, the same age as Lilly. Believing computer science would be a real plus in his law enforcement career, he works evenings at the police department so he can attend classes full-time during the day. Gilbert knows Lilly's age because they attended elementary school together. An exceptional student and an unusual child, she had made a big impression on young Gilbert. But it now appears that she doesn't remember him. Embarrassed that he is the oldest in all of his classes and the same age as his instructor, he is reluctant to remind Lilly that they had once been classmates. If she doesn't remember those days, it is fine with him.

The research team begins its work in the spring of 2000 as Gilbert is completing his third year at Hofstra. In preparation for their first meeting, Lilly distributes background papers describing her project. Like many milestone innovations, Lilly's core concepts are not complicated. Her algorithm is built around the idea that word choice in the composition of a document is based on the personality and demographics of the writer. For this reason, she believes it will be possible to profile authors based on their written words.

Using a list of one thousand carefully selected keywords, she set up a computer to scan documents written by a group of volunteer student authors and count the number of times the keywords were used. Keywords used most frequently by female authors were designated female 'features. ' Those used most by males, were male features. She programmed the computer to classify as 'female-authored,' those documents using more female than male features. 'Male-authored' were those using more male than female features. This was the *classification* component of her learning algorithm. It was that simple and that brilliant.

———◆———

Although he spends almost as much time assisting in Lilly's research as he does on his coursework, Gilbert finishes the school year with high grades. They earn him an invitation to join the Hofstra chapter of *Kappa Mu Epsilon,* the national mathematics honor society. The four other members of the research team are also invited. The ceremony takes place at an evening candlelight dinner ceremony attended by the full chapter membership, most of the mathematics and computer science faculty, and a few professors from other departments. Lilly, a dais speaker that spring evening, is seated next to one of the few non-technology faculty members in attendance, Professor Fernand Pierre-Paul. Lilly and her academic colleagues have no way of knowing that Pierre-Paul, a rising star in the field of forensic psychology, is the alter ego of a notorious Haitian drug lord.

At the mixer following the dinner and initiation ceremony, Lilly visits the table at which her research team is seated. She is accompanied by the fastidiously dressed and heavily cologned Pierre-Paul. As Lilly introduces the professor, Gilbert, now called Gil by the team, is struck by the softness of the professor's carefully manicured hand. Pierre-Paul's hand is so small that he is barely able to return Gil's grip as the two shake hands. The professor greets and congratulates the team in a rich bass-baritone voice that is out of sync with his small stature and slight frame. It reminds Gil of the mesmerizing and chilling character, *Mephistopheles,* he had seen in a performance of the opera, *Faust,* at the Hofstra theatre. The professor thanks the group for the contributions to science he is sure they will make in the course of their careers. With dramatic eloquence no less compelling than that of the operatic Prince of Darkness, he pledges his support and assures everyone that his office door will always be open to them.

Pierre-Paul's conversation and demeanor are congenial. But, everyone notices how he positions himself so that he stands squarely between Lilly and her research team. It is a power move that takes Lilly out of the conversation. With a vaguely condescending manner, he comments at length on Lilly's work. He expresses his hope that the goals of her project will be achieved.

Strange behavior, Gil muses. Isn't the professor aware of the groundbreaking nature of Lilly's work? Hasn't he heard that her experiments are already the talk of the machine learning world? Gil has always thought a PhD committee member is supposed to be a mentor who supportively guides his candidate through the challenges of dissertation research—someone who protects her from those who might unfairly criticize or block her growth. But here was the little professor ever-so-slightly diminishing his candidate in front of her students. Like an animal spraying his surroundings, he also seems to be marking his turf. And he is doing so more aggressively than one might expect in an educational setting. Maybe there is more to this than academics, Gil thinks.

———•◆•———

Over the summer break, Gil takes no classes. But he continues to assist Lilly on her project, meeting with her and other team members every other Saturday afternoon. On the day of their first meeting in July, he helps his sister move into her new apartment and can't make the scheduled meeting time. But because Lilly urgently needs data he has compiled on the results of recent modifications to the classification algorithm, she asks if he can drop his results off at her parents' home in St. Albans when his sister's move is completed. Even though Lilly still lives in the Greenwich Village apartment she used as an NYU undergrad, she frequently spends evenings and weekends at her parents' home because of its proximity to Hofstra.

Upon his arrival that evening, Gil is welcomed into the Rodride home by Lilly's mother, a shorter, slightly plump, but just as pretty version of her only child. Shy and soft-spoken, she has Lilly's same full mane of hair and a slightly darker complexion. Gil introduces himself as a member of Lilly's Hofstra research team. Instead of walking him around the side of the house to the backyard where Lilly said she would be working, Mrs. Rodride escorts him through the crowded, hot living room in which a dozen or so men stand in a circle, their glasses raised. One of them, his shirt opened and untucked, a handkerchief tied around his neck as a sweatband, leads the others in a rousing toast in French.

"Sommes-nou Française ou ne le sommes-nous pas?" (Are we French or aren't we?)

"Yes, Ro-Ro!" "*Oui, Monsieur!*" "Of course!" "Cheers!" the men surrounding him respond enthusiastically.

One of them offers a second toast.

"*Pour notre famille coloniale française!*" (To our French colonial family)

As Mrs. Rodride stands with Gil waiting for an opportunity to lead him through the crowded room to the backyard, the toasting continues. Each toast is more passionate than the one before it. By the time all the men have spoken, a few are almost in tears. Before they are done, glasses are filled several times.

After the final toast, the men separate into several animated conversations. One involves a spirited game of dominos, with players loudly slapping their tiles to one of several card tables set up in the room. The tall, light-skinned man who led the toasts, walks into the adjoining dining room with one of the guests. He seats himself at the head of the dining table and directs the younger man to sit facing him at the far end of the table. When signaled by a nod of his host's head, the younger man begins, in an earnest and hushed tone, a short statement in Martinican Creole. The host listens intently to his guest's remarks, nodding occasionally. At their conclusion, he offers a few words of his own to which the guest responds with a broad smile. The appreciative guest thanks his host as he stands and backs out of the dining room.

The tall Martinican signals for someone else to join him at the table. But before anyone is able to do so, Lilly walks into the room from a hallway leading to the backyard. Motioning to Gil to join her, she says: "Excuse me, Papa, I would like to introduce you to someone. I didn't remember it until he reminded me today, but he and I were once classmates at P.S. 40."

As her father turns in his seat to face Gil, Lilly continues, "This is Gil Hunt. He is now a student at Hofstra and is working with me on my research."

"I'm pleased to meet you, sir," Gil says, extending his hand. The strapping Martinican, who looks to be in his late sixties but still very fit, shakes Gil's hand firmly. Without smiling, he responds, "Will you be staying a while longer?"

"Yes, sir," Gil replies.

"Good," Lilly's father answers, "then we can talk later."

"We'll be out back, Papa," Lilly says as she escorts Gil out to the yard.

"Looks like I barged in on some kind of a celebration," Gil comments as he and Lilly settle into large wooden lawn chairs situated near a vegetable garden that takes up almost half the yard.

"Next Tuesday is Bastille Day," Lilly replies. "It's a big day for these Martinicans. As you saw, they're very patriotic and sentimental about it. Even though they all speak English pretty well, when they get together, they usually speak Creole. But because they were toasting Bastille Day, they used their best French.

"They're all settled here in America, yet they hang onto their French culture. Most of them are now American citizens, but they think of themselves as having dual citizenship. Many of them live very modestly here in the States so that they can save their money, buy property, and build nice houses back in Martinique. When they retire, they look forward to moving back and living like big shots."

"It's interesting that these men bond more on national than racial identity," Gil observes. "But despite their French roots and their Martinican pride, they are Black men in America. They must be aware that the issues they face as men of color, the discrimination they face on the job, or the hassle they get from white cops isn't because they're French. It's because they're Black. Here in America, they face more challenges because of their color than because of their national heritage. Doesn't that affect their sense of identity?"

"These are mostly older guys who came along a generation before the black power and black nationalist awareness of the sixties. So they don't relate well to that kind of thinking," Lilly answers. "They've all faced plenty of discrimination here. Sometimes it's even worse for them than for African Americans because of the language barrier. But because they also often face discrimination from African Americans, their default allegiance is usually to France or other French colonials."

"The attitudes and behavior I've seen here are fascinating," Gil replies. "But quite different from the British West Indian mentality, at least the part of it I grew up in. My family and our neighbors always thought they were smarter, more cultured, and of higher social standing than most other West Indians and Americans. But they never seemed to have the same kind of passionate, emotional connection to their Trinidadian cultural identity as what I've witnessed tonight. Trinidadians in the States tend to be very ambitious strivers, working multiple jobs, dabbling in real estate and other entrepreneurial ventures to build a nest egg. But I never see tears of passion for the Trinidadian flag. The mindset I mostly associate with Trinis is striving ambition, doing things the proper way, and righteous indignation when earned respect is not received."

"A few years ago, I made my first Trinidad carnival trip as an adult. Through the Trini mother of my coworker, Angie, I booked a carnival package that included air travel and hotel accommodations. For a long time, Angie's mother, Pearl, had been trying to match me up with her daughter. But at the last moment, Angie had to back out of the trip. It was just as well because even though I had known and liked Angie for many years, neither of us had romantic interests in each other. Her no-show meant I wouldn't have to worry about getting boxed into any awkward situations by a well-meaning but meddling mother playing matchmaker for her daughter."

"But Pearl didn't see it that way," Gil continues, turning to glance through a dining room window at the Martinicans still raising their glasses in endless toasts. "Most of the people in the tour group were traveling with a spouse or partner and were paired off in their hotel room assignments. However, at trip time, there were still two single, un-assigned travelers and only one remaining double room. At LaGuardia Airport, the tour representative gingerly approached me and the other single, a zaftig, dramatically attired middle-aged woman named Rhoda who had the demeanor of someone intent on enjoying every moment of her first-ever carnival. After carefully sizing us up, the agent bluntly asked whether we would mind sharing a room. Although surprised by the unusual but intriguing request, I was in a hedonistic carnival spirit and agreed. With a mischievous smile and a wink, my prospective roommate wisecracked: 'We'll have to mark off sections of the room and the bed that belong to each of us. But I guess I can make it work with this handsome young hunk.'

Lilly smiles at the kind of suggestive comment that would be difficult for her to make. "It's nice when you're able to let it all hang out," she says, winking at Gil and raising her open hands above her head as if she is testifying in church.

"Rhoda and I shared a laugh, shook hands, and introduced ourselves," Gil continued. "But Pearl had heard the entire conversation and erupted in indignation. She was infuriated that a 'decent young man' like me might be coerced into a compromising situation with a 'brazen American hussy' who would be a party to such an outrageous arrangement. As if she were responsible for the protection of my honor and virtue, Pearl read the riot act to the embarrassed agent. He apologized and promised to make sure we were both accommodated with a private room even if he had to pay for it out of his own pocket."

"As it turned out, Rhoda and I had rooms next to each other. But we spent so much time together, we might just as well have been in the same room. Whenever possible, we avoided Pearl's ever-present surveillance. I didn't want to be the target of her next outburst if she thought I had weakened and succumbed to Rhoda's advances. After Carnival, Angie got a big laugh hearing about her mother's efforts to keep me pure and available for her daughter. But Pearl's over-the-top, almost cartoonish antics and her attitude of superiority are defining characteristics of many West Indians from British colonies. For sure, it's the attitude of many in my family."

"Interesting contrast," Lilly responds, "more practicality than passion—more striving than patriotic."

"I suppose so," Gil answers. "Though offensive to many outside the culture and to some inside it, Pearl's attitude of self-confidence and ambition and her desire for status have propelled her and many like her to achieve great things here in the US."

Lilly notices Gil staring at an odd latticework of old venetian blind slats and pipes that had been wired together to support several tomato vines in the vegetable garden. "Although these guys may have nice houses out here in St. Albans," she says, "there's something about a simple, homemade, hardscrabble apparatus like this that keeps them grounded. Stuff like this keeps them in touch with the humble circumstances over which they triumphed to be here in America. They're still coconuts at heart, and in some ways, they will never change. This," she adds, smiling and pointing to the clap-trap tomato-vine support, "is pure coconut!

"Sometimes, though, I have to draw the line with my father. A few weeks ago, he dragged an old radiator out here, turned it on its side, and was getting ready to use it as a planter. When I explained how tacky it looked, he reluctantly threw the radiator in the trash. Occasionally, he listens to me."

"Your father is obviously a pretty important man in this community. The only thing missing in that series of audiences he conducted at the dinner table tonight was the kissing of his hand."

"That's the way it is with these guys. They revere him. As soon as someone arrives here from Martinique or Guadeloupe, the first thing their family does is to get an introduction to my father. Whenever someone has a family dispute, trouble with the kids, or marital problems, they come to see him, and somehow he is usually able to help them. When someone needs work, they talk to him, and more often than not, he opens a few doors.

"Before we moved to Long Island, we lived at 1771 Madison Avenue in Harlem, almost the center of New York's French Colonial community. That building and most around it were filled with families fresh from Martinique, Guadeloupe, and Haiti. In those days, the neighborhood was the arrival area for all new French West Indian families. This central location was a short distance from the many West Indian food markets on Park Avenue where produce and special delicacies from the islands could be purchased. Shortly after the first wave of them arrived in the early 1900s, the men formed *The Society of French Colonials* and held monthly meetings in 1771's basement recreation room. During meetings, they always mounted a large French flag on the wall and pledged their allegiance to it. Even though they no longer meet at 1771, they still get together regularly, especially on days like Bastille Day.

"My father never had much schooling, and he doesn't have a prestigious job. He's been working for the same property management unit of a Midtown Manhattan commercial building for almost twenty-five years. He's the building superintendent now, the guy who opens and locks the doors each day, the man who makes sure that everything in the building is always working and clean. But for most of his years there, he was a janitor. Now he's responsible for seeing that the janitors and repair staff do their jobs.

"He's always worked hard, saved his money, and kept his nose clean. He's a naturally smart and tough guy, and with his age and life experiences, has developed the kind of wisdom these Frenchies seem to appreciate so much."

"Some of the guys kept calling out 'Ro-Ro' during the toasts," Gil says. "What's that all about?"

"My father's first name is Roger. His Martinican nickname is Ro-Ro. But only a few men who are close to him in age and have known him for many years, back from their Martinique days, can call him by that name. You probably noticed that almost everyone addressed him as Mr. Rodride or Monsieur. Name respect is very important in this group."

Lilly and Gil finally get around to her project. By the time they finish discussing the analysis he had done on her latest experiment and reenter the house, all her father's guests have left. Mr. Rodride asks Gil to join him at the table for one more round of refreshments, pointing to the now-vacant chair at the other end of the table. As Gil sits, the

Martinican motions to Lilly, who hands him two rock glasses. Into each, he pours three fingers of whiskey, neat, from a bottle of Four Roses bourbon that stands in the middle of the table.

"So you were classmates, and now she's your teacher? Got the better of you, eh?" Rodride asks in his heavily accented English, the trace of a mischievous smile on his ruggedly handsome face. His daughter cringes as she and her mother peer at the two men from the kitchen. "She's a very smart girl," he proudly adds, now beaming.

"That she is, sir. I'm lucky to be able to work with her."

Although Lilly's father understands that his daughter and Gil are teacher and student, to Gil their conversation has the distinct feeling of a father evaluating the suitability of his daughter's suitor. While Gil enjoys the characterization, the situation is awkward for Lilly.

Satisfied with Gil's responses and demeanor, Rodride raises and drains his glass. Gil attempts to follow suit but needs two tries before he can finish his drink. He struggles with the heat and intense nutty taste of the straight whiskey. While he enjoys alcoholic beverages, usually beer, he rarely drinks straight liquor, and his throat is on fire. Lilly's father, unaware of Gil's discomfort, or maybe because of it, pours another round in each glass. Gil tries to nurse his drink as he responds to his host's questions about where he lives and works.

Gil is suddenly aware that he has a problem. Trying to match the hard-drinking old Martinican was not a good idea. The two double shots of bourbon on an empty stomach have his head spinning, and he doesn't want to stagger as he leaves the table. With Lilly anxiously watching, Gil makes it to his feet, thanks Lilly's father for his hospitality, and reaches the door without incident. Mr. Rodride bids him good night.

Before Lilly begins walking with Gil to his car, Rodride whispers in her ear, in Creole, "This guy is ok. He looks like more of a man than that little schoolteacher, the one with the soft hands. The little turd!"

While Gil hadn't gotten sick in front of Lilly and her family, he isn't in the best condition to drive. Lilly takes the wheel of his car and drives the fifteen minutes to his Hollis Queens apartment. A couple of hours later, after some food and black coffee, Gil is able to drive Lily back to her house and return safely to his place. In the coming months, he and Lilly laugh and joke about how he barely survived his initiation into the drinking rituals of the *Martinican Don* and his faithful subjects. But it will take a little more convincing to get her to tell him what her father confided to her as they left the house that night. Gil thought she didn't want to embarrass him with the wisecracks the Frenchman had probably made about him, the big army veteran who couldn't hold his liquor.

Trouble in Mind

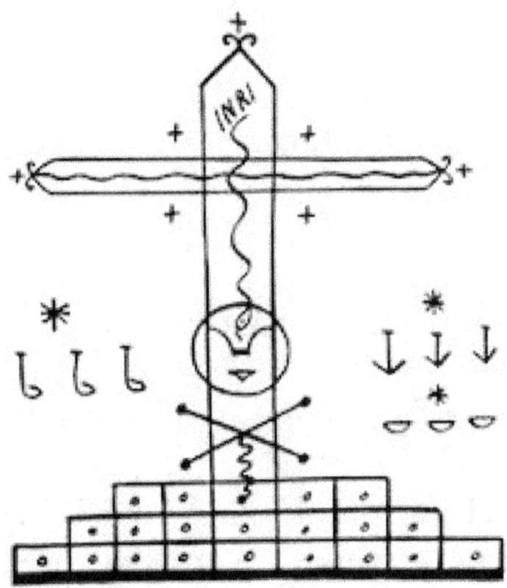

"Stay the hell out of my business!" Jacques yells into his cell phone as he paces in his ViVi Michel den. "You've been interfering with my marriage since day one. Your daughter is a grown-ass woman. She and I can make our own decisions without you. For the last time, back off!" he warns Myou Léon, who had called to protest his escalating physical abuse of her daughter.

On her last visit home, Catheline wore dark glasses and heavy makeup to hide a black eye and a bruised mouth. Myou had seen too much violence in Catheline's short marriage and would tolerate no more of it. "The next time I see you've hurt her, I won't let her come back to Haiti," Myou pushes back.

"You do that, it will be the last thing you ever do!" Jacques shouts, sputtering with rage as he terminates the call.

Refusing to be intimidated, Myou quickly calls back. Without letting Jacques get in a word, she attacks hard.

"You're nothing but a punk! A little man who is tough only when he's beating on a woman or riding Sonny's coattails and those of his *Dechoukaj* thugs. Maybe it's my fault for raising my daughter to be a lady who doesn't know how to deal with a pig like you. But I grew up in the streets, and I've seen your kind of gutter behavior all my life. Your bullying may intimidate Catheline, but it doesn't scare me one bit. So here's the deal, you lay a hand on her once more, you'll never see her again!"

"I've warned you for the last time!" Jacques yells, throwing the phone against the nearest wall, shattering it to pieces.

⬤◆⬤

Aside from the troubled relationship with his disgruntled and resentful trophy wife, Jacques had consolidated his position as the preeminent drug merchant in Haiti. Though only twenty-five, he had survived the Millevoix presidency, weathered the ups and downs of local politics, and the shake-up within the *Medellín* Cartel after the killing of Carlos Escobar. He had come out on top in deadly skirmishes with other ambitious smugglers trying to cut into his action. And he had bribed enough Haitian officials so that he was able to build an airstrip outside of Port-au-Prince that allowed for unrestricted traffic of kilo-loaded planes from Colombia.

Ex-president Henri Millevoix is now back as the army's top general. Since 1994, Jacques has been paying him three to four million dollars per year to allow the movement of more than seventy-thousand pounds of Colombian nose candy through Haiti each year. His two main smuggling techniques, the tried-and-true bag-switching routine and the now-perfected embedding of product into asphalt and cement shipments, are pulling in thirteen million dollars per year.

With strategic bribes and the exchange of favors, Jacques stays close to the levers of power in Haiti's continually changing political landscape. He assisted in the election of new President Jean-Bertrand Aristide. He later survived a coup in which Aristide was removed from office in 1991 and then restored to the presidency in 1994. Generous portions of his payments to Millevoix are earmarked for the president.

Because of his friendship with Aristide, Jacques had been named godfather to one of the former priest's children and had even been feted at the National Palace. He had completed his PhD in record time. His rapid academic progress had been accelerated by generous gifts to the university. Immediately after being awarded his degree, he had been hired as a visiting lecturer by Hofstra and was building a reputation in his psychology specialization.

Only his personal life is at loose ends, as his promiscuity and abusive behavior continue to strain his marriage. Catheline tries to endure her mistreatment by focusing on the materialistic aspects of her life. Such distractions usually get her through a few more months of the troubled marriage and allows Jacques to believe he has survived the latest crisis. But when outside women begin brazenly calling their home, Catheline reaches her breaking point. Instead of confronting Jacques and risking another violent response, she waits until he is away on one of his twice-monthly trips to New York to make her move. She picks the kids up from their nursery school, drives straight to the airport and boards a plane to Miami, where she and the kids remain with her mother in Little Haiti.

By the end of 1999, Catheline has filed for and been granted a divorce. Jacques deeply resents that she has been awarded custody of the boys. But he tries to live with the situation since at least she lets them visit him frequently. But when he gets word that she is spending time with a new guy in Miami, often accompanying him to the *Neptune,* an illegal Little Haiti gambling joint, Jacques strikes back. Deciding that he doesn't want the wrong type of man in his sons' lives, he refuses to let the boys return to the States at the end of their most recent visit.

Two weeks later, Catheline and her brother slip into Haiti unannounced. She picks up the boys from school and heads to the airport for their return to the US. When alerted in the US by one of his men who arrives at the school to find that the kids have already been picked up, Jacques immediately sends word to Port-au-Prince Airport security that no one should be allowed to take his kids out of the country. He gives the same instructions to his contacts at the Dominican Republic border. He alerts his people at the various harbors to be on the lookout for anyone trying to leave the country by boat with the boys.

Jacques had left Haiti a few days earlier and had not planned to return so soon. But he couldn't ignore this brazenness from his ex. There is no way he could allow her to breeze into town with her brother, kidnap the kids and take them back to the States without his approval. He had given explicit instructions to the school never to allow his children to be picked up by anyone not approved by him in advance. Also, pickups were always to be made in a vehicle driven by one of his guards. He had set up these ground rules to not only prevent Catheline from taking off with the boys but also to safeguard against the kidnappings and ransom demands that had become commonplace in Haiti.

Jacques is still fuming when he takes his seat in first class the following morning. He has with him only a small leather shoulder bag, which he places on the seat next to him under his folded sports jacket. His wraparound sunglasses and panama straw hat, the brim pulled down front and back, partly shield him from the intrusive stares of the crowd now filing past him into the packed coach section. If he had his way, these people with their noisy children, tacky carry-on bundles, and greasy food containers would be boarded through another door to the rear so they wouldn't disturb the peace and quiet of first class.

Jacques knows he will have to teach some people a few lessons, starting with the sloppy administrators at the *Union School*. He pays top money to keep his kids in a safe and secure environment where this kind of mess is not supposed to happen. He will also have to deal with Catheline and her smart-ass mother.

He is sure that Myou is the real culprit behind the abduction, as it is unlikely that Catheline and her brother would have pulled this off on their own. It is that troublemaking Myou, a nickel-slick, small-time hustler in Miami's Little Haiti, who cooked up the whole idea. She had been a thorn in his side ever since he met her daughter. He is sure that if it weren't for her, Catheline would be no problem. She might even try to come back to him, and under the right circumstances, he would consider taking her back.

Sonny meets Jacques at the airport and takes him directly to the school as the situation with his kids will have to be taken care of before he goes home. As they speed away from the airport in a black Cadillac Escalade shielded with dark tinted windows all around, he checks his telephone messages and asks Sonny whether there are any new leads on the whereabouts of his children. The big man has nothing to report but tells Jacques he is confident the boys are still somewhere on the island with their mother and her brother.

A half hour later, the big SUV pulls to a stop behind the administrator's Peugeot. Jacques is angrier than ever at still having no news about his children. He steps out of the Cadillac and walks impatiently by the guards at the front door who know better than to challenge him. Without saying a word to the nervous secretary, he barges into the schoolmaster's office.

After parking the car, Sonny rejoins Jacques, who now confronts the frightened administrator.

"Where in the hell are my children?" Jacques yells, his face not more than six inches from that of Dr. Jean-Claude Bol, Union's principal.

"I apologize for not being able to answer that question, M. Maurice. When they were released to their mother after school yesterday, our people thought she was authorized to pick them up. Usually, there is no problem with either parent picking up their children."

"Well, this isn't the usual case, so I don't want to hear about what you usually do." In his anger, Jacques spits out each word with a spray of saliva into the administrator's face.

"There are a lot of people who would abduct and hurt my kids and make me pay a lot of money to see them again. That's why I pay this expensive tuition—so I won't have to worry about that kind of bullshit.

"You better hope I find my children, unharmed, and very soon, or your days at this school and maybe even on this earth are numbered. If I decide to let them continue here, I will hold you responsible for their whereabouts and well-being at all times. If their safety is ever again in doubt, if for even five minutes they can't be located on the school grounds, or they take too long in the bathroom, you will have to answer to me. And when I finish with you, you'll regret the day you were born! Do I make myself clear?" Jacques demands of the terrified educator now cowering before him, his head awkwardly lowered, his eyes closed and his hands clasped at his chest.

"Then look at me when I talk to you, motherfucker ... and answer me like a man!"

"Yes, I understand," his stricken victim replies in a hoarse voice cracking from panic and humiliation.

"And what I said goes the same for that dumb-ass secretary of yours, those sorry guards, and everybody else who works here. You'll all pay the price if I ever have to come back here again to deal with this kind of shit!"

Jacques leaves the office and steps back into the big Cadillac in time to answer a call from one of his men. A few moments earlier, Catheline had dropped off the kids at the Ranch without a word to the guard working the gate. There was a male in the car with her, the same one, likely her brother, who had been seen with her a day earlier in a Port-au-Prince market.

——◆——

Myou Léon had worked hard all her life. Splitting her time between orderly work at a nursing home and flipping burgers at the airport. She had scratched and saved enough to open a video arcade in Little Haiti and a travel agency that specialized in travel to Haiti. Despite her grueling work schedule, the ambitious young businesswoman showered as much attention as she could on her two children. She always stressed to them the importance of education. Her friendly talk to everyone, including the neighborhood prostitutes, and her willingness to front empty-pocketed Haitians trying to return home for a family funeral endeared her to the community. When every business on 54th Street in Little Haiti was robbed, her small office was never hit. Still, there were always challenges. When her husband, who operated a local restaurant and also ran the *Bolita*, an illegal lottery, was gunned down in front of their home with the engine still running on his Mercedes, she soldiered on.

She thinks she had passed through most of her trials in life and can now enjoy watching her grandchildren grow up. But as she prepares to leave her office to pick up her daughter and grandsons at the airport, Catheline calls to tell her that she has been unable to get the boys out of the country. She has just dropped them off at their father's home and will be returning to Miami with her brother on the next available flight. As Myou locks the door to the small travel agency, disappointed that she will not be seeing the boys any time soon, a Toyota sedan screeches to a stop at the curb in front of her office. From the open passenger window, a gunman fires six shots, dropping Myou in her own doorway, her keys still in the door. As the Toyota roars off, shocked neighbors and passersby rush to help the tough, still-young grandmother who lies dying in the street.

By the time an ambulance arrives, all the life has drained out of Myou's body. It is never proved that Jacques ordered the hit. But Catheline never again speaks to him, and as the boys grow older, they find many excuses to avoid him.

Ten

Lilly's Request

"Gil, I need a favor," Lilly says as the two walk to their cars after a late afternoon research team meeting. "Next Friday, at our annual ball, my sorority is honoring me as *Soror of the Year* in recognition of my computer profiling work. Unfortunately, the guy who was going to be my date got called out of town. It's an important event, and I'd prefer not to attend alone. Would you be my escort for the evening?"

"I'd love to be your date, even if I'm only backup," Gil answers. "Give me the details, and I'm at your service, ma'am."

Though Lilly doesn't mention Professor Pierre-Paul, Gil assumes it is he who backed out of the engagement. Because of the professor's position as her PhD advisor, Lilly had always attempted to be discreet, but it was always clear to Gil that the two were in some kind of a relationship.

Lilly has been somewhat down the past few days. Gil assumes the pressure of her upcoming PhD dissertation defense and a grueling summer of project work has thrown her off her game. He now understands what may have indeed been bothering her. Although he doesn't like seeing Lilly in distress, a part of him welcomes the situation. It will give him a chance to spend time with her that has nothing to do with school or work. He will try to help make the event very special for her.

While Gil is correct in sensing that Lilly has been disappointed by the escort situation, there is more to her recent low spirits. There is a bigger problem that also involves the professor.

Things have gone well for the team over the summer. Good progress has been made incorporating personality dimensions into the profiling algorithm. But one profiling feature, 'honesty,' poses particular challenges. Because it is such an essential aspect of moral character and a critical factor in all ethical, religious, and social value systems, it is, by far, the most challenging personality component to profile.

While many people can accept not being thought of as open, agreeable, or even conscientious, and might enjoy being typed a loner, a rugged individualist or a non-conformist, no one ever wants to be thought of as untruthful. For most, to be tainted with even a hint of dishonesty is an anathema. This sensitivity made it hard to assess authors without shaming them. Test authors were assigned code names so that their identities were never revealed, and their test scores and labels were kept confidential. Still, many were unable to answer questions that might make them appear the slightest bit dishonest, even if only anonymously and to a computer. The team's challenge was to devise and administer questions that did not intimidate or embarrass an author, while still accurately assessing his or her message as to its sincerity, straightforwardness, and adherence to known facts.

Lilly knew she might not receive forthright responses to such overt questions as: 'Are you honest?', 'Have you ever stolen anything?', or even 'Have you ever lied on an employment application?' For this reason, she included in her test veiled-purpose queries such as: 'Do you like to take chances?' or 'Do you feel guilty when you do something you should not do?' These covert questions were more likely to yield candid answers and accurate personality insights.

By the beginning of the new school year, Lilly and her team had completed the training and testing of her algorithm. It classified features such as 'gender,' 'English as a native language,' 'openness' and 'honesty' with a high probability of accuracy. All other features it classified with reasonable probability. Lilly was pleased that her algorithm could profile so many dimensions and characterize what she considered the most critical of personality aspects, honesty.

As she put the final touches on her dissertation and planned for its defense before her committee, she and her team began using publicly available documents to profile authors not previously involved in the testing. Some were written by known public figures, including a few members of the university faculty and administration. Because staff members or committees often prepared these documents, profiles could not always be attributed to the document signer or issuer.

But there were surprises. Lilly is shocked when a document composed by Fernand Pierre-Paul returns a profile indicating, with high probability, that he had not been open or honest in his writing. His was a memo that had been prepared in response to one of Lilly's research reports. It had been pulled from her bulletin board and submitted to the classifier by one of her team members. Believing the communication might have been edited or written by a staff member, she again profiles the professor. This time she uses a letter he had written in his own handwriting a few months earlier. Because the message was of a personal nature, she is confident it will be a more accurate indicator of his thoughts and state of mind. She submits it without the involvement of any other team members. And she makes sure the profile results aren't saved in the computer or shared with anyone. To her dismay, the new message is also classified as dishonest.

Lilly knew all the reasons why she should not be upset by the situation. Her algorithm simply reported that, based on two hundred and fifty words selected from a single document, it was probable that the professor had not communicated honestly. That meant there was some possibility that his words were truthful. And there was also the chance that on another occasion, he might test out with different results.

After a few frustrating hours of trying to rationalize away the results of her own algorithm, Lilly gets a grip on herself and realizes the game she is playing. Because she doesn't like a particular outcome, she is questioning the process she has worked so long to create. As a person of science, she knows she shouldn't let emotion cloud her reasoning. Since she has several more personal letters from the professor, she decides to run them all through the classifier and let the results speak for themselves. She is shaken but somehow not surprised when the algorithm classifies them all as dishonest.

------◆------

The ball is a festive evening of great music, good food, and the company of elegant sorority women and their dapper, black-tie escorts. Although Gil rarely attends formal events, he is glad he decided to buy his own tux. A rental suit would not have done justice to the affair, Lilly's award, and her gracious acceptance remarks.

Although she is usually conservatively attired for her academic duties, wearing pants suits or slacks and a blouse, and an occasional skirt or even jeans, tonight Lilly pulls out all the stops to create a glamorous look. Her beauty and femininity, always in check on campus, are on full display for this event. Her simple but elegant pale green gown exposes her shoulders and reveals curves usually hidden in her borderline-nerdy campus attire. Her dramatic french roll hairdo and elbow-length gloves, adorned at one wrist with a pink rhinestone bracelet, add a classic touch that sets her apart from everyone else.

Even though she lectures twice each week to her two computer science classes, Lilly has never before addressed such a broad and prestigious audience. The assembled are members of the sorority's alumni chapters in the New York metro area. All are all high achieving professional women, most of them older than Lilly. Her impassioned remarks calling for young women of color to escape stereotypical career paths and break into science and technology fields are a big hit with her enthusiastic audience and their escorts. Following her comments and the singing of the sorority hymn by the members, everyone enjoys more socializing and dancing. At the end of the ball, Lilly and Gil join a few of the sorors and their guests at a private after-party atop the Washington Square hotel in which the affair had been held.

It is almost 4:00 a.m. when Gil and Lilly finally arrive at the door of her apartment.

"You'd better come in for some coffee before you hit the freeway back to Queens," Lilly urges Gil. "I don't want to hear about you wrapped up around a telephone pole after falling asleep on Grand Central Parkway."

Gil accepts Lilly's invitation and steps into her small but comfortable apartment, seating himself on a sofa facing a large picture window that overlooks a now-deserted Macdougall Street and Washington Square Park. As Lilly brews coffee, Gil undoes his bow tie. He is happy to finally own and wear a self-tie bow tie, as he never thought a man could consider himself well-dressed if he wore a clip-on bow tie.

As she serves his coffee, Lilly again thanks Gil for being her date.

"I wouldn't have missed it for anything," he answers. "When I first met you at P.S. 40, back in the day, I would have never guessed that all these many years later, I'd be escorting you out to receive a science recognition award.

"Well, maybe I could have anticipated that you would someday be receiving awards because I always knew you were that smart. But I never would have guessed that I'd be with you when they handed you one."

"That's nice of you to say, Gil. But do you really remember those elementary school days? Although I remember a few things, most of everything from back then is a blur. Though I seem to remember you used to go by another name."

"Yeah, Wellington. Wellington G. Hunt III. I didn't like the name too much at the time. Sounded like somebody's stuffy old bank president. A few grades after I met you, I began using my middle name.

"But I recall those days well," Gil continues, "especially that very first day I saw you. It was already several weeks into the 1987 school year, and you almost had to be dragged into our seventh-grade class. You were like a coil of bristling energy trapped in a new school dress. The class snickered and stared when Mr. Thorne introduced you, and you responded with a glare that let everyone know you were no pushover. I remember thinking how pretty you were and how that defiant look on your face matched the intensity of your bright red dress.

"I guess what made the experience so memorable is what happened when Mr. Thorne invited you to the blackboard. There was this game he used to play with us—he claimed it was to sharpen our thinking. Each Monday, a class member would write a current-events question on a corner of the blackboard, and it would stay there until someone answered it. The person who came up with the answer would write the next week's question.

Gil pauses momentarily to sip from the coffee cup Lilly has refilled. He resumes his story with added vigor as he tastes the shot of Drambuie she has added.

"Since you seemed pretty nervous with your parents still hovering in the hallway outside the classroom, Mr. Thorne probably thought he would loosen you up by inviting you to post the question for the week. You didn't look very pleased but went to the board and wrote something I'll never forget. Do you remember what it was?"

"I'm starting to recall the situation, but I haven't the slightest recollection of what I wrote."

"'Before which body did Oliver North testify?' was exactly what you wrote."

"I remember how the class stared at those odd words, no one having any idea what they meant. Previous topics had always been about sports or pop culture; we weren't prepared for anything so heavy. I remember wondering what could make you come up with such an off-the-wall question. And how could we answer a question we couldn't even understand?

"No one ever responded to your posting or offered even a reasonable guess. At first, we reacted as if you were confused and didn't know what you were writing. But as the days passed, it began to dawn on some of us that the confusion might be ours, not yours. We were the clueless ones.

"A week or so later, none of us had come up with any guesses. Mr. Thorne invited you again to come to the blackboard to answer the question yourself. You wrote: "The Tower Commission.

"Since your words didn't register with us, Mr. Thorne asked you to explain. You told us how the Tower Commission was a special investigative unit appointed by President Reagan to look into allegations that the US illegally sold weapons to Iran and used the proceeds to fund Nicaraguan freedom-fighters. You explained that North was a member of Reagan's national security staff and that he had to testify about the weapons before the commission."

Lilly could no longer hold back her amusement and laughed as Gil recited her comments word for word, even imitating her delivery from so many years ago. "This is amazing! I can't believe you remember all this."

"Mr. Thorne enjoyed the whole thing," Gil continues. "He watched us sit stunned and still befuddled. But this time, not a snicker could be heard from the class.

"He thanked you for the question and your eloquent answer and asked how you happened to know so much about the situation. You told us that the topic had been all over the news for the past few weeks. You explained how every time you turned on the television or looked at a newspaper, there was a conversation about the investigation. You said the wide news coverage made it impossible to miss the story.

"Mr. Thorne stuck the knife in when he pointed to the class and commented: 'Well these people somehow managed to miss it!' He reminded us that we were so busy watching baseball and dumb TV sit-coms that we didn't have time to listen to the news or read the papers. He chided us that we needed to do something about the situation.

"If Mr. Thorne was trying to embarrass the class into taking our studies more seriously, it sure worked for me. I remember all this so vividly because the whole episode was a big wake-up call for me. Although I was always a decent student and got good grades, I was never as curious or motivated to learn as you. Before you showed up, I was willing to loaf along, doing no more studying than was necessary to keep up with the class and stay out of trouble. But after you flexed all that intellectual muscle, I decided I wanted to be smart also. I wanted some of your magic. Even though I would never have admitted it at the time, you became a sort of a role model for me.

Lilly shifts nervously in her chair, both flattered and embarrassed by Gil's vivid recollection and impromptu tribute.

"That was the first time you were my role model," Gil continues. "Now with all your great machine learning work, you've done it again. This time I don't have a problem acknowledging it or thanking you for it."

"I'm happy that I've been able to offer inspiration," Lilly answers. "But we've been reminiscing now for almost two hours. Coffee or no coffee, I don't want to put you out and make you drive all the way out to Long Island with no sleep. That couch you're sitting on is a convertible bed, and you're welcome to pull it out and get some shut-eye before you leave."

Gil accepts the offer. As he pulls open the bed, Lilly brings out linens. A few minutes later, he is relaxing in the comfortable convertible bed, the living room now dark except for the faint beam of light from a streetlight that finds its way through an opening in the curtains of the big picture window.

Gil is not sure how long he has been lying in the dark, reflecting on the events of the evening when he realizes that Lilly is standing next to the sofa bed looking down at him. He hadn't heard her come out of her bedroom, as perhaps he had momentarily drifted off to sleep. But there she stands, wearing a short nightgown or a slip. Without saying a word, she lifts the covers and slips into the bed next to him. As he lies on his side looking at her, she nestles close to him, pressing her back against his bare chest. Reflexively he reaches around her and pulls her even closer to him. Although he is suddenly on fire, his body tingling from head to toe, she relaxes and even sighs. He is wearing only skimpy briefs, so she must know how aroused he has become, but it doesn't seem to bother her at all.

After laying there for a long few long minutes, enjoying her fragrance and the warmth of her body against his, he moves his hand to the shoulder strap of her garment and slides it off her shoulder. She places her hand over his and turns her head so that her cheek presses against his lips. She whispers: "Let's just sleep tonight."

No other words are spoken by either of them. Lilly dozes off and begins breathing deeply, but Gil is too excited to sleep and doesn't drift off again until morning light begins to show. It is several hours later when he awakens to bright sunlight streaming through the picture window and the sounds of Lilly fixing breakfast. After showering in Lilly's frou-frou bathroom and enjoying her steak, eggs, and grits breakfast, he gathers himself to head for home.

Once again, she thanks him for being her knight in shining armor. Gil brushes off her comments, replying in seriousness that the pleasure had been all his. As he leaves, he expresses his thanks to the moron who cancelled his date with Lilly and made such a memorable evening possible. He tells her of his hope that there will be more cancellations.

Eleven

Juliette's Dilemma

Back in more carefree days, before he was overtaken by the politics of revenge and retribution and the demands of hustling, Sonny enjoyed visiting the *Centre D'Art*. He had always been fascinated by the beautiful sculptures, paintings, pottery, and clothing created by local artists for tourists eager to take home a piece of exotic Haitian culture. He was amazed at how these inspired, but mostly untrained artisans could create such expressive and compelling art.

Because he has grown up in Haiti and could enjoy its beauty and cultural richness in his daily comings and goings, Sonny has never thought much about buying local art. Occasionally he might spot a piece he would enjoy owning, but in the past, he never had the funds to make even a small purchase. Now that he always has money in his pocket, he can afford to buy whatever catches his eye.

Today as he strides through the colorful rows of outdoor stalls, Sonny is struck by the dramatic and expressive paintings on display in one of the booths. He pauses to absorb the full impact of each piece.

He attempts to engage the artist and discuss one painting. But the busy artisan, wrapped in a colorful shawl with a baby strapped to her back, seems always occupied with other customers. Sonny finally interrupts her. When she turns to him, her face partially hidden under the floppy brim of her wide straw hat, Sonny recognizes her. It is the *Dechoukaj* victim who had lived with him and Jacques for several months, and who suddenly disappeared as if she had dropped off the face of the earth. Sonny calls her name.

"Juliette...?"

Getting no response, he says: "Juliette, it's me, Sonny. I know it's been a few years now. You and your sisters stayed with Jacques and me for a while."

The young artist finally answers: "Yes, Sonny, I remember you. I don't mean to be rude, but I've got my hands full working this booth and servicing these customers all by myself."

"I understand," Sonny replies. "It's a nice surprise to see you. Maybe I can come back when you're not so busy, and we can talk for a few moments. I've always wondered what became of you and your sisters."

"The bazaar closes in an hour," Juliette responds. "Come back, and we can talk then."

Sonny returns an hour later and helps Juliette move the few remaining unsold pieces to a small storage shed not far from her booth. When the last piece is stored, she walks with him to a bench in the adjoining picnic area. As they sit, Juliette transfers the baby from her sling to her lap.

"So tell me what you've been in the years since I last saw you," Sonny begins. "Tell me about your sisters and this new addition you're holding, and about all this artistic talent I never knew you had."

"There's not much to tell," Juliette replies, not as happy to see Sonny as he is to see her. "I always appreciated what you did to get the girls and me settled, but things got very uncomfortable at the LeBlanc house. I had to get out of there in a hurry. I took an apartment in Port-au-Prince with a guy I had been seeing. We'd planned on getting married, but it never happened so I concentrated on my art and the girls. Just when I'd given up on the idea of children of my own, little Euphrasie here came along.

"The girls are still with me and doing fine. They're now finishing high school and want to go to college. As for the art, I've always been interested in drawing and painting. Even though I'm pretty much self-taught, I've had an opportunity to work on my skills a lot over the years. The patrons here at the bazaar seem to like my work. That's about all there is to it."

Sonny understands Juliette's reticence to reconnect with him, as there was only hurt in her life the last time they were around each other. She had nothing positive to look back on, and no pleasant memories to recall.

She never knew that he lead the attack that wiped out her family and destroyed the life she had known. But he had always been troubled by his role in the shameful event. The abuse she had to endure at the LeBlanc home and his failure to help her because he was usually stoned only added to his remorse. Though not given to self-recrimination, the memories of the suffering he had caused her weighed on him. Her unfortunate situation had come to symbolize all the pain and suffering he caused those punished in the name of *Dechoukaj*.

Even though it appears that her life has taken a turn for the better, it is clear that there is more to Juliette's situation than she cares to share. Although Euphrasie is a toddler, she has been either strapped to her mother's back or seated in her lap with a cover over her tiny legs throughout Sonny's visit. Noticing her turned-in feet when she kicks the hot blanket off her legs, Sonny senses that the baby probably can't walk. He had only seen feet like that once before on a lame beggar who used to push himself about the waterfront on a small cart; his deformed feet uncovered to evoke sympathy and donations from passersby.

Sonny wants to talk more but accepts Juliette's reticence. When she refuses his offer to drive her home, he thanks her for the brief visit and bids her goodbye. Since he has already arranged for Jacques's weekend security, his presence is not required at the mansion that night. With no immediate obligations, he looks forward to an evening of peace and quiet at his Jérémie getaway.

Sonny tries once more to reconnect with Juliette a few weeks later when he again visits her booth, this time buying two of her paintings. She is happy to sell him the pieces and tells him how honored she is that he would want to display her work in his home. But beyond that, she shows no interest in any further communication. He never again visits her at the market.

Expecting that their paths will not likely cross again anytime soon, Sonny is surprised several months later to drive past her as she sits in the shade of a large mango tree at the side of a highway north of Port-au-Prince. Fanning herself with her hat, her baby sitting on her lap and a small bundle at her feet, it appears as though she might be stranded. Circling as soon as he sees her, Sonny pulls up and asks whether he can offer her a ride.

This time she accepts. As she cools off in the air-conditioned comfort of his Jeep, Juliette tells him that she had been walking with a group heading to a campground near the town of Archahaie, where they would spend the night. The next morning they would continue to the site at which a new *houmfort* was to be established and a new *houngan* appointed. One of her customers had invited her to attend the dedication. He promised that, as part of the ceremony, the *houngan* would attempt to summon the *loa, Papa Loco,* the spirit of healing. If he could be invoked, she would then be able to ask health favors for Euphrasie, that her deformed legs and feet be healed.

The ceremony would involve a series of voodoo rituals performed according to long-established traditions. Although Juliette had never participated in one of these dedications, she remembered her father telling her about the venerable process. It had been handed down by generations of Haitians for as long as anyone could remember.

Juliette admits to Sonny that her idea of pilgrimaging to the campground on foot was overly ambitious. Euphrasie is bigger than ever, the heat is unbearable, and her bundle had become very heavy. Juliette didn't know the members of the group very well, and when she began to slow them down, she told them to go ahead without her. She thought she could catch up after a short rest, but after sitting for a few minutes, she realized she didn't have the energy to rejoin them. Reluctant to hail a tap-tap and risk a ride with a strange driver, she believes it is a miracle that Sonny should happen by in this somewhat remote area some five miles outside the capital.

As he drives back toward the marchers, Sonny resists the urge to ask how it was that her man, presumably the baby's father, allowed her and his daughter to travel on foot without him for such a long distance. He catches up with the group and follows them to the campground. As he helps Juliette out of the car, he asks if he can remain with the group that evening and go with her to the ceremony the following morning to lend support to her healing request. When she agrees, he excuses himself and calls the mansion on the radio-phone he now carries at all times. He wants to be sure that everything is in order and that security is set for the evening and the following two days until he and Jacques will leave for New York to oversee a large delivery.

At sunset, the pilgrimage of more than one hundred sets out on foot, laughing, joking, and singing their way for the remaining two miles to their destination. They carry food, supplies, and treats in bundles on their heads, in backpacks, and on several small pushcarts. Sonny totes Juliette's bundle and even offers to carry Euphrasie.

What a strange turn of events, he muses as he walks with Juliette and her group. It was only a few months ago that he had been battling to eliminate every vestige of voodoo from Haiti, now here he is preparing to take part in one of its ceremonies. Maybe his patron *loa* has guided him down this path, he wonders, as he touches the *Belie Belcan* amulet hanging from his neck.

As dusk closes in, a man stationed at the roadside directs them to a winding country road. The unpaved trail will take them the last half mile to the compound that has been donated as the site for the new *houmfort*. In a brief arrival ceremony before going inside, a guest *houngan* and *mambo* make a signature of *Loco* on the ground. Each pilgrim throws water on it three times.

Once inside, everyone works late into the night. They cut brightly colored paper and palm leaves into fine strips that they make into large balls resembling ostrich plumes. They use these to decorate chairs and containers designated for the various *loa*. When all the decorations are in place, a necklace of beads and snake bones is made for the new *houngan*. Each element of the necklace represents a different *loa*.

The following day, a sumptuous meal is prepared and eaten on the grounds of the new *houmfort,* which is now decorated throughout with the colorful plumes created the night before. The ceremonies begin with the dedication of drums and homage paid to *Papa Legba,* the special god that serves as the intermediary between other *loa* and humanity. Legba speaks all human languages and has the power to grant or deny humans permission to talk with *loa*.

Guests are then summoned, with shoes off, into the crowded *houmfort*. One of the officiating *mambo*s places a red and yellow scarf on Juliette's head, tying it with a special knot. A similar bandanna is tied around Euphrasie's head, the child still strapped to her mother's back.

Jules Oscar Herard, the senior officiating *houngan,* is seated facing the altar. Next to him sits the young man who is to be elevated to *houngan*. Before him on the altar is the recently made stone and bead necklace. Near the altar is a long table that holds food and drinks for *Legba* and all the *loa* to be honored. When all guests and participants are in place, Jules Oscar covers his own head with a ceremonial scarf. He begins a long chanting litany, honoring many Catholic saints and voodoo *loa*.

Each of the many Haitian gods summoned has purview over some specific aspect of human affairs. In addition to *Legba,* one of the other important *loa* celebrated is *Erzulie,* the revered and feared spirit of love, help, goodwill, health, beauty, and fortune but also of jealousy, vengeance, and discord. Also honored, of course, is *Loco,* the *loa* Juliette hoped would be able to heal Euphrasie. Only *Ghede,* the spirit of death, is not honored. Since this ceremony is intended for the living, *Baron Samedi* must not be present. In fact, if he somehow manifests himself, he will have to be driven away.

After sprinkling water in the direction of the four quarters of the world, Jules Oscar continues the ceremony, consecrating two chickens to *Papa Legba*. First, he kneels and kisses the sign of *Legba* on the bare earth. Then, with drums picking up the intensity of the ceremony, he breaks the wings and the legs of one of the chickens. He holds the throat of the bird so that it does not disturb the ceremonial chanting and singing with cries of pain. After wringing the chicken's neck, he places it atop the *Legba* signature. In its death agony, the unfortunate creature leaps up and crashes into a shuddering Juliette before dropping at her feet. Even the stoic Sonny winces at the ceremony's casual brutality, an unmalicious, almost gratuitous inhumanity that makes it all the more frightening. To him, all the bloodshed is out of step with the otherwise joyous and hopeful mood of the event.

With the similar killing of the second chicken, the full ceremony has begun. Jules Oscar bows twice toward the altar then takes a white pigeon lifting it to toward the heavens before killing it to usher all *loa* into the *houmfort*. There follows tribute to a series of gods. These *loa* will be invoked to respond to the specific requests of one or more of the pilgrims. When the *houngan* recites *Loco's* name and salutes the white pot on the altar dedicated to him, several *mambo*s and other servitors become excited, a sign that the *loa* is now present. Having become 'horses' of *Loco*, the *mambo*s begin dressing a table on which they place a sacred stone dedicated to *Loco*. At this point, Jules Oscar himself is possessed; *Loco* has taken over his body. It is a sign that the *loa* is preparing to grant favors asked of him by the supplicants.

A schoolteacher who is losing her sight is called to the altar. She has come to the *houngan* to find out what she must do to regain her vision. The *houngan* again summons *Papa Loco*, and the call is answered. Through Jules Oscar, *Loco* demands specific articles and then tells the *houngan* which ceremony should be performed. When Jules

Oscar begins to conduct the rites, *Loco* again takes possession of his body and performs the ceremony himself. By thus 'tying the points,' the *loa* grants the schoolteachers request and executes the cure.

Loco can also be cruel and unresponsive. The next supplicant is a woman nearing middle age who wants help conceiving her first child. When she is summoned to the altar by Jules Oscar, *Loco* refuses to recognize her. Through the *houngan*, he tells her to wait for another time.

Finally, it is Juliette's turn. *Papa Loco* gives instructions to Jules Oscar that the healing ceremony for Juliette will have to be performed under a tree that has been dedicated to him. Singing and chanting as a group, everyone moves outside as directed, bringing *Loco's* white pot from the altar and hanging it on the tree. The *houngan* makes Juliette kneel beneath a large tree branch and orders the two *mambos* assisting him to pass a live chicken around her head and shoulders. He then makes a cross of cornmeal on Juliette's head and instructs her to move around the tree trunk, dancing as the mood hits her. After a few moments of spinning in one direction, she is ordered to reverse directions. Finally, the chicken that has been passed around her is handed to Jules Oscar, who kills it with a long curved knife. The bird is returned to the two *mambos*, who begin pulling its feathers, throwing them up and letting them float to the ground. Juliette's request is completed when some of the food from the long table next to the altar is placed in the hollow of the tree for *Loco*.

The ceremony moves back inside to pay tribute to *Ogun*, the warrior *loa* of fire, politics, and war, to *Damballa*, the creator of all life, and finally to *Brave Guedé*, the messenger of all the gods. All *loas* honored and the requests of all supplicants heard and addressed, everyone dances, sings and celebrates through the night. The following morning, the festivities finally over, the new *houngan* in place and the *houmfort* officially dedicated, the assembled pilgrims depart for home.

Sonny offers to drive Juliette home, but she asks to be dropped off instead at the *Centre D'Art*. The big man thought it odd that after almost two days away from home with a baby in tow, Juliette would want to go to the artist's market instead of home. But since her request was no more unusual than coming to the healing ceremony unaccompanied by the baby's father, he offers no comment and begins the drive to the market.

"How are you and the baby this morning?" Sonny inquires as he pulls out onto the highway.

"I'm ok, I guess," Juliette responds. "But I'm not sure what to expect from Euphrasie, though. She seems to feel fine this morning, but there's no change in her legs as of now. Were we supposed to see a change this quickly, or will the healing take longer?" she wonders aloud. "Or will there ever be any healing at all?" There is a note of frustration and disappointment in her voice.

"Even though I come from two generations of voodoo, I've never understood it or had any real interest in learning about it. I tried to get into the spirit of yesterday's ceremony. But I have to admit that when others became possessed by *Loco* or one of the other *loas*, I felt nothing. No passion, no nothing. The only thing I felt was compassion for all the birds and animals that were sacrificed. Every time another one was killed, I was more repelled. To me, the whole thing seemed like some kind of barbaric ritual. A life of indifference and disbelief has not prepared me well for whatever good might have come out of the pilgrimage."

Sonny understood Juliette's feelings of doubt and disappointment. He had also tried to get into the spirit of the ceremony but started with an even greater disadvantage. His was a lifetime not only of doubt and questioning but outright rejection of anything even associated with voodoo. He didn't question the power that the ancient religion held over people. Still, he always believed that the power of voodoo was the power people invested in it, not any magical powers intrinsic to voodoo itself. His attitude was summed up in the words of wisdom given to him by Angel Baptiste, one of the old-timers who used to work the fishing boats and repair fishnets with him at the waterfront.

"Voodoo can't hurt you," the grizzled old sailor used to say. "But it can make you hurt yourself!"

Sonny subscribed to Angel's view of voodoo and had always stayed away from the old tradition and all other forms of black magic. His only involvement with voodoo was his *Belie Belcan* amulet. Even though according to voodoo tradition (in the Dominican Republic), *Belie* was said to have the power to protect people from demons and evil, he wore the charm only because it was a gift from Angel's Dominican wife. Sonny had known her since his childhood, and she had always treated him with the affection of the mother he had never known. In a twist on Angel's take on the power of voodoo, Sonny wore the *Belie Belcan* because he believed such a unique gift from a special person would always protect him. Thinking he was protected, he lived as if he really was.

Sonny shares none of his doubts about voodoo and the healing ceremony. Instead, he comments: "Now don't get down on yourself or the ceremony. Give it a while to work. If it doesn't, other things can be done."

"I know there are other options," Juliette responds. "Medical options. One involves manipulating and massaging the feet and ankles to stretch the tendons and ligaments so that the feet can assume a more normal position. But this should have been done right after birth while the tissues were most flexible. Unfortunately, Euphrasie was not born in a hospital. Neither the midwife who assisted in the delivery nor I knew anything about the condition. By the time I saw a doctor, it was too late to manually correct the condition, clubfoot—how I hate those words—without expensive surgery. On a young person, corrective surgery is usually successful, but there are few doctors here who specialize in that kind of work. Most people who need the procedure get it done in the States."

"So there you are," Sonny encourages her. "There is a way out."

"I'm not so sure about that," Juliette responds. "The baby's father thinks the condition was caused by my father's lifetime of voodoo practice. He believes the condition is punishment from an angry or disgruntled *loa*, possibly from the Almighty himself. Although I never practiced voodoo and don't even believe in it, he blames me for carrying the curse and afflicting his daughter with the punishment. It was he who made me take part in the healing ceremony. Since he believes voodoo is the root cause of the problem, he thinks it is my responsibility to use voodoo to solve the problem."

"Even though he didn't join you in the ceremony and support your healing request?" Sonny asks.

"That's right. He feels the deformity resulted from the curse on my family. But because he despises voodoo and refuses to be tainted by its evil, he believes there is nothing that can be done. We'll have to live with the situation.

"He doesn't even want to hear about the medical procedure. Every time I bring it up, we have an argument. We've had so many that we don't even live together and never have. He pays the rent on my apartment and comes to visit now and then, sometimes staying the night."

"Wait a minute," Sonny interrupts, "this doesn't make any sense. If he can afford to pay for an apartment that he doesn't even live in, can't he afford to pay for an operation that would help his own daughter walk? And if he could do something that would make his daughter and everyone else happy, why wouldn't he?"

"That is a question I've asked myself many times," Juliette responds. "But unfortunately I don't have a good answer. I don't think he wants to find happiness."

"But he's punishing his own child!" Sonny exclaims. "What kind of a man can do that?"

"I can't answer that. I'm trying to save up enough for the operation by selling my art. But it's difficult because most of what I earn at the market goes to pay for my sisters' schooling. The baby's father pays for the rent and the food. The rest is up to me. After the operation is done, I'll figure out what to do with the rest of my life. For now, I'm stuck. To survive, I have accepted the role of a concubine."

With Juliette divulging details of her life that she had never intended to discuss with Sonny or anyone else, they have been sitting in Sonny's Jeep in the *Centre D'Art* parking lot for almost an hour.

Sonny offers a suggestion. "How about this?" he ventures. "I still have the house Jacques and I moved to when we left the LeBlancs. He's got his own place now, a big mansion here in Port-au-Prince that he bought last year. I spend a lot of time up here, but the Jérémie place is my getaway. Nobody is ever there but me and an occasional guest.

"Why don't you, the baby, and your sisters stay at my house for a while until you can get the operation done? You can sell your art at some other market, and I'll be happy to help with the cost of the operation. Consider it a gift with no strings attached."

"It's wonderful of you to make such an offer," she responds, the smile on her face the first Sonny has ever seen from her. "But I must decline. It would cause a major problem with the baby's father, and he would take it out on me. He's vindictive, unpredictable, and he's got a real mean streak."

"But he doesn't have to know where you are unless you choose to tell him."

"It won't work," she repeats with a look of painful resignation.

"Why not?" responds a puzzled Sonny. "Except for Jacques, nobody here in Port-au-Prince knows anything about that house."

"Because Jacques is the father!" she finally replies after a long pause.

Recoiling from the bombshell that has just exploded in his face, Sonny stares at Juliette, unable to accept what he has heard.

How is it possible that he could be unaware of such a significant piece of Jacques's life? While he had no way of knowing whether she spoke the truth, Sonny trusted Juliette. And the baby suddenly looked a lot like Jacques. The awful story made Sonny realize he was not as close to Jacques as he had always thought, nor had he been quite the mentor he had always believed himself to be.

Although Jacques had shown a cruel and vindictive streak in recent years, Sonny liked to remember how his one-time protege had earlier been empathetic and unselfish and had advocated on behalf of those threatened by *Dechoukaj*. In his wildest dreams, Sonny could never have envisioned Jacques as someone who would be abusive to his own child and its mother.

After a long silence, Juliette continues: "Jacques always knew I was suffering with M LeBlanc. I was completely inexperienced and didn't know how to protect myself from the old man. But Jacques used to talk to me and reassure me that things would work out. When he started bringing MDMA to Haiti and making money, he got me the apartment in Port-au-Prince. I moved out of the LeBlanc's around the same time you and he moved to your house in Jérémie. I appreciated the lifeline he had thrown me, and I fell in love with him. He was my first real boyfriend, and I believe I was his first girlfriend too.

Her eyes welling up, Juliette continues her painful disclosure. "But a permanent relationship just wasn't in the cards for us. As Jacques started making money selling drugs, he lost his humanity. I became fed up with his callous treatment, but before I could cut things off, I got pregnant. Things got really ugly when the baby was born with deformed feet. Jacques became a different person overnight, showing a meanness and cruelty that I could never have imagined. He even suggested that maybe the baby really was LeBlanc's. He said that only to hurt me since he must have known that he was the first man I had ever been with."

Sonny is dumbfounded. He doesn't know what bothers him most. Is it Jacques's mean and cruel treatment of Juliette and the callous disregard for his own daughter, using her as a tool to punish her mother? Or is it the dishonest and deceitful way he has kept his despicable behavior a secret?

Sonny stares at Juliette in silence. "Juliette," he finally continues, "I've done a lot of things in my life I'm not proud of. In the name of what I thought was justice, I've often lived by a brutal and unforgiving code that caused me to treat people cruelly. I may have been fooling myself, but in my own way, I thought I was helping Haiti to become the nation it originally set out to be. At no time did I ever intend to hurt anyone for selfish gain or out of hatred or meanness. I suppose many who have brutalized others in the name of *Dechoukaj* might offer the same excuse. I can only say to you that I'm truly sorry for what happened to you and your family, for what you went through at the LeBlanc's, and for what you're now going through with Jacques."

Sonny was in unfamiliar territory. A creature of the streets who usually reacted instinctively to circumstances, he was not generally inclined to introspection. But because of his long and complicated history with Juliette, he now found himself not only reacting to his environment but also contemplating his impact on it.

"Since Jacques is Euphrasie's father," Sonny goes on, "I can see that it wouldn't be wise for you to stay at the Jérémie house. But there's got to be a way to get you out of this mess. Over these last few years, you've had more than your share of bad luck, none of it deserved as far as I can see. Try to hold on a little longer, and we'll come up with a way to work this out. I pledge this to you in the name of all those I have hurt."

Sonny's Trip

Jules Colixe doesn't see it, but things aren't quite right in the LaGuardia Airport customs area. Several characters loitering in the waiting room are not what they appear to be. As passengers file in from the afternoon Port-au-Prince to New York flight, a shabbily dressed man snores on a bench. Another in dark wraparound glasses sits with a leader dog, and a young woman stands in line with a swaddled baby in her arms.

The young courier waits for the crowd to thin before entering the area so that he can spot anyone that doesn't fit into the usual customs routine. Wearing a Negro Leagues baseball cap and a long-sleeved denim shirt, as he had been instructed, the young Haitian waits to be interviewed and have his passport stamped. When he sees the customs agent he is looking for, a stocky, brown-skinned man with rolled-up sleeves and a union button fastened to his necktie, he leaves the line and heads toward the help desk where the agent meets him.

"May I assist you, sir?" the customs man asks, following a pre-arranged script to the word.

"Yes, I need help with this form. I don't understand what I'm supposed to do."

Precise questions and answers are required to proceed with the bag switch. Colixe understands that any deviation is a signal that something is wrong and that he should pick up his suitcase and leave the area without completing the interview or attempting to make the exchange. In such an event, he is to return to the terminal and call his handler for instructions. He has made more than thirty of these runs over the last two years. Although nothing has ever gone wrong, he always follows the protocols to the letter as he knew the risks involved.

Everything proceeds as planned as he and the customs clerk continue their choreographed conversation. After responding to all questions, Colixe walks toward the inspection area carrying the replacement bag that had been placed under the table for him. But when the clerk attempts to take the cocaine-filled case to the rear of the room, all hell breaks loose. The sleeping vagrant, the woman carrying a fake baby bundle, and the man with what now appears to be a drug-sniffing dog spring into action flashing badges. Shouting that they are federal agents conducting a random drug check, the sleeper collars Colixe, the woman stops the clerk, and the man with the dog throws the suitcase onto an inspection table. He pries open its latches to reveal twenty-five kilos of cocaine hermetically sealed in heavy-duty plastic tubes. When one of the containers is cracked open, the dog begins barking. The drugs are impounded, and both Colixe and the clerk are arrested, cuffed, and hustled into a waiting police vehicle.

The loss of a cocaine shipment with a street value of five hundred thousand dollars is a major blow to Jacques. But an equally severe setback is the agents' discovery of a small notebook Colixe had carelessly left in the suitcase. It contains several names and telephone numbers. Three are the wholesale buyers the courier planned to meet. The fourth is Jacques Maurice. Things could only be worse if Jacques had been arrested with his courier.

Previously unknown to US NARCs, Jacques is now linked to the cocaine shipment. The agents will likely lean hard on Colixe and force him to admit Jacques had hired him to bring in the coke. In return for leniency in the inevitable trial and sentencing, Colixe will probably also provide information about other recent shipments.

Although only two of the names in Colixe's notebook are prior customers, all three will now face heavy scrutiny from DEA agents. There is little chance they will be able to receive new shipments any time soon. And if Jacques is to continue his hustle, he will have to operate under a new identity and no longer use the bag switch. Worst of all will be his 'radioactivity.' Word will soon get around that several wholesale dealers got burned because of the failure in Jacques's operation. While street demand is still high, Jacques's existing and potential customers will be spooked by the LaGuardia bust. They will be wary of future dealings with him regardless of any new identity he assumes. In the coming months, NARC vigilance will be intense in the New York area, especially on products and travelers coming into the States from Haiti. Jacques will somehow have to convince his customers they will not face unnecessary risks in future buys from him.

Shipments of asphalt from Trinidad that passed through Haiti on the way to the States had been a useful smuggling cover. But Jacques is sure that until things cool down, any future asphalt transactions will likely be examined much more carefully. Unwilling to risk the interception of another large shipment on a risky option, he discontinues any further use of asphalt.

Scrapping the bag switching and asphalt routines puts a severe crimp in Jacques's operation. He has few alternative smuggling options, as most products grown or produced in Haiti for export to the US, such as cocoa, coffee, mangoes, and clothing, are not suitable for hiding cocaine. And he is sure that any products passing through Haiti on the way to the US will get heavy scrutiny from the NARCs. He concludes that, for the foreseeable future, his shipments will have to make one or two intermediate stops before landing in the States.

He will begin by hiding his product in the frame of a motor vehicle and moving it in a circuitous, multi-continent route before landing it in the States. After several conversations with a North African business contact, Jacques decides that his initial 'carrier' vehicle will be transported first to France, after faking a stop in Algeria. With new vehicle identification documents, it will be driven from the South of France to the northern border. It will finally be shipped to Canada and driven south across the Canadian-US border into New York. There, the drugs will be recovered and sold to wholesale buyers.

Sonny is unknown to anyone in US NARC circles and will pose as Charles Jolebois, an Algerian businessman taking his newly purchased vehicle on a vacation through several countries. With his heavy weed-smoking days behind him, Sonny is back to his old self. Jacques is sure he can count on him for such a critical mission.

Jacques orders a new 2001 Ford Expedition. After delivery to a Miami buyer and shipment to Haiti, a top-notch auto body man is brought in from the States to hide the drugs in the SUV's huge body. Jacques won't be satisfied with stashing the coke in hard-to-find but already existing compartments in the engine area, floor, or doorposts. A diligent NARC will find even the most remote nooks and crannies. Instead, Jacques intends to cut open the vehicle to expose dead spaces where drugs can be hidden. When all such areas are loaded, he will have them sealed, re-welded, and re-painted so that there will be no evidence that the compartments ever existed. Even drug-sniffing dogs won't be able to detect the coke. To recover the drugs, the vehicle will once again have to be cut open. Only those who had hidden the contraband would know where to look.

After the body man inspects every square inch of the Expedition and reports on the storage space available, Jacques estimates that one hundred fifty kilos can be hidden in it. At current rates, a cargo of this size will have a wholesale value of three million US dollars. As the product then works its way down through the drug chain, the street value might exceed six or seven million, depending on how the coke is cut. But Jacques concerns himself only with getting his product to the wholesale buyer. Dealing with unpredictable and unstable street pushers will be somebody else's headache.

With the help of an Algerian contact, Mohamed Belkheir, Jacques arranges the first leg of the trip, shipment of the Expedition to the French port of Marseille. Belkheir is a member of *Le Pouvoir* (the power), a group of Algerian power brokers that rules the North African country, even picking its presidents. Jacques met Belkheir when he and several other Algerians visited Haiti on a state-sponsored visit. At the request of new Haitian President Jean-Bertrand Aristide, Jacques had entertained the delegation lavishly, providing them with meals, drugs, and female companionship. Belkheir is now ready to return the favor.

The Algerian puts Jacques in touch with a high-level government administrator. The official agrees to create an import/export paper trail to make it appear that a Miami buyer had sold the Expedition to Charles Jolebois in Algeria, who then shipped it to Marseille. The paperwork will indicate that the vehicle has never been in Haiti or owned by a Haitian national. Jolebois' travel papers will depict him as a Haitian who emigrated to Algeria with his family as a child. After his father's death, he operated the family antique shop for many years. He now wishes to move to the US at the end of a short vacation in France and Canada. He will indulge himself with the purchase of a big, comfortable American-made SUV that accommodates his burley six and a half foot frame. Travel papers will also be created for Edouard Monde, who will accompany Sonny on the six-week trip. Monde will provide backup and an extra pair of eyes to safeguard the vehicle and its precious cargo. He was one of Sonny's crew that provided security at Jacques's mansion. He will pose as Jolebois' cousin.

———•◆•———

After almost two months of bodywork on the Expedition and preparation of travel documents, Sonny stands on the main deck of the *MS Invictus* as it eases out of PortMiami on its fourteen-day journey to Marseille. The big container ship, loaded with more than 90,000 tons of commercial cargo, mostly automobiles and machinery, carries only twenty passengers. Sonny and Jacques had watched as the Expedition was driven into its container, strapped in place, and hoisted into the cargo hold by a giant crane on the *Invictus*'s deck. Sonny had earlier signed a seal that was fastened to the container's bolt-on cover. It will remain in place throughout the crossing to ensure that no one tampers with the container or its contents.

Rainy weather and overcast skies capture the all-business atmosphere of the 1940s-era cargo vessel. On this ship, passengers will enjoy no cruise ship amenities. Like Sonny, most of the travelers are accompanying valuables they want to be able to check on from time to time during the crossing. A one-hour time slot will be provided each day during which passengers, accompanied by a crew member, can visit the cargo area to inspect their property. One man and his two assistants are babysitting a collection of expensive antique vehicles that are to be delivered to a wealthy Austrian Baron living in Monaco. Each of the Baron's cars is stored in its own shipping container.

Among the ten passengers is a young family of four that has brought no cargo other than their luggage. They had chosen to travel on the *Invictus* because of its low fares. With no recreational facilities anywhere on the boat except for a dartboard in the small dining room, the young parents will have their hands full keeping their two little boys from succumbing to cabin fever. The only woman traveling alone is an artist from Marseille who now lives in Monte Carlo. As passengers are loading, she introduces herself to Sonny as Miranda Jacinthe. She explains that she is accompanying a vehicle she purchased at an auction while vacationing in California.

A few hours later, still dressed in the motorcycle jacket and headscarf she wore at boarding, the tall Frenchwoman once again approaches Sonny as he stands at the aft end of the big ship watching the coastline of Miami disappear into the horizon.

"Monsieur Jolebois. Monsieur Jolebois," she repeats before Sonny realizes that someone is addressing him in French. He is not yet accustomed to his assumed name and makes a mental note that he will have to be more alert if he intends to make it all the way through Europe and back to the States without blowing his cover.

"I'm sorry," Sonny responds in English. "I was caught up in the shoreline scenery and a little bit lost in thought." Like many Haitians, he speaks French-based Kreyòl as a first language and understands little French. He is fluent in English.

"It's nice to get away," Miranda answers in English. "But sometimes it can be disorienting to step out of our everyday routines."

"I suppose so," Sonny says to the olive-skinned artist who seems determined to engage him. Although he had talked with her for a few moments during boarding, she hadn't registered with him as they had only exchanged polite chitchat. If they never spoke again for the rest of the voyage, it would be fine with him.

Few people mattered enough in Sonny's world to warrant a real conversation. Those who did were a small clique of friends and acquaintances he had known for many years, none of them white. He had no particular ill-will for *blancs*. But because they had never been a part of his world, he found it difficult to relate to them, their culture, and their values.

Miranda wanted to talk and, in some way, connect. She seemed appreciative that he had assisted her during boarding. He had carried two of her heavy bags up the slippery gangplank when the all-day rainfall suddenly turned into a downpour.

Since this will be a two-week trip with many unavoidable interactions, Sonny decides to give her at least the courtesy of occasional brief conversations. But as always, he will be careful. Although it is unlikely she is surveilling him, too much is at stake to let his guard down with her or anyone else.

The French artist strikes Sonny as intelligent, witty, and maybe even attractive. But it is difficult for him to be sure about her looks. As hard as he might try, he never quite appreciates European standards of beauty. He believes it places too much emphasis on Caucasian facial characteristics and big busts. Many who meet those standards seem top-heavy, with the rest of their bodies straight as a board. To him, the full facial features, curved hips, and ample behinds of Black women are essential elements of feminine beauty.

"Since the shuffleboard and skeet shooting gear hasn't yet been set up on deck, and the outdoor cocktail bar won't be open any time soon," Miranda quips with a smile, "I'm going down to the cargo hold to check on my toy. How about you?"

"My vehicle is stored in a container, so there's nothing much to see. I watched the crew load it onto the ship a few hours ago."

"Well, mine isn't in a container," Miranda responds. "I thought about that. But as much as I want to keep my car safe, I wouldn't want to be unable to see it for the whole two-week crossing. Want to come check it out with me?"

"OK," Sonny answers. With nothing else to do, for the moment, he eases up on his effort to keep his distance.

They ride the lift down a couple of decks to the cargo level. After walking past several rows of vehicles, Miranda stops at a cream-colored sports car decorated with a hood ornament in the form of a big lunging cat. The sleek roadster is adorned with chromed wire wheels, white-walled tires, and a caramel-colored convertible top that matches its leather seats. Sonny has never seen anything like it in Haiti. Even parked and motionless, it has the look of speed—as if being driven any slower than one hundred kilometers per hour would be a sacrilege.

"What kind of car is this?" Sonny asks as he stares at the exotic machine.

"It's a Jaguar XK-150S. It was Jaguar's marquee sports car back in the fifties. It was bought new in 1958 and taken to California by a Brit who babied it like it was one of his children. Everything on it is original, and the former owner claims the car has never seen a drop of rain or felt a flake of snow. I saw it at an auction I attended on a whim. I hadn't planned on buying anything but fell in love with this big cat. In celebration of a very successful year with the sales of my art, I decided to treat myself to it. I was so excited, I drove it all the way from California to Miami with the top down. It was an unforgettable adventure.

"Since you're vacationing in France, why don't you stop by my place in Monte Carlo for a day. We can take the Jag out for a drive and a picnic. I'm only a two and a half hour drive along the coast from Marseille."

"I'd like to," Sonny answers. "But I've got a commitment to be in Lyon the day after we arrive in Marseille. And from there, I'm headed to Paris, where I've got a full schedule. Thanks for the invite, but I'll have to take a rain check until the next time I'm in France."

Sonny and Edouard will indeed head immediately to Lyon upon their arrival in France. But they have no plans other than to get the Expedition off the streets and into the garage of their rental house. They will stay in Lyon for three days before driving north to Le Havre. There they will once again enclose the SUV in a storage container and load it onto a ship bound for Halifax, Nova Scotia.

It will be a shame to leave the South of France without enjoying the beauty of its coastal countryside or sampling the excellent cuisine for which the region is famous. But Sonny knows his main job is to protect the Expedition and get it to the US without revealing that its journey had begun in Haiti. That means keeping a low profile and driving the SUV carefully and during off-hours to avoid heavy traffic in cities like Paris.

The game plan is for Sonny to remain in France long enough to support his driving vacation story. But he will have to make sure the vehicle isn't damaged or stolen. Even a minor fender-bender would risk discovery of the contraband. For the few days it will be parked in the garage of the Lyons home, it will have to be guarded at all times. And while Sonny has known Edouard for years, he doesn't want to tempt fate by leaving him alone with the SUV. A seven-figure payday might be too much for his young travel partner to resist. That kind of money could buy a lot of anonymity in some exciting destinations around the world. For a million other reasons equally pressing, Sonny knows he will have to be on his toes throughout the trip. There will be no joyriding in the Jag or hanging out with Miranda in Monte Carlo.

Sonny and Edouard share a tiny cabin above the *Invictus*'s engine room. With double-decker bunk beds, a single porthole overlooking a narrow catwalk, a few clothing hooks, and a small two-drawer storage chest, most of their belongings remain inside their duffel bags throughout the voyage. They spend little time in the cramped cabin other than when they are sleeping.

There is little to do on the long crossing other than walk the decks, look for the occasional porpoise or converse with other passengers at mealtime. Sonny is glad he brought along a few books. He had never been exposed to reading and had never developed the habit. But the unpredictability of post-Duvalier Haiti had convinced him he needed to know more and be better informed. In several recent visits to the artist's market back home, he had stopped into the *Revolution Bookseller*, each time buying a book. His *Dechoukaj* experiences spurring an interest in the politics of empowerment, the three he purchased were: *The Wretched of the Earth* and *Black Skin, White Masks*, by Frantz Fanon, and *The Autobiography of Malcolm X* by Alex Haley. He enjoys a few pages from each, daily. On pleasant days, he reads out on the open deck. In bad weather, he takes his book to a quiet corner in the dining room.

Ever since learning of him, Sonny had been intrigued by Fanon, a Martinican medical doctor, psychiatrist, and revolutionary who died at age thirty-six after fighting in Algeria's war for independence. The only other book Sonny had ever read had been about Haiti's revolutionary hero, Toussaint Louverture. It seemed fitting to read Fanon's book on a trip to the very same country in which Fanon fought as a liberator. He knew little about Malcolm other than the fiery Muslim minister's reputation as a powerful force for empowering inner-city Blacks in 1960s America.

"What's with all the books?" Edouard asked when he saw Sonny take the three volumes out of his bag on the first day of the voyage.

"It's about time for me to do some reading," Sonny responded. "There are way too many things I never learned. Now's a chance to do some catching up."

"You gonna read all three?" Edouard asked.

"Who knows? But however much I read, at the end of this trip, I'll know more than I do now. If you're interested, you're welcome to look at whatever I'm not reading at the moment."

Sonny hadn't expected Edouard to take him up on the offer and was surprised by his comment a few days later as they strolled on deck.

"I started one of Fanon's books yesterday, and I like his message. He's a smart guy, but some of his ideas on colonialism are difficult for me to understand. I also read a little of Malcolm's autobiography. He speaks in the language of the common man, so his book is an easier read for me. I love how he inspired so many young African Americans. It's a shame that neither he nor Fanon made it to age forty."

"Yeah, that's so often the tragedy of a revolutionary's life," Sonny responds. "They're revered by their followers but hated by the powerful and dangerous forces they oppose. They live close to the edge. Like Toussaint, they often aren't appreciated until after they are dead and gone.

"But dreams are hard to kill," the big man continues. "Even though Fanon and Malcolm died too soon, their dreams live on. Fanon helped Algeria become independent, and we're still reading his books. Malcolm has always been a symbol of the struggle for human dignity."

"Reading about these guys and all they did in their short lives makes me wonder what we accomplished with *Dechoukaj*," Edouard responds. "If it made any difference, I can't see it."

Sonny had long accepted the reality that his *Dèchoukay* campaigns had punished and settled scores without improving conditions in Haiti. But he had never before acknowledged the failure to anyone.

"You're right. When Baby-Doc fell, we had an opportunity to make real change, but we didn't seize the moment. The *Brigades de Vigilance* didn't get the job done, and the army filled the vacuum. Instead of taking the battle to the new oppressors, we stopped marching and gave up the fight. It was then that the military consolidated its position. We squandered the opportunity of a lifetime," the big man added, solemnly.

"So, what about our dreams, Sonny? Do we still have any for Haiti? Or are they now only about getting a big payday from this truckload of drugs we're babysitting?"

"You and I are just surviving," Sonny answers. "We may not be poor farmers trying to grow a few yams on a tiny plot of worn-out soil in Haiti. Or fishermen hoping for a catch from the depleted waters back home. But like them, we're only surviving. For now, our dreams for Haiti are on hold, if not dead."

The unexpected conversation with his young travel mate leaves Sonny in a contemplative and reflective mood. Later, in his private thoughts, he acknowledges a failure even worse than *Dechoukaj*, his role in allowing and enabling Jacques's slide into a world of drugs and crime.

He had never expected his young protégé to be a choir boy. But he had always hoped the youngster would grow into someone who stood for something—if not patriotism, at least a cause or a principle of some kind. In the past, Sonny had chosen to believe that Jacques only needed more time to make his way in the field of teaching, that selling drugs was just a means to that end. But it had become clear that Jacques's teaching was not based on any notions of service. It was only a cover. The young drug lord wanted to represent himself as a respected member of academia while he made his fortune selling narcotics. He valued learning only for his personal fulfillment and never appreciated teaching as a high calling or a service to his fellow man.

The more Sonny thinks about it, the more he realizes he deserves much of the blame for what Jacques has become. He hadn't spent enough time encouraging a younger Jacques to live up to his full potential. And he had set a poor example with his own behavior, especially his heavy weed smoking. Instead of reading to the boy and helping him with his schoolwork, he exposed him only to the brutality of *Dechoukaj*. And he hadn't been much of a role model as a breadwinner, either. When he took Jacques along on his weed purchases, the boy learned there was a lot more money to be made selling drugs than repairing fish nets or working at some other menial job.

Sonny's biggest regret is not putting a foot into Jacques's ass the first time talk of selling drugs ever came out of his mouth. Because the boy had been through such a tough childhood, Sonny never came down hard on him about anything. Instead, he helped him build a drug empire. It pains the big man to admit that, even now, his shameful enabling continues as he lounges on the *Invictus* guarding Jacques's multi-million-dollar drug shipment. Tough love might not have changed things. But it would have been worth a try before the ambitious young dealer trapped himself in a world he can no longer escape.

Sonny also regrets not earlier learning about men like Fanon and Malcolm. Reading about them sooner might have given him a better understanding of the world, where he fit in, and how he could have made things better for Jacques and maybe for Haiti.

For as long as he could remember, Sonny has always lived in a small world, a creature of survival and low expectations. His has been a life of avoiding pain instead of seeking knowledge, purpose, and fulfillment. If slaves like Toussaint and Jean-Jacques Dessalines could teach themselves to read and write, expand their worlds and become great leaders, how is it that, until now, he has never found the inspiration to read and grow?

Although street smart, handsome in his smooth, dark skin, his strength reinforced by a calm determination when he faced danger, Sonny had always sensed that something was not quite right in his life. Even though he commanded the attention and respect of those around him, he lived with a vague sense of unworthiness. In light moments he would sometimes refer to himself as a lost Mandinka warrior that had been abandoned by his tribe and exiled to Haiti.

Sonny had never given much thought to these feelings, and until recently had hardly been aware of them. It had never occurred to him that his childhood on the streets might have been a factor, that growing up without the protection and security of family might have long ago planted within him the seeds of self-doubt. Or even that his physical deficiency had affected his sense of self-worth.

The stigma of damaged manhood had come into Sonny's life many years ago with a childhood infection under his foreskin that festered too long without proper treatment. When medical care was finally administered, a neighborhood healer botched a circumcision that left him with a cluster of scar tissue around his afflicted phallus. From then on, he was self-conscious of his body and never allowed anyone to see him unclothed. Although his equipment was fully functional, he would have sex only in the dark, a quirk that made it difficult to establish real intimacy since it seemed that he preferred his sexual contact to be furtive and secretive.

Sonny was coming to the painful realization that he hadn't gotten anywhere near the best out of himself. His harsh self-assessment was reinforced as he learned how the heroes of his books had made their extraordinary contributions despite severe handicaps. Leukemia ended Fanon's short life, and Malcolm spent years in prison for his early life as a pimp and drug hustler. Sonny was beginning to understand that he had allowed his vision and sense of purpose to be stifled by the kinds of challenges over which others had triumphed. Because of this limitation he had been unable to strike a more significant blow in Haiti's struggle for self-determination.

With all his reading and introspection, Sonny appreciates the crossing in a way he could never have anticipated. He is only sorry that he doesn't have more books. He has almost finished the three he brought and wants to continue reading on the return voyage. Perhaps he will be able to find a good bookstore somewhere on the drive to Le Havre.

◆

Sonny has seen Miranda a few times on deck and in the dining room, each time exchanging a few light pleasantries about the weather or the ship's progress. For most of the voyage, she has sensed and accommodated his desire to be left alone. But tonight, she joins him at his table and engages him in a dinner conversation about their backgrounds and childhoods.

Miranda had enjoyed a comfortable middle-class upbringing and had studied art at the prestigious *Ecole Normale Supérieure* in Paris. Based on the chronology of events she related, he concluded she was the same age or perhaps a few years older than him. He was impressed by how well she had taken care of herself.

"Since we'll arrive in Marseille tomorrow morning, what do you say we celebrate our last night on this cruise with some fine cognac?" Miranda asks as they step out of the dining room at the end of the final dinner meal of the crossing.

"That would be great," Sonny replies, "but I don't believe they serve drinks on this old seagoing warehouse."

"They don't, but I've got a bottle of Napoleon in my cabin that I've been saving for a special occasion. I guess our final night on the *Invictus* is as good a reason as any to crack it open," Miranda continues as they stroll the main deck toward the cabin area.

"I'm right here," she says as she stops and unlocks a cabin door. "Come on in."

It has been a while since Sonny had enjoyed fine cognac. A taste of Napoleon would be a welcome treat after challenging himself with so much reading and self-examination. He nods and follows Miranda into a more spacious stateroom than the small cabin he shares with Edouard.

"Have a seat," Miranda says, pointing to the couch below a porthole that opened out onto the deck. "I'll be right back with some glasses," she adds as she steps into an adjoining room before closing the door behind her. Sonny sits alone for longer than he thinks it should take to fetch a couple of glasses. He wonders how he could now be sitting in Miranda's cabin after trying so hard to avoid her.

The door then opens, and to his astonishment, Miranda steps back into the stateroom completely nude, holding a snifter of cognac in each hand. Sonny stands as she walks toward him. Without a word, she hands him one of the generously filled snifters and clicks her own against it.

"I guess you know how hard I've been trying to keep my distance," Sonny finally manages after a long pause and a deep swig of his cognac.

"Yeah, and for most of this voyage, I tried to help you. But to hell with that," Miranda says as she places a hand on Sonny's chest and gently pushes him backward. The big man could have resisted but instead lets himself fall back onto the couch. Miranda steps closer, and still holding her drink, deftly climbs onto his lap. She straddles him, her knees flexed outside his legs so that she faces him, her bare torso only inches from his own. She takes a sip of her brandy and, with her free hand, begins undoing the buttons on his shirt.

"As an artist, I'm always trying to please people. I provide them with beautiful sculptures so they can live their dreams of being surrounded by art and culture. But I, too, have dreams. I dreamed about you for a long time, even before this cruise.

"I dreamed about what these hands could do to me," she says, her voice now deep and hoarse as she takes one of his hands and draws it to her breast. "And what this body could do to mine," she continues, releasing his hand and moving hers across his bare chest.

How in the hell had he not noticed this smoldering, dark-haired beauty, Sonny asks himself? Her deep complexion, full lips and nose, and her lush hips and thighs tell him that somewhere in her family's past at the southern-most tip of Europe just across the Mediterranean from Algeria, Libya, and Egypt, their French blood had somehow mixed with the blood of Africa.

If he hadn't been able to see this unusual woman until she gave him no choice, what else is he missing as he looks at life through blinders, his ability to live and fully experience his surroundings blunted by whatever it is within him that stifles his imagination and sense of purpose?

But tonight is not the time for introspection. He can focus only on Miranda and every brash and amazing aspect of her: her soulful beauty, her bold sexuality, and even the hair on her arms and legs that he finds so unbelievably sensual and which, in her avant-garde bodaciousness, she flaunts. When the last button on Sonny's shirt is opened, Miranda pulls it from his shoulders and flings it aside as she rises from her perch on his lap. With her glass still in her hand, she walks across the room and sits on the edge of her bed, wordlessly offering Sonny the opportunity to leave if he feels so inclined.

He stands and drains the rest of his cognac as he approaches her. He pulls her up into his arms with the intensity of someone who has come alive after a long sleepwalk. The following hours are a blur of passion and urgency, the likes of which Sonny has never before experienced or dreamed possible. Sharing an intimacy that was at the same time gentle and rough, he and Miranda lose themselves in perfect harmony, thrust for passionate thrust.

The nightstand lamp that casts a pleasant glow over the stateroom remains on for several more hours. On this occasion, Sonny is not troubled by the light. Somewhere in the middle of the night with the big man finally asleep and Miranda ready to drift off, the lamp is finally turned off.

Long before dawn, Sonny wakes in a start, an internal alarm activating all his senses. But he quickly realizes there is no danger or cause for concern. With the woman who has brazenly elbowed her way into his world still asleep in his arms, he relaxes and lets the tension flow out of his body. Fully enjoying the moment, he never wants it to end. It takes every ounce of his willpower to get out of Miranda's bed and back to his own cabin, where he and Edouard ready themselves for docking and getting the Expedition on the road. He doesn't want to even think about the missed opportunity to picnic with Miranda and enjoy a few carefree days on the Riviera. That will have to wait for another time.

Before he leaves Miranda, Sonny gives her the *Belie Belcan* charm that has hung from his neck for so many years. If Miranda had dreamed about him even before they met, maybe his guardian *loa* has directed them to each other. Grateful for his guidance and protection, Sonny now wants Belie's magic close to Miranda. When he fastens the chain about her neck, he says only that the charm is a loan and that he will soon return to Monte Carlo to reclaim it.

By noon the Expedition is parked safe and sound on the Marseille-Fos port dock next to the *Invictus*. After loading their gear and a final goodbye to Miranda, Sonny and Edouard head north out of the port city for the three-hour drive to Lyon. Before turning onto highway A6, Sonny notices a bookstore. Spotting a parking space on the street that will give Edouard and him a clear view of the vehicle while they are in the shop, Sonny parks and enters the well-stocked old-school *Librairie Ville-Marie*. With its wood paneling, carpets, and winding stairways to second-floor balcony bookshelves, the old bookshop looks as though it has been selling books for hundreds of years.

Unfortunately, most of the books in Sonny's area of interest, the politics of Black activism and self-determination, are in French. The only book in English that interests him is Eldridge Cleaver's *Soul on Ice*. It describes Cleaver's 1960s evolution from street thug and rapist to *Black Panther Party* Minister of Information.

After a stressful drive through heavy midday traffic on streets and roads not designed for vehicles the size of the Expedition, Sonny and Edouard arrive in Lyon. Sonny promises himself that when they depart for Le Havre three days later, they will leave early. This will avoid all rush hour traffic and allow them to arrive at the Le Havre dock with enough time to pack the Expedition in a container for the departure to Novia Scotia.

The home in Lyon is a disappointment. It is comfortable and has a large garage where the Expedition will be safe for the three-day stopover. But Sonny had hoped to stay in a centuries-old stone structure with a tiled roof and beamed ceilings, the type always pictured in European travel posters. Instead, their bland rental house is part of a subdivision of cookie-cutter one- and two-story homes, none of which are more than thirty years old.

Sonny makes only one trip to the local food market. He spends most of the stopover reading under a mimosa tree in the colorful, flower-filled backyard. He and Edouard cook most of their meals on an outdoor charcoal grill. At the end of the three-day stay, he has almost completed the Cleaver book. It is interesting and well-written but not as inspiring as his earlier reads.

Their six p.m. departure keeps them out of the hectic traffic of Paris and other large cities along the way to Le Havre. Twelve hours later, the Expedition is once again sealed in a protective container and stored in the hold of the cargo ship *St. Nicholas* for the twelve-day crossing to Nova Scotia.

With no new books to read and no one among the small group of passengers as interesting as Miranda, the trip to Canada is a tedious slog with lots of sleeping and walks around the deck. After arriving in Canada and clearing customs, Sonny and Edouard are back on the road heading from Prince Edward Island to New Brunswick on the mainland. They continue down the Atlantic coast, finally reaching the customs station at the US–Canada border southwest of the city of Saint Stephen. The Expedition is searched, but no drugs are found, and no connection to Haiti is made. The long, transatlantic trip through France and Canada has proved its worth.

After passing through Maine and New Hampshire on endless stretches of boring interstate freeways, Sonny and Edouard stop at a *White Castle* in Lowell, Massachusetts, a few miles Northwest of

Boston. There they meet up with Eric Dissageport and Allain Price. The two have driven up from New York to accompany them and their precious cargo the last few miles through some of the tougher sections of Brooklyn to the warehouse where the coke will be recovered. After sending his shipment halfway around the world, Jacques doesn't want to risk a holdup or carjacking when the drugs are so close to home. Over double sliders, fish sandwiches, fries, and coffee, Sonny lays out the final leg of the trip. Eric and Allain will follow the Expedition in their Jeep Cherokee. They will be armed with handguns concealed in holsters under the dashboard, and an automatic rifle hidden under the rear seat cushion. Sonny and Edouard will continue to travel unarmed. Sonny doesn't want to risk having the Expedition impounded if a weapon is discovered during a routine traffic violation police stop.

If for any reason, the police stop the Jeep, the Expedition will continue unaccompanied for the rest of the trip. If they stop the Expedition, Jacques will be called so that appropriate legal resources can be called in. If the Expedition is stopped by anyone other than police, Eric and Allain will intercede and resolve the situation, hopefully with only a show of force and no gunfire.

Everything proceeds without a hitch until they reach the Bedford-Stuyvesant section of Brooklyn. Although it is almost one a.m., there are many cars still on the streets but no pedestrians. At a stoplight at the intersection of Nostrand and Lafayette Avenues, not more than a few blocks from their final destination, two teenage boys appear from nowhere and approach the SUV's driver and passenger doors. Flashing pistols that seem too large for their scrawny adolescent bodies, they order Sonny and Edouard out of the vehicle. Because the Expedition is behind another car, Sonny can't run the light. Before he can warn the young carjackers about the danger they face, gunshots ring out from behind the Expedition. Eric and Allain have opened fire.

The vehicle in front of Sonny immediately speeds off without waiting for the light to change. Sonny follows suit as both teens run from the gunfire. The boy on Sonny's side staggers as he disappears into an alley off Nostrand. The big man can't see whether the other boy is also hit. In this depressed, inner-city neighborhood, late-night shootings frequently occur with no immediate police response. Tonight is one of those nights.

Sonny speeds the last few blocks to their destination as Edouard calls ahead to make sure the gate and warehouse doors will be open. Less than five minutes after the gunfire, he pulls into a warehouse on Park between Kent and Franklin Avenues. Moments later, the Jeep screeches to a stop next to the Expedition as the big doors close.

—◆—

As always, bringing the drugs into the US is only half the problem. Selling them without getting busted, set up, or sold out by a compromised customer, double-crossed by a partner, or ripped off by a competitor is an even bigger challenge, especially with such a large shipment. Jacques had become a major New York wholesaler, and with no recent deliveries of his product, street demand was high. NARCs were aware of the drought and were on the lookout for the arrival of drugs from new sources.

Jacques had a couple of options. He could break up his shipment, selling portions to several different customers. This would keep him under the 'large-deal' threshold above which the DEA focused most of its attention and firepower. But on the downside, more transactions meant that more things could go wrong. Smaller transactions with less sophisticated, cutthroat players conducted in bad neighborhoods could be dangerous. A single large deal with a well-financed, big-time player was neater and cleaner. But large transactions were also risky. They were the kind that most interested the NARCs who were nothing if not patient. The relentless agents were willing to invest months, if not years, orchestrating traps, doing business with lower-level dealers to build relationships and working their way up to the kingpins and major dealers.

Although *Molly* was no longer a key component of his business, Jacques had kept in touch with Carlos Marquez, his original New York MDMA supplier. He had always liked Carlos and admired his smooth, hip style of conducting business. He had incorporated much of Carlos's swag into his own dealings.

Many of Carlos's deep-pocket, yuppie clients had expanded their tastes and were now into cocaine. They viewed coke much the same as *Molly*, a sophisticated and acceptable way of getting high that didn't involve the devastating and debilitating effects of drugs like heroin. To these high-flying achievers, Smack was a crutch for the poor and ignorant. Many of Carlos's clients were into cocaine but didn't care for doing business with the sources of coke in New York. They had been pushing him to become their supplier.

At first, he resisted, not wanting to incur the risks and costs of building the necessary infrastructure. He had never been greedy and was happy to be one of the main MDMA dealers in New York. But his *Molly* sales had flattened and, in some cases, even declined. He was beginning to lose his well-heeled crowd of partying young professionals.

Over breakfast at a small eatery not far from the *Blue Note* jazz club where they had started their business relationship, he tells Jacques he is interested in moving into cocaine. He wants to become one of his wholesale customers.

The timing couldn't be better. It has been a month since Sonny had brought in the shipment from Europe, and Jacques wants to get rid of it. It is now sitting in a safe house he maintains in Harlem and isn't earning him a penny. He and Sonny had moved the drugs during a Friday rush-hour trip. They drove a circuitous route from the Brooklyn warehouse through Queens and across the Tri-Borough Bridge into Harlem. Sonny used every trick in the book to avoid a possible tail without getting stopped for a traffic violation. At the end of a wild ride, he pulled into the garage of the safe house, a four-story brownstone just north of Fifth Avenue on 129th Street. It was the only house on the block that had a built-in, street-facing garage. Jacques rents out the top three floors and keeps the ground floor, basement, and garage for his own use. One of Carlos's accountant customers handles the property management for him.

The setup is perfect for Jacques. It allows him to come and go without ever using the front door unless he wants to leave the car and catch a cab or the subway. He is just another rarely-seen apartment dweller lost in a crowd of busy and often overlooked New Yorkers. The few people that have seen him in the building don't even know he is their landlord. Shortly after purchasing the place, he installed a working fireplace that could be moved to reveal a large walk-in safe. He used the hidden safe to warehouse his product from the time it arrived in the US until it could be sold to a wholesale buyer. Only he and Sonny have ever set foot in or even knew of the existence of the safe house.

If the deal can be arranged with Carlos, it will be Jacques's biggest by far, almost three times his largest previous sale. After the Colixe bust and notebook discovery, several of his regular customers were on the DEA watch list and were no longer buying from him. Because he had shut down the bag switch and asphalt routines, he'd had nothing to sell his customers who were still in the market. It has been almost a three-month drought, and Jacques needs cash.

A week after their breakfast meeting, Carlos calls Jacques and offers to buy his entire new shipment. With the backing of several of his deep-pocket investment banker Molly customers, he has pulled together the buy amount and has already begun setting up his distribution network. Jacques is relieved to be able to do his largest deal ever with someone he has known and trusted for years. But there are always concerns. In large drug transactions, even between parties that know each other well, there is the chance that one of them has been compromised and, under pressure from the law, is consummating the deal only to entrap the other party. If it meant escaping the prospect of long jail time, parties to an agreement could usually be expected to turn on each other.

Jacques believes there is an additional advantage in dealing with Carlos. Knowing the pill-dealer so well and having observed his behavior in many situations over the years, he is confident he would have discerned any subtle changes in demeanor that might suggest betrayal. Seeing none of those signs, he follows his tried-and-true hustler intuition and proceeds with the deal. He agrees to sell Carlos the entire one-hundred-fifty kilos for $3 million. Because of the size of the buy and the inexperience of his new customer, he knows he will have to use heightened security to counter a level of DEA surveillance that neither of them have yet experienced.

Jacques secures weekend use of a small farmhouse outside of Peekskill, New York. A ninety-minute drive northeast of Manhattan, the remote farmhouse is situated on an isolated stretch of road two miles from the nearest intersection in one direction and three miles from US 9A in the other. With lookouts posted at these points, any incoming traffic can be detected long before it reaches the farmhouse. If unexpected visitors pass a lookout point, there will be adequate time to make a hasty escape using an unimproved dirt road that can only be negotiated by a competent driver using a sturdy four-wheel-drive vehicle. Jacques arranges the use of such a vehicle for the day of the transaction and advises Carlos to do the same. He also requests that Carlos limit his party to four people. He promises to do the same.

The transfer goes off without a hitch. As planned, Jacques posts men at either end of the road leading to the farmhouse. Along with Sonny and two others, he arrives with the cocaine three hours early. He receives Carlos and his party at the appointed meeting time.

Jacques and Carlos greet each other on the old-fashioned wood porch. They joke about how, with all the necessary precautions, it is not as much fun to do a big coke deal as it was to transfer a few packages of pills at the *Blue Note* surrounded by great food, music, and company. The pleasantries quickly over, one of Carlos's men checks the purity of two samples, one from each of the two drug–stuffed duffel bags. When he is satisfied that everything is in order, Carlos hands Jacques an attaché case that contains three hundred packets of hundred dollar bills, one hundred bills to a packet.

The entire transaction done in less than an hour, Carlos and his men depart with their drugs. Ten minutes later, after locking up and dismissing the outposts, Jacques, Sonny, and their two guards also leave. This time they take the dirt road and work their way southeast until they hit US 9A heading back to the city. Once on the freeway, Jacques breathes a huge sigh of relief. He is once again flush, has a new pipeline, and an important new customer. He had paid his dues with penny-ante weed and *Molly* deals, bag-switch schemes, and nerve-racking mule-smuggling where, at any time, some poor bastard might bring down an entire mission by prematurely shitting out some coke or overdosing from a pellet that ruptured in his stomach. As he reflects on the events leading up to today's transaction, he sees the deal with Carlos as a water-shed moment in his career From here on out, he will concentrate only on large, multi-kilo deals. They could be as dangerous and stressful as the smaller deals, but the return is a hell of a lot better.

The Truth

Lilly hasn't slept well in the weeks since her profiling tool labeled Fernand's letters as 'untruthful.' As she lies in bed fretting through the remaining hours of another long night, she wonders how much she really knows about Fernand other than the few scraps of information he had provided her. In the two years since they met, he had thoroughly worked his way into her life but had shared little about his own. She knows only that he was born in Haiti, has no family, and had received his academic degrees in Haiti. Although he often travels, whenever he is in New York and not busy, she is with him unless she is teaching or working on her research. His frequent absences had made sense when he explained how he split his time between Haiti and New York, lecturing at both Hofstra and his alma mater back home. But she is now disappointed with herself for allowing such a secretive and guarded man to take up so much of her life.

She had once accompanied him to Haiti for a long holiday weekend in 1997. But his Cap-Haïtien home on Haiti's northern coastline gave no clues about his life. With not a family memento or picture to be seen, the comfortable house looked sterile. The mystery surrounding him had increased when he reneged on his commitment to escort her to her sorority awards banquet, claiming he had unexpectedly been summoned to an urgent meeting in Haiti.

As the events of her two-year relationship once again play out in her mind like the rerun of a troubling movie, she recalls how she had not even been attracted to Fernand when she first met him in 1995. An alarm had gone off when he began making advances toward her, but she didn't rebuff him. She feared he would perceive her rejection as a lack of appreciation for his role as her mentor and PhD adviser. His smooth, engaging manner, persistence, and intellectual prowess wore her down, and she allowed a relationship to develop. Shame now gnawed at her for having compromised herself to advance her academic career.

Unwilling to wallow in self-pity, Lilly needed to reassure herself that Fernand hadn't made a fool of her. She wanted to push back but wasn't sure how. Confrontation didn't seem to be a good idea, at least not at the moment. Nor would it make sense to try to discuss her concerns with him if he had already established a pattern of untruthfulness. Resentful of his inattention and deception, Lilly decided she could no longer allow events to overtake her. Somehow she would pierce the shield of secrecy surrounding the enigmatic professor.

She started by using his cell phone to track him. As an undergraduate and later a Hofstra lecturer, she had partnered with AT&T to research the use of location-aware devices such as mobile phones to create real-time geographical position profiles of users. Although it had not yet reached consumers, technology now existed that allowed such profiles to be used together with telephone calling patterns to monitor the location and movement of mobile phone callers. Using her contacts at the telephone company, her data mining skills, and her ability to hack into almost any database, Lilly believed she could track Fernand's cell phone call history and pinpoint the GPS latitude and longitude coordinates of all his calls in recent months.

Although she was accustomed to surprises and revelations about the professor, what she discovered over the next few days was both shocking and disturbing. Other than when he was with her, rarely was Fernand ever where he claimed to be. Most of his calls in Haiti came not from his Cap-Haïtien home but from the ViVi Michel region just outside the capital city. The only call activity from his home occurred the weekend she spent with him there many months ago.

Often when he claimed to be in New York and too busy to be with her, he was actually in Haiti. There were also occasions he claimed to be in Haiti but was really in New York. Using satellite imagery accessed through a prototype map rendering application, Lilly was able to view the ViVi Michel location from which Fernand made most of his calls. Zooming in on the map, she saw a detailed image of the property's many luxurious amenities. Only one other location revealed heavy call traffic from him, a warehouse in Port-au-Prince not far from police headquarters.

There were so many questions and loose ends. What was going on in Fernand's life that caused him to be so deceptive and secretive? Why did he claim to live in a home in which he never spent any time? Even though he said he owned the Cap-Haïtien residence, when Lilly queried the Haiti Central Government tax rolls, she found he was not listed as the registered owner. The house was actually owned by a Jacques Maurice, a Haitian national who also owned the ViVi Michel estate and several other properties around Haiti.

How could Fernand afford to travel so much and live in relative opulence on the modest salary of a university professor? True, he had two teaching positions, one in the US and one in Haiti, but both were part-time. Was he ashamed to admit he was from a wealthy family that subsidized his extravagant lifestyle? Or could he be a philandering husband who married into wealth?

After a review of all available public data, she realized Fernand Pierre-Paul was a cipher, completely unknown in Haiti except for the BA, MA, and PhD degrees awarded to him in Haiti. Fernand and this Jacques Maurice shared some kind of a relationship, but she would need to do more digging to figure out what it was.

The smile is missing from Lilly's face when she sits down with Gil a few days later for their biweekly one-on-one meeting. Her eyes are puffy, and she shows none of her usual energy and enthusiasm as she invites Gil into her office. After a routine review of the status of profile testing and a short discussion of his own coursework, Gil abruptly changes topics.

"I don't want to pry, but you haven't been yourself the past few days. Is anything wrong?"

"Is it that obvious?" Lilly answers, taking a deep breath and releasing it with a long sigh as she slumps back in her desk chair. "Yeah, something's not right. But I'd rather not get into it at the moment."

Like the persistent cop that he is, Gil is not ready to give up easily. "So what do you say we get out of here and meet someplace off campus where we can relax, get a bite to eat, and kick it around like two old classmates?"

"That's not a bad idea," Lilly replies. "These office and lab walls are beginning to close in on me."

"Let's meet at the *Steer Inn* on Babylon Turnpike at five," Gil adds as he rises. "It's only ten minutes from here, south on Nassau Road, and left on Babylon Turnpike. You can't miss it."

"Ok, see you soon."

Gil is seated in the popular eatery an hour later with a few minutes to spare before Lilly shows up. He had a good feeling about the house he had just seen on Manhattan Avenue, a quiet tree-lined street in Roosevelt, a Black community a few miles from Hofstra. He had decided to give up his small apartment in Queens and move closer to school and work. What he liked most about the Roosevelt house was the sound of the breeze blowing through a large maple tree on the front lawn. He could hear the gentle rustling of leaves through the front windows of the master bedroom. Having grown up in crowded city neighborhoods, he had never experienced anything like it. If it worked out that his purchase offer was accepted, he would look forward to the night he could fall asleep to such relaxing sounds.

Lilly arrives at five p.m. sharp, relieved to be out of the office and in the company of someone she likes and trusts. A smile is back on her face as she joins Gil in a booth for two. She has never been in the neighborhood roadhouse, which is popular not only for its good food and drinks but also for the live blues music it features on weekends. After tasting her vodka and orange juice and ordering dinner, she begins to unwind.

"It's hard to discuss my situation," she begins, "because I know that if I am to be a serious scholar, I shouldn't allow my academic work to be confused by my personal feelings and emotions. I know it, but I've done it just the same and created a mess."

"I'm guessing you've already figured out that Fernand and I are involved," she continues.

"Yes, I've picked up on that," Gil responds.

Lilly describes how the memo from Fernand was taken from the bulletin board and submitted to her algorithm as team members were gathering input documents to test the capability of the software to determine author truthfulness. She described how she wasn't too concerned when that single document was flagged because she knew that interoffice correspondence was often written by support staff.

"But I became alarmed and almost unglued when I submitted many of Fernand's personal letters and all were designated as untruthful.

"What has been especially troubling is that Fernand's memo is not the only occasion of his untruthfulness. I could have easily dealt with that one incident. But if I have any confidence in the tool I worked so hard to create, I have to face the fact that all the letters he wrote me over the past two years have also been untruthful."

Lilly goes on to describe what she has discovered about Pierre-Paul's comings and goings in Haiti and his strange association with the mysterious Jacques Maurice. The agitation in her voice increases as she unburdens herself about the unpleasant events of the past few days.

"Fernand is a blank slate in Haiti," she continues. "The only public records I could find about him come from the university, and even they are skimpy, confirming only that his degrees were conferred by them. But what about the rest of his life? The trail starts and stops at the university.

"And what's the tie-in with this Maurice character? Between the two of them, there's obviously some wealth. But where does it come from? Fernand isn't making big money as a teacher, so Maurice must be the deep pockets. If so, why is he taking care of Fernand?"

"Maybe there is a way to figure out what's going on," Gil interrupts as they begin their dinners. "It's possible that everything you describe might be legit, but it feels like one or the other of these guys is dirty. Maybe both. There are FBI databases that can easily be checked to see whether either of them has a criminal record in the US. But getting information about them in Haiti could get complicated.

"Most countries have their own versions of a national crime database, some a lot better than others. When I was in the academy, I remember hearing about the FBI's International Operations Division, which was set up to tie all these databases together. To make it happen, FBI legal attachés from the division, I think they're called 'legats,' are assigned to each foreign nation that shares data with the FBI.

Feeing that additional libation will help settle Lilly's jangled nerves, Gil pauses and signals for another round of vodka and OJ, this time doubles.

"I'll start by doing some digging here in the US," he continues. "We'll see where that takes us. Based on what I find, I'll work through the Haiti legat to see what's going on with Fernand and Maurice in Haiti. I should know something soon."

⸻◆⸻

"Lilly where are you?" Gil almost barks into his cell phone a few days later when Lilly picks up his call. "I've been trying to reach you for the past couple of hours. I need to meet with you as soon as possible."

"I'm out at Jones Beach. Been here all afternoon," Lilly answers. "Things were quiet on campus. It's a nice day, and since I had no appointments or classes, I decided to close up shop, come out here, soak up some rays, and try to shake off the blues. It's working. I've been reading, enjoying the sound of the surf, and not paying attention to the phone. So what's going on?" she asks. "What's the urgency?"

"I'll tell you as soon as I see you. Is anyone with you?"

"No, it's just me. It was a spur of the moment thing. I don't even have on a bathing suit. I'm wearing what I had on at school."

"Ok, I'm heading out now. I'll meet you in forty-five minutes at the main snack bar. Go there right now and wait for me. I want you in a public place where there are plenty of people around. If possible, stay off the phone, but if you must talk, don't tell anyone where you are."

"What's all this about, Gil? You're scaring me. Is what you've found out that bad?"

"Everything's under control. But I've come up with some troubling information about our guy. Just do as I say, and everything will be ok."

"All right, I'm on my way," Lilly responds calmly even though her heart pounds.

She relaxes a bit when she sees Gil striding purposefully along the boardwalk. His look of strength and confidence comforts her. She stands to get his attention as he enters the busy eatery and walks toward her. When they sit, he reaches across the small table for two and places his hands on hers.

"Can I get you something?" he asks. "When we met at the Steer Inn on Wednesday, you didn't eat much. I know stress can kill the appetite, but you've got to stay strong. You're going to need all your strength in the coming days."

Gil leaves the table and returns a few minutes later with chili-cheese fries, cokes and hot dogs slathered with mustard, onions, and more chili.

"Your professor seems to have a clear record here and in Haiti," Gil begins as they start on their food. "In fact, he's so clean, it looks like he hardly exists. Other than his position at Hofstra, he's doesn't have much of a footprint except for the apartment he rents in Hempstead. It's like he came out of nowhere with only a passport and a pocket full of university degrees. Back in Haiti, only the University of Haiti knows anything about him. They seem to think highly of him, but won't say why.

"It's a different situation with this Jacques Maurice. Here in the US, he has no record, but some guys I know who work narcotics in New York City say his name came up in a drug bust at LaGuardia a few months back. Maurice was never arrested, but his name was in an address book carried by a courier who had come in from Haiti carrying a half-million dollars worth of cocaine. Maurice's passport has not been used in the US since that bust, and no one has seen him around New York in almost six months.

"Maurice is a pretty well-known and powerful figure in Haiti, but no one wants to talk about him, at least not on the record. He's said to be a big drug lord, the biggest on the island. He specializes in moving Colombian cocaine through Haiti to the US and seems to have a lot of juice in Haitian government circles. His cozy relationship with President Aristide allows him to run his drug enterprise with no interference from the police or anyone else."

"Ok, so Fernand is clean, and Jacques Maurice isn't," Lilly interrupts. "But what do they have to do with each other? Why is Fernand spending so much time with a coke dealer?"

"Take a look at this," Gil answers. He pulls two four-by-six-inch photos from his jacket pocket and places them on the table next to each other facing Lilly. One is labeled 'Jacques Maurice,' the other 'Fernand Paul-Pierre.' Maurice wears a short, neatly trimmed goatee and a half smile that could be a smirk, while the clean-shaven, serious, and bespectacled Pierre-Paul is attired in a conservative three-piece suit. Although Maurice's picture is dated six years earlier than Fernand's, the two look like clones of each other.

Lilly gasps but says nothing for a few moments as she stares in silence at the snapshots.

"At first glance, these two could be twins who took separate life paths: the cocky, ambitious street kid who found his way into the drug world, and the serious scholar who dispenses knowledge," Gil explains. "But the FBI face-recognition analyst who pulled these photos from passport databases claims that, based on current feature recognition technology, he is 99.9% sure that the two photos are of the same man.

"I'm sorry to be the person who has to break this to you, Lilly, but your colleague is leading a double life. Just as he's laundered drug money to get it out of the States and back to Haiti, it looks like he's also been trying to launder his image with this teaching cover. And it's obvious that cover identity never existed until Jacques Maurice paid or somehow coerced the University of Haiti to issue his degrees to an assumed name. Based on the fallout from last spring's drug bust, we may have seen the last of Jacques Maurice around these parts. All we may be left with is Fernand Pierre-Paul."

"Damn," whispers Lilly. "I was ready for a dose of unpleasant news, but nothing like this."

"I know this is a lot to have to digest in a hurry," Gil says, "but we've got to make plans for our next steps. You could be in danger. And by the way, Maurice is recently divorced and has two small children."

Her heart once again pounding and her stomach now churning, Lilly stares at Gil, for the moment unable to speak. "Look, I'm not pleased to know my guy is a drug dealer, and I'm sure as hell not anxious to stay in this kind of a relationship, but after all this time with him, what's the sudden danger for me?"

"You mentioned that you had been tracking him through his phone and asking a few questions about him back in Haiti. If he has gotten even a whiff of that, you're in trouble. But even if he can't be sure it's you who's doing the digging, you're still in trouble. He'll go after anyone he thinks might be able to take him down."

Again placing his hands on hers, Gil continues: "Where is Pierre-Paul right now?"

"He's been in Haiti this week. I talked to him a couple of days ago. He said he'd be back in the US within a week."

"Have you ever posed any of your questions directly to him? Could he possibly know of your suspicions?"

"Until recently, I've never tried to dig into his Haitian origins. I've always accepted things as they are. Even though I've had my doubts about him, especially after he stood me up for the banquet, I've never challenged him on anything or asked him any questions."

"That's good," Gil responds. But it doesn't mean you'll ever be safe around him again. I don't think he'd be surprised that someone, probably a cop, might be checking on his Jacques Maurice identity since that name popped up in the New York bust. I'm sure that his Aristide administration contacts have alerted him that many inquiries have recently been made about him, directly and through the Haitian legat.

"But the uncovering of his other identity is something else. As far as he knows, there are only two entities that could know about his dual identity. The University of Haiti, for sure, since they created the alias for him. And you," Gil adds, pointing at Lilly. "Knowing your forensic skills, he could be worried that you've figured out his game."

"It's possible that someone else might have sought a match in a face-recognition database," Gil continues. "But they would have had to start with some knowledge of the two parties they were trying to match. The technology is not yet there to start with one face like Maurice's and query all the international databases searching for a match.

"It is still a laborious process to prove a match even when starting with two images. That means only the university, or you could have outed him. The university people are right there in Maurice's backyard. They know who they're up against and are well aware of the long list of competitors, rivals, and other enemies who have disappeared after crossing him. They wouldn't dare spill the beans on him.

"He's probably not sure about you but might want to silence you before you're able to provide too much evidence about him or testify against him in the kind of a brutal US court trial he would never see in Haiti."

His hands still pressed against Lilly's, Gil pauses to take stock of her. She seems to be weathering the ordeal, at least so far. "I know it sounds unbelievably cold-blooded to think that after you two have been so close, he might turn on you and hurt you, but anything is possible in a situation like this.

"Ok, you've heard the worst," Gil continues, "so now let's talk about what we're going to do. But first you've got to take a bite of your food before it's cold," Gil adds as he takes one of the hot dogs from Lilly's plate and holds it up to her mouth. Lilly adds a dollop of chilli and bites into the dog.

"Yeah, I know I've got to get my nourishment," Lilly responds, attempting to force a smile as she takes the hot dog from Gil's hand and nibbles at it.

Gil pauses to dig into his own food.

"As soon as I received these two photos and got confirmation that they were the same guy," Gil continues, "I met with the inspector who heads my precinct. I informed him that we've got Haiti's biggest drug lord waltzing in and out of town and masquerading as a college professor right under our noses. That same morning, we met with the Nassau County police chief and some of the guys from the New York City Narcotic Squad who were on the bust when Maurice's name first came up. The chief thinks a pretty good case can be made and is ready to have Maurice arrested as soon as he sets foot back in the States.

"I've gotten a commitment from my boss and the New York team that before any moves are made against Maurice, you and your family must be out of harm's way.

"So here's what we're proposing. This afternoon, you'll check into South Nassau Communities Hospital under cover of some kind of emergency surgery like an appendectomy. We'll also send your parents away for a few days, maybe to Martinique, and we'll watch their home while they're gone. You'll be under 24-hour protective guard until

Maurice is picked up. That will happen as soon as he shows up at his apartment, tries to visit you, or sets foot on the Hofstra Campus. We'll also keep our eye out for him at the local airports, but who knows what route he'll take coming back into the country.

Gil rises and walks around the table to sit next to an obviously shaken Lilly.

"Now I know you'd rather not have to cool your heels in a hospital for a week or more while we wait for Maurice to show up. But if we sent you out of town with your parents, it might tip Maurice off that we're planning an operation. So we need you to stick around. If this works as expected, we should have him in custody within a week to ten days."

Lilly turns away from her mostly uneaten food and moves closer to Gil. Her eyes welling up with tears, she rests her head on his shoulder as he pulls her to him.

"Gil, I appreciate what you and your people are trying to do," Lilly says, straining to keep her composure. "The sooner I can get away from Fernand, the sooner I can get on with my life and work. And if he can be prevented from ruining any more lives with drugs, so much the better.

"But I assure you, he's not going down without a fight. I've never seen him in his drug lord mode, but from being around him at Hofstra, I know he holds grudges and forgets nothing. And if he's as powerful in the drug world as you describe, he's still going to be a force to be reckoned with even from behind bars. I'm guessing that if he thinks I've had anything to do with his arrest, he'll be coming after my parents and me real hard. He'll still have the network and resources to wreak havoc and get his revenge no matter what prison he's in."

"Everyone understands Maurice is a powerful and dangerous man," Gil acknowledges. "And no one is taking his threats lightly. But this will be a major bust, and the government will assign plenty of resources to make sure you and your parents are out of harm's way. Maurice won't be the first tough guy we've locked up who promises to get even and blow up the world. But once they're behind bars, these guys usually change their tune.

"And to get to you, he'd have to get through me. That won't be easy because I'll be there 24-7 to keep you safe, and I'm not going anywhere. I'm sorry you're stuck in this mess, and I'll do whatever it takes for as long as it takes to get you out of it. You had no way of knowing this guy was a drug dealer and killer."

"I appreciate that Gil, but it sounds like the only way I'll be safe is to assume a new identity and go into some kind of a witness protection program. I've worked hard to establish myself in my field, and I don't want to go into hiding. I'm going to have to think about this.

"And it's going to be an even tougher sell for my father. Yes, he and my mother have talked for a long time about retiring back to Martinique. But he's a proud man and won't appreciate being run out of town. He didn't get to be such a respected man in the French West Indian community by running from trouble."

"I understand," Gil answers. "But we don't have to come up with the long-term plan today. All we have to decide right now is what we're going to do tonight, tomorrow, and every day for the next week or ten days until this guy shows up and we can get him off the streets. We can't delay a minute on that. We can discuss the long-term plan later. You give me the ok, and we can have your parents on the next plane to Martinique or wherever else they want to go. And we'll get you situated in a room at the hospital."

"When you put it like that, I guess I don't have much choice. Let me call my parents, and then we can head to the hospital. But if I'm going to be holed up there for a few days, I'll have to get someone to pick up a few things from my apartment."

"Let's not get anyone else involved just yet," Gil cautioned. "I'll go by your place after you're settled and pick up whatever you need.

"You've done plenty already," Lilly replied. "I can't expect you to go running around after my laundry."

Gil stared at her for a moment, a look on his face somewhere between amusement and puzzlement. "Lilly, in case you haven't figured it out yet, I've been crazy about you ever since our grade school days at

P.S. 40. I didn't know what to do about it back then, and in a minute, you were gone. But providence somehow caused our paths to cross once again. Even though there's another guy in the picture, I'm lucky to have you back in my life, and I'm not ever going to let you slip out of it again, even if it means I have to do your laundry for you."

"But, Gil, I need underwear, toiletries, personal items. You don't want to be digging around in that kind of stuff, do you?"

"Lilly, I'm a cop," Gil responds in mock seriousness. "We know how to find things. I understand if you don't want me rooting around in your stuff. So make up a list of what you need and mark the items you don't want me to see. I'll close my eyes when I get to them."

"Ok, officer, you win. I'll come peaceably," Lilly answers, somehow even managing a smile as she begins dialing her parents. Gil had talked her down off her ledge, and she was already starting to feel that things might work out.

Fourteen

Revanj pou Myou

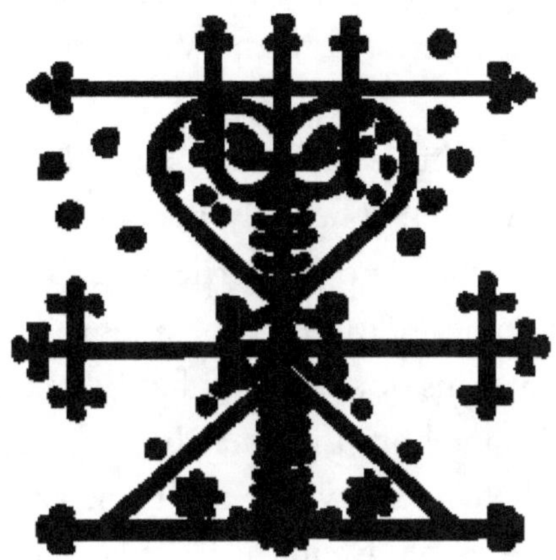

Jacques's hustler intuition tells him loud and clear that trouble is brewing. He knows that inquiries have recently been made about him at both the University of Haiti and Haiti's Tax Assessor's office. And someone from the New York City Narcotics squad has been digging into Haitian criminal databases for information on both Jacques Maurice and Fernand Pierre-Paul.

He knows the New York City police have been tracking him ever since his name showed up in the address book at the LaGuardia bust. And there's no telling how much Jules Colixe has spilled his guts after his arrest. But why is anyone checking on Fernand Pierre-Paul? How have his two identities become linked?

The woman who called the school for background information on Fernand Pierre-Paul claimed to be doing research for a magazine article about recent PhD degrees awarded in the Caribbean. She left no contact information, but her call came from Nassau County in New York. The university told her they could provide no information without Dr. Pierre-Paul's authorization.

The assessor's office informed Jacques that it had released ownership information on several of his properties that a caller had identified by address. Because property records are public information, they had no choice but to comply. The caller, also from a Nassau County area code, was particularly interested in the ViVi Michel and Cap Haitïan properties.

Jacques is puzzled. Why would anyone in Nassau County be concerned about ViVi Michel? The only person in the US who knows anything about any of the Haiti properties is Lilly. But she only knows of the Cap Haitïan home and thinks it belongs to Fernand.

Jacques now knows his dual identity has been uncovered, probably by US NARCs. But somehow, Lilly may have pieced together his story, as well. Maybe it is she who knew first and tipped off the NARCs.

He had already stopped traveling as Jacques Maurice, but if the cops are onto his game, he can no longer enter the US as Pierre-Paul either. There is no way he can return to New York now.

Having been through many battles against those who would displace him as Haiti's top drug man, Jacques reacts quickly and instinctively. He has one of his lieutenants follow up with the prospective buyers he had been cultivating in New York, and he arranges a leave of absence from Hofstra. He will also have to deal with Lilly.

He had talked with her a few days ago, but she hadn't mentioned being contacted by whoever was inquiring about him. He called her twice today, but she didn't pick up or return either call. And then a few hours ago, there was a flurry of messages that she had checked herself into South Nassau Communities Hospital and was about to have her appendix removed.

The sudden illness seems strange for a person like Lilly, who is always so fit and healthy. It doesn't feel right when he calls the hospital and is told that even though she has only been admitted for observation, she is unavailable to speak with him. His suspicions grow when he calls her parents and can't reach them either. It is beginning to look like the dogging of his trail by the unidentified woman from Nassau County might have something to do with Lilly's sudden illness and unavailability.

He knows what he has to do.

"Sonny, I've got a problem, and I need your help," Jacques says to the big man over breakfast the following morning at the mansion. "You already know about my teaching at Hofstra. And you know that I've tried to keep my business and academic lives separate by teaching under a different name, Fernand Pierre-Paul."

Sonny nods.

"I went to a lot of trouble and expense to have my degrees issued to my alias. And until recently, no one outside the university knew that Jacques Maurice and Fernand Pierre-Paul were one and the same. People at Hofstra know only Professor Pierre-Paul—our customers and everybody here in Haiti know only Jacques Maurice. But there's this woman at Hofstra, Lilly Rodride, you met her once at my apartment, she's become a problem for me. She thinks because we've had a little fling, she's entitled to dig into my affairs. It looks like she may have already connected my two identities. I don't know what she's figured out about our business, but she might be talking to the cops. She hasn't said anything to me about what she knows, but I have the feeling she's just playing it cool for the moment. She's nervy and smart, but maybe not as smart as she thinks.

"She doesn't know I'm onto her half-assed detective work. She uses phony names in her sleuthing. But all her calls have Nassau County area codes. A few even have Hofstra phone numbers, and it's always the same female voice. She has no idea how quickly I find out about any inquiries made about me in Haiti. So that gives me a little bit of an edge in dealing with her. But the bottom line is that this woman must be dealt with before she upsets our apple cart. I want her to disappear, and I want you to take care of it. I'll be returning to start the fall semester next week. Before I get back to the campus, I want her gone."

Sonny is floored. He can hardly believe his own ears. Just like that, Jacques wants a woman killed because he suspects she might have discovered the truth about him. And the little bastard wants him to do the dirty work. Jacques wants him to take the life of a schoolteacher whose mission is to impart knowledge to young people, the kind of work that Jacques had always talked about but had never taken up as a serious calling. Having met the gifted young scholar and seen her work her magic in the classroom, Sonny is sure her only offense is trying to figure out what kind of a character has worked his way into her life.

Sonny knows that Jacques had long ago become a cold-blooded killer. Since most of his killings had grown out of drug battles and turf wars, Sonny had always accepted the violence as part and parcel of their brutal business. As far as he is concerned, anybody in the drug world has to know that their life could end at any moment. And most in that world deserve nothing better. Even outside the drug world, Sonny had turned a blind eye to much of Jacques's cruel and callous behavior. As hard as it was, he had resisted the impulse to turn on his former protégé for the shameful way he treats Juliette and Euphrasie.

But he is now convinced that Jacques has lost his mind along with his last shred of decency and humanity. How else could he think it was ok to use drug-world rules of engagement to get rid of a girlfriend just because she knows too much about him?

Aside from the insult of being requested to perform such a despicable act, the request confirms for Sonny how little his own life and safety mean to Jacques. To be asked to commit a brazen murder on the busy streets of Manhattan, and risk being captured or killed at the scene by police, tells him that Jacques views him as disposable.

Jacques waits for Sonny's answer, knowing that this kind of assignment will be tough for him. He knows it is not that the big man can't handle the rough stuff. Sonny had already ended many lives in *Dechoukaj* and other battles over the years. The big man is not afraid to fight an adversary to the death with his bare hands.

As Jacques sees it, Sonny has this weird sense of conscience and morality that sometimes make it difficult for him to use force and intimidation to achieve his objectives. For a guy as big and tough as Sonny, this is a kind of weakness that Jacques can never understand or accept.

Even though Jacques sees Sonny's scruples as an Achilles' heel that is out of place in their world, he has always kept the big man close to him for one crucial reason. Of all those around him, he knows Sonny is the only one who couldn't be bribed or tricked by an enemy to double-cross or betray him. Sonny is the only person in the world from whom he could expect that kind of honesty and integrity. Despite all his wealth and the people he can buy, Jacques knows that, in some ways, the big man is still his only protector.

But he believes it is time to force Sonny to get off the fence in terms of commitment. He needs the big man to be willing to take on any assignment with no moral equivocation. If he can't count on that, he will have to take a hard look at whether he still wants him around.

Sonny knows what Jacques is up to and surprises him by accepting the assignment. He has no intention of going through with the hit but isn't ready to say so just yet. He has long known it would only be a matter of time before Jacques's corrupt nature and murderous ways would drive them apart. That time had finally come. But he will need a few days to get his ducks in order before making the split. For the moment, he will have to play along with the request.

For the next hour, Sonny goes through the motions of mapping out a plan to follow Lilly home from Hofstra after one of her late classes. He will tail her on the Long Island Railroad into New York and then on the subway ride to her apartment building. He will make the hit on the subway stairs so that it will look like a street mugging.

Two days later, as Sonny drives Jacques to their Port-au-Prince warehouse to organize the next New York shipment, he revisits their unfinished conversation.

"Jacques, about that schoolteacher hit. I'm not going to do it. Not that hit or any other."

"I've gone as far as I can go with you and all your non-stop violence and grudge-settling. I'm getting out of this life. I'll stick around long enough to train up one of the other guys to do the things I've been doing. Then I'm gone."

"What the hell are you talking about, Sonny?" Jacques shoots back. There is a surprising note of hurt in his anger. "You think you can walk away from me and this business just like that?"

"Hell yeah. I can, and I will. And while we're talking about hits," Sonny goes on, "I've taken out a contract that you need to know about. It's already bought and paid for, and it's on you! Here's how it works. If anything happens to that teacher or me, the contract automatically kicks in.

"It may be somebody in a crowded airport with a poison dart. Or it might be a guy in the next car with a bazooka that sends a missile through these bulletproof car doors. It could even be a girlfriend who poisons you, or the butler who blows you off your toilet with a shotgun blast in the face. One way or another, if I get hit, so do you. There will be no getting away from it. And as an extra incentive, a big bonus is paid as soon as the hit goes down. To keep things on track, the contractor expects to hear from me on a regular schedule. The first time he doesn't, the hit is on. So you better hope that nothing bad ever happens to me or prevents me from making that call, even if you have nothing to do with it.

"Now, don't get me wrong. Even though I never wanted to see you in this kind of life, I'm not trying to do anything to interfere with your business, and I won't get in your way. If you don't mess with me, you'll never have to worry about any trouble from me. In fact, I wish you the best of luck."

Jacques is speechless, an unusual situation for him. But Sonny can feel the intensity of his anger. As Jacques seethes in the back seat, Sonny pulls up to the gate of the electrified security fence that now surrounds the warehouse. From a secure guardhouse inside the entrance, a sentry sees Sonny at the wheel of the Escalade and opens the motorized gate.

When the gate is open enough for the big SUV to drive through, a large commercial truck barrels around a nearby corner and speeds through the open gate behind Sonny. The driver of the truck slams on its brakes, but the vehicle's momentum causes it to bump the rear of the Escalade. A machete and club-wielding mob of at least a dozen jump from the truck. In unison, they repeatedly shout the Kreyòl words: *"Re-vanj pou Myou!"* (Revenge for Myou!) as they surround the Cadillac.

Sonny pushes the accelerator pedal hard to the floor as Jacques screams at him to drive the remaining fifty yards to the warehouse's rear door so that they can get inside the building before the mob pulls them out of the Cadillac. Wheels screeching and gravel flying, Jacques jumps out of the still-moving vehicle as it approaches the building. But as he reaches for the warehouse door, he is caught.

Sonny lunges for the attacker whose raised machete is trained on Jacques's hands. But Sonny's right leg collapses as someone slashes at his knee. He stumbles to the ground from another blow to his temple. As he falls, he sees a machete blade swing down toward Jacques's hands. Lethal blows continue to rain down on Jacques as the attackers chant: *"Sa se pou Myou!"* (This is for Myou!). Sonny blacks out without ever hearing Jacques utter a sound.

The attack is quickly over as soldiers scramble out of the army head-quarters building immediately across the busy street and run toward the warehouse. The mob knew no one would expect such a bold attack in broad daylight and so close to army turf. They were confident they could pull off the raid if they worked swiftly. Benefiting from the element of surprise, they are back in the stolen truck speeding away from the warehouse within seconds of the strike. Moments later, they abandon the truck and disappear into the neighborhoods.

The arriving soldiers call for an ambulance and a vehicle to search for the killers. But it is evident from Jacques's dismembered body that he is beyond medical care. Sonny is unconscious but still clinging to life. Because the mob was so focused on Jacques, with each attacker determined to strike a death blow of his own, they didn't punish Sonny as much as they would have if they'd had a few more moments. Jacques was their primary target. They didn't have time to finish Sonny off before the soldiers were on the scene.

—◆—

Sonny spent several weeks in intensive care drifting in and out of consciousness before doctors knew whether he would survive his wounds. He had sustained a concussion, damage to his right eye, a punctured lung, severe lacerations to his back and shoulder, and his right knee had been shattered. He had to undergo four surgeries to stop the bleeding in his brain. Only because of his strength and robust constitution was he still alive.

It is five weeks before Sonny regains the alertness to recall how the attack had gone down. Depressed and still in pain from his many wounds, he is overwhelmed with grief to learn that Jacques is dead. Despite their falling-out, Sonny is ashamed that he has survived.

He begins working hard on his physical therapy, not so much to restore his fitness but to relieve the boredom of the long hospital days and to keep himself from dwelling on how he had failed his friend. Even though his strength and vitality begin to return, he finds no joy in living. He continues to mope through his days until he finally receives a visitor, the only one he will receive except for Natalie, the housekeeper who takes care of his Jérémie home.

To his surprise, it is Miranda. They had talked a few times in the months since his trip to Europe. But when he was no longer able to answer his mobile phone, she began calling his home, pleading with the elderly Natalie for information about him. Worried about his continuing depression, Natalie finally told Miranda about his injuries, his hospitalization, and his low spirits. Miranda was on the next plane to Haiti.

"Hey, big guy!" Miranda announces with a broad smile as she is escorted into Sonny's room. "It's bad enough that you ran off without doing me the courtesy of a picnic, but now you're hiding out in the hospital without a word to me," she continues as she touches the part of Sonny's face not covered with bandages. "What kind of a way is that to treat your old travel partner?"

"I guess I wanted to get a little more of my strength back before I called you," Sonny responds as he tries to return Miranda's smile.

Sonny can hardly believe she has come all the way from France to visit him. She tells him she will remain in Haiti until he is discharged and then will take him back to Monte Carlo for some extended rest and physical therapy.

The big man doesn't argue with her. He is not used to being taken care of, but he enjoys Miranda's attention. He arranges for her to stay at his Jérémie home for the week or two until he is discharged and can travel. For the rest of his hospital stay, she spends the days talking with him and helping him through his exercises, and the evenings in the yard of his house, capturing her impressions of Haiti's beautiful scenery in a sketchpad.

"So, what happened to you?" Miranda finally asks as they sit together one afternoon on the patio outside his hospital room. He has almost fully recovered and will be discharged the next day. The bleeding in his brain has finally been stopped, and he no longer wears a full head bandage. He will have to wear a patch over his right eye a bit longer. Although he has more stitches in his body than a rag doll, his many lacerations are healing, and he has regained full lung capacity. But his right knee is in bad shape, and it is likely he will always walk with a limp. For now, he has to use a cane. The doctors have suggested a replacement knee, but Sonny isn't ready for a titanium implant.

Despite their intense previous encounter on the *Invictus*, Sonny had never discussed anything about himself with Miranda. She knew him only as Charles Jolebois, the Algerian art dealer who was moving to the US. She had been attracted to him on impulse and hadn't had the time to learn much about him. The only question she had about him at the time was how he could have spent so many years in Algeria speaking only Haitian Kreyòl and English.

Because of his brush with death and all the prodding, poking, and medication he endured during his recovery, Sonny has come to accept his own vulnerability and mortality. He responds to Miranda's question more forthrightly than he might have under other circumstances. He knows that if he is ever to come out from under the heavy funk that now grips him, he will have to talk to someone. Since Jacques is gone and he has no one else, Miranda will have to be his confidant. So the man of few words goes against his usual tendencies. On one sunny afternoon out on the patio, he tells Miranda everything about himself.

In all his thirty-two years, Sonny has never cried or shed a tear over anything, at least not that he can remember. Even though he doesn't break down as he talks to Miranda, he comes close. When he tells her about his last words to Jacques, his broad shoulders shudder, and tears stream down his face.

"All I ever wanted to do was to help that boy," he almost pleads. "With all his smarts and energy, I wanted to see him achieve his full potential. I believed he could reach goals and accomplish things that most of us can only dream about. But now he's gone. Never to see his sons grow up or play with his grandchildren, and never to look back in pride at his accomplishments. He'll never be able to sit down with me when we're old and gray and share stories about all we had to over-come to make it through our crazy lives. Was I that bad a role model?" Sonny asks.

Without waiting for, or even expecting an answer, Sonny continues his stream of questions: "Or is this just a totally messed up world where random shit happens for no rhyme or reason, where people like Jacques are dealt a bad hand and from birth are on a path to ruin?

"What other kind of a world could it be when the last thing a young man hears in life are the awful words I spoke to Jacques. Could it have been any worse for him than for his closest friend to turn his back on him and threaten his life?

"I knew there was no chance Jacques could ever change his ways. And I knew I had to get away from him before there was no hope for me either. We both knew that if I couldn't pose some kind of a threat—a serious ongoing threat, he'd have had me killed as soon as he could. That's what he had become.

"But it wasn't my contract or even the drug business that ended his life. What finally did him in was payback for his murderous ways from an angry community of Myou's many friends and neighbors who looked up to her as a guardian angel. They had always believed Jacques was behind her killing and had vowed to avenge her death.

"But why in the hell did things have to be that way?" Sonny demands, slamming his fist to the table on which his cold and untouched lunch still sat. "Why did this man's life have to go so wrong?"

After a long silence, Miranda finally speaks. "I can't answer your questions, Sonny. And words can't express how sorry I am about your loss and Jacques's death. Both of you had misfortune in your lives and had to deal with situations you often couldn't control. Like everybody that walks this earth, you both made mistakes, and there were things you could have done better. Unfortunately, Jacques's mistakes were big, and his penalties severe. But you can't beat up on yourself. Nobody made Jacques choose to live such a violent life."

"Maybe not," Sonny countered. "But wasn't he one of God's children? Didn't he start life as an innocent baby? What kind of a just and merciful God would put so many stumbling blocks in his own child's life? How could he fill that child's life with so many bad options and then punish him for selecting one of them?"

"I don't know the answer to that either, Sonny. But you can't torture yourself like this. You did the best you could for Jacques, and it wasn't all bad. For all the years you guys were in each other's lives, you were always there for him. You always protected him, and he must have known it. Even in the brutality of *Dechoukaj*, he saw you were trying to strike a blow for Haiti. He must have respected you for it. But could it be that you expected too much from him?

"He was smart and had his own academic dreams. But he was burdened with your dreams as well. Maybe you put too much on him with all your expectations of him becoming a great teacher.

"It's hard enough living up to one's own aspirations, let alone the hopes and dreams of others. To his credit, he followed through to get an education. But the pressure to become a great teacher might have killed his passion for it. And maybe, having lost his passion, he was ripe for a different life. The drug world might have been his escape.

"What should give you comfort is that at least he's now at peace. He'll never again have to agonize about who might be plotting to kill him and take over his empire. He will never have another worry or another sleepless night.

"You poured a lot of your energies into Jacques, and things didn't work out. But you are still here, and you probably have a few unfulfilled dreams of your own. Yes, you've been through a lot, and you're lucky to be alive. But you're still a young man, and you have a lot to live for. There are many ways you still can matter.

"I don't think it was an accident that we met," Miranda continues. "Last night at your place, I watched the old classic film, *Casablanca*, and it made me think about us because we met near the real Casablanca. In one of the movie's great scenes, bar owner Rick runs into an old lover when she happens into his establishment with her husband. Later that same evening, drunk, depressed, and alone after the painful encounter, Rick muses to himself about the misfortune of coming face to face with the lost love of his life who is now married to another man. He asks himself: 'With all the gin joints in all the towns in all the world, why did she have to walk into mine?'

"Rick's words reminded me of how excited I was to see you for the first time on the gangplank of the *Invictus*. I remember wondering, with all the old cargo ships on which I could have traveled, how did I happen to find you on that one? Rick was heartbroken seeing the woman he had loved and lost, but I was thrilled to have finally come face to face with the man of my dreams. I know it may sound silly to have such thoughts, especially since I just spoke of the dangers of unrealistic aspirations. But I'm an artist who reacts to the world with intuition and strong emotions. For better or worse, I am ruled by my passions and dreams.

"All this is to say that I don't think it's your destiny to be locked into a world of depression and self-blame. I believe we were destined to meet, and that all this has happened for a purpose.

"I'm still not sure how things will work out. But I'm happy with the journey so far. I wouldn't trade our time on the *Invictus* and these days here in Haiti with you for anything in the world. We both have many dreams yet to realize."

Monte Carlo Reset

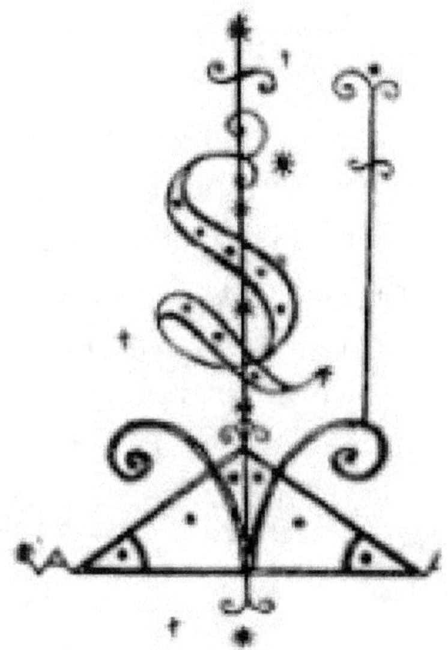

When Miranda first suggested a trip to Monte Carlo, Sonny didn't like the idea. He feared a long journey in confined quarters would be painful for his slowly healing knee. But Miranda convinced him that a change of scenery and surroundings would help snap him out of the depression that had gripped him since Jacques's death. Unlike their previous travel together, this would not be a long ocean voyage.

Miranda booked the fastest available air passage so that Sonny could resume his exercise therapy as soon as possible. Their flight left two days after his discharge from the hospital. It wasn't far into their flight when Miranda began to administer her own brand of therapy.

"Do you know what I'm most looking forward to on this trip?" she asks.

"What might that be?" Sonny replies.

"For big Sonny to come out and play!" she answers as she reaches into his lap and grasps his crotch.

Though he is no prude, Sonny is speechless as Miranda stares at him with a mischievously seductive smile, unconcerned that other passengers are watching her antics.

Reveling in her cut-up persona, she continues to hold him, asking: "Can he?"

Beginning to understand and appreciate the lusty artist's unique blend of sensuality and humor, the big man bursts into booming laughter that stretches rarely exercised laugh lines in his usually serious face.

"Big Sonny may be the only part of this old Mandinka-warrior body that hasn't been busted up. I'm guessing he'll be able to rise to the occasion," He replies, enjoying his play on words.

"Oh, I'm so happy," Miranda responds in mock relief. "After that addictive dose of him on the *Invictus*, I wouldn't want to spend the rest of my life on withdrawal."

Sonny planned only a two-week trip but ended up staying almost two months in Miranda's world of art and culture. It couldn't have been more different from the life he had known in Haiti. Monte Carlo was an affluent city of old money situated in the tiny principality of Monaco on the Mediterranean Sea. The elegant, old-world architecture of its homes and public buildings was like something out of a travel magazine. New York might have more skyscrapers, people, and energy, and Haiti might have more natural beauty, but Monte Carlo was in a class of its own. Even the pace of life was unique, a relaxed atmosphere of luxury and ease. Monaco's nickname: 'Richman's Paradise City' was well deserved.

Miranda's sprawling, ultramodern home featured a cavernous, stand-alone studio that was bigger than the living quarters. The huge workspace was needed to accommodate the larger-than-life sculpture that was her specialty. The dramatic and voluptuous pieces in various stages of completion throughout the studio exemplified the artist's outsized spirit and passion. To move and shape the enormous blocks of all varieties of stone, she employed heavy-duty winches and jackhammers powered by motorized air compressors. Her work required a combination of artistic creativity and industrial engineering know-how.

Sonny came to life in Monte Carlo. Watching Miranda work her magic in the studio, dining in the city's many great eateries, and spending relaxing evenings at home with her was just the tonic he needed. They finally got their chance to picnic, enjoying several leisurely afternoon drives along the scenic French Riviera with the top down on the Jaguar. They stopped at Miranda's favorite spots, ate picnic basket lunches, and enjoyed spectacular views of the Mediterranean.

Sonny loved the beaches, particularly *Plage du Larvotto*, one of the most popular in Monte Carlo. With its crystal clear blue water and gently rolling waves, it rivaled the beauty of *Anse d'Azure*, his favorite back in Haiti. The only difference was in the crowds. People packed the *Larvotto's* expanses of smooth pebbly sand and the cafés and shops surrounding it. The *Anse*, like many other beaches in Haiti, was isolated. Surrounded by densely vegetated hills and cliffs that jutted abruptly out of the sea, one had to climb and hike to get to the site. To the delight of young Haitians like Sonny who frequented the spot as a boy, the waters of the *Anse* hid the remains of a sunken World War II German U-boat.

A highlight of his visit was the evening he spent with Miranda at the legendary *Grand Casino*. They dined on the terrace of the *Le Salon Rose* restaurant and played blackjack in the elegant gambling house itself. Sonny even bought a suit to complement Miranda's high-fashion evening attire.

He hadn't yet thought about returning to Haiti when the real world intruded into his respite. It came in the form of a telephone call from Natalie informing him that Carlos Marquez, Jacques's old *Molly* supplier, had been trying to reach him. He assumed Carlos wanted to arrange for a new shipment of the cocaine Jacques had begun supplying him. Carlos didn't know Jacques was dead and called Sonny when he couldn't reach his old friend.

The big man had no intention of ever selling drugs again, but he returned the call when Natalie told him about some business Carlos said needed to be attended to regarding a Harlem property. Sonny had only been to the safe house a couple of times and had almost forgotten about the place. He recalled that the brownstone had been acquired through a limited liability company in which he and Jacques were the only members. With Jacques gone, he was now the sole owner.

Sonny returned Carlos's call and told him of Jacques's death. Next, he contacted the accountant Jacques had hired to run the property and lease the apartments. He scheduled a New York trip to meet him and take care of any loose ends. Since he no longer intended to be involved in the drug business, he wanted to make sure there was no troublesome contraband on the premises that could cause problems when he tried to dispose of the property.

Once the outside world began to intrude into Sonny's paradise getaway, it continued with a vengeance. The following day, Natalie called in a panic to relay a chilling message. When she arrived at the house that morning, she found a note pinned to the front door with the following message:

PAY US OUR MONEY!

M

001-57-381-6632

The terrified housekeeper told Sonny she was afraid to return to the house. The big man immediately called the number on the message and was told by M that he and Jacques owed a balance of $600,000 on their last buy. According to M, the original cost of the shipment he took through Europe in the Expedition was $800,000. M claimed that, at the time of the buy, Jacques had only $400,000 in ready cash. Because of his long history with the Cartel, they fronted him for the remaining amount due. But the unpaid balance was now more than six weeks old and had ballooned to $600,000. It didn't matter to the Cartel that Jacques was dead. They would keep increasing the amount owed and, if necessary, kill every living soul in the city of Jérémie to collect their money. Sonny told M he would need a few days to pull together the funds and would then call to arrange a meeting to make the payoff.

Sonny again calls the Cartel a few days later. This time he talks to Phillipe Estrada, the *guy* who had helped Jacques and him pull off the Fort Greene deal, their first smuggling effort when they used human mules. Sonny tells Phillipe about Jacques's death and the threatening messages he has received. He reminds Phillipe that in all the years he and Jacques did business with the *Medellín,* Jacques had never asked to be fronted for any purchase. Nor had he ever been late in any payment or out of compliance with any commitment to the Cartel. Now that he is dead, how is it that the Cartel claims he has an unpaid debt?

Phillipe is unable to answer Sonny's question and responds that he has not been involved in any recent business with Jacques. He promises to get the details as soon as possible. But he cautions Sonny that the Cartel is relentless about collecting debts. He counsels Sonny that it will be wise to pay the full amount due before any further penalties accumulate. Questioning the organization, he cautions Sonny, will likely not end well. Phillipe promises to call Sonny as soon as he has any information.

But the big man is not ready to end the call. "Something stinks here!" he tells Phillipe.

"Now it's possible that Jacques was fronted on this last purchase, something that had never before happened. But that's probably not what really went down. I believe you've got somebody in your organization who's in business for himself. When he found out Jacques was dead, he stole $400,000 of the money Jacques had already paid and is now trying to make it look like we stiffed the Cartel."

"Wait a minute, amigo," Phillipe shoots back. "We don't make those kinds of mistakes, and none of our people would even think about stealing from us."

"Bullshit," Sonny fires back. "I'm going to check to see whether an extra $400,000 can be found in any of Jacques's accounts or his personal effects. If so, I'll settle up the full amount with you people. If not, you get nothing, and I never want to hear anything from any of you ever again!"

Before Phillipe can respond, Sonny continues: "Listen, Jorge... Jorge Arenas is your real name, isn't it? I know a lot about you, more than you'd ever guess. Jacques, rest his soul, started collecting information on you back when we did the Fort Greene run. He'd been collecting it ever since. In his wisdom, he had the feeling that the day would come when we'd need leverage over someone in your organization. He created his own information network in your country and hired the best people he could find to track you and learn everything there was to know about you and your family. He always kept his network strong and up-to-date, and I plan to do the same.

"We know shit about you that you may not even know, all the dirt about you, your parents, your grandparents, aunts and uncles, your children and nephews, even your neighbors and your girlfriends. I could tell you a few stories about that wife of yours that would shock the hell out of you.

"In case you think I'm talking through my hat, we picked up your sister's youngest daughter, Sophia, outside her school in Ibaqué two hours ago. She's unharmed, and in fifteen minutes, she'll be allowed to call her mother to pick her up at the MacDonald's on 60th Street. We'll drop her off there to meet her mother. I tell you all this to let you know how serious I am. I'm finished doing business with you people. If any of you ever again disturb me, my home, or anybody I know, whatever is left of the next person we pick up from your family won't be dropped off at any McDonald's.

"Now I'm pretty sure I'm not going to find that $400, 000 you claim Jacques didn't pay you. But if the *Medellín* must be paid, and you can't find the insider who's stealing your money, then pay them your damn self! I know what's in your accounts, and I know you can afford it.

"So listen, the bottom line is I never much liked or trusted any of you sons of bitches from the beginning. I only went along with buying from you because Jacques wanted it. I should have stopped him before the first buy, and I'm sorry I didn't. I know I can't shut down the Cartel, but I can put some serious hurt on you and everybody in your family. And I sure as hell will if I ever have to cross paths with you or any of your pals again.

"Oh, and by the way, through you, we've been able to zero in on a few other *Medellín* big shots. I know you wouldn't want any of what we know to be leaked to, say, the CIA, with a trail of breadcrumbs leading to you. So that's it, amigo. You watch your back because I'll be watching you from here on out!"

Sonny knew it was a risky move. But he had no choice. He was sure that the Cartel hadn't fronted Jacques a penny. But if he let them shake him down, they'd never leave him alone. They probably knew Jacques was dead and may have cooked up the ruse to force him to buy more drugs. He would have to hold firm and not cave in to any threats. But to be safe, he'd stay out of Haiti for a while.

A week later, still using a cane but now much stronger, Sonny stood in the hidden safe at the Harlem safe house. Miranda had pleaded with him not to leave so soon. She tried to convince him that he needed more rest and healing. But there was no holding the big man back. She begged him to return to her as soon as possible and, once and for all, leave the violence and uncertainty of his previous life behind him. Sonny assured her that was his goal, but he had to first take care of several pressing issues in Haiti and the States. Before he left, she put the *Belie Belcan* back around his neck. She was sure he would need it more than her.

Sonny found $1.4 million in cash in the safe but no drugs. It had not been quite three weeks after the $3 million Carlos Marquez score that Jacques was killed. Immediately after Carlos had paid him, Jacques had rushed back to Haiti to prepare his next delivery. It had been a long dry spell after the LaGuardia bust. Now that he had worked out a new smuggling approach, he wanted to restore his cash flow. As soon as possible, he had planned to start a few new vehicles on their travels.

Before he'd returned to Haiti, Jacques had deposited as much as possible of the $3 million into the various accounts he used for laundering his US revenues. He had brought some cash with him and had left the remaining $1.4 million in the safe. After his next shipments were sent off, he'd intended to get back to the US with a new identity and take care of the rest of the cash. But the fatal warehouse attack had ended those plans.

Sonny met with the accountant and took care of all matters relating to the brownstone and the limited liability company. With the three upstairs apartments still rented, he decided to stay in the main floor apartment until things cooled off in Haiti. While he waited, he would take care of some unfinished business.

First, he called Jacques's ex, Catheline, who told him that Jacques's estate had gone into a trust for their children. She and the boys would move back to the mansion. Since Sonny would no longer be staying there, his own house in Jérémie would need a security upgrade. He hired a contractor to install an electrified fence and security cameras, and he retained a monitoring service to keep an eye on the place.

⬥

A few days later, Sonny stands at the LaGuardia Airport American Airlines arrival gate as travelers deplane the morning flight from Port-au-Prince. He watches patiently, finally spotting the passenger he is looking for. Juliette Michel smiles as she pushes Euphrasie in a fold-up stroller. The baby is now almost two years old. A bar attached to her shoes looks as though it is intended to apply pressure to straighten her still turned-in feet. After the voodoo healing ceremony in Archahaie,

Sonny had done some reading and learned that almost all infants born with clubfoot were cured entirely with non-surgical therapy in the first months after birth. It still baffled and saddened him that Jacques had stood in the way of such treatment.

While recuperating in the hospital, Sonny had called Juliette to let her know of Jacques's death. He offered to send her money since Jacques would no longer be paying her rent. He also told her that as soon as he was back on his feet, he wanted her to bring Euphrasie to New York so that she could finally be attended to by a doctor. Over the telephone, he introduced Juliette to Miranda, who invited her for a visit later in the year so that the two could do some artist-to-artist mentoring.

After stopping by the Harlem townhouse to drop off Juliette's bags and allow her a chance to freshen up, Sonny sets off with his two guests for an appointment at the Clubfoot Treatment Center of *New York Presbyterian Children's Hospital*. In the days before Juliette's arrival, he had ordered and accepted delivery of bedroom furniture for the guest room in which she and the baby would stay. Juliette offered to help him with the cost, but he wouldn't accept anything from her. He told her that he wanted her to focus only on restoring her baby to full health.

After examining the baby's feet and legs, an orthopedic surgeon tells them he is confident Euphrasie can be healed through a combination of physical therapy and surgery to release her abnormally tight ligaments and tendons. The operation will be followed by a cast and splinting to maintain the correction. The entire treatment will take two to three months.

As the doctor explains the option, little Euphrasie, free for the moment from her corrective braces, walks happily but unsteadily around the examining room teetering on the outside edges of her turned-in feet. She has to hold the furniture to remain standing but is excited to be able to roam about on her own. When she wants to move quickly, she gets down on all fours. But for the sheer joy of accomplishment, she seems to enjoy standing and walking, however difficult and painful it might be.

Perhaps because of her own situation, Euphrasie is fascinated with the cane Sonny still uses. She even tries it for herself later that evening when Juliette takes off her shoes and allows her to move around the brownstone in her bare feet for a few minutes before bed. Sonny plays with the cheerful baby and tells her that they will heal together in the coming months so that she won't need a walking stick, and neither will he.

Euphrasie's treatment program begins two days later. She seems to enjoy the fuss and attention she receives, perhaps realizing, with an infant's sixth sense, that she is being healed. At her first session, one of the therapists flexes, stretches, and rotates her feet about her ankles. After a half hour of therapy, he applies plaster casts that extend from her toes to the top of her thighs. The casts are intended to retain the correction achieved during therapy. They will remain in place until the next session a week later. The process will be repeated each week.

It is anticipated that in each session, additional correction will be made so that in a month or two, the clubfoot condition will disappear. At that time, treatment will transition to an extended maintenance stage to prevent relapse. This will involve wearing a prosthetic twenty-three hours a day for two to three weeks and all night every night for three to four years. The device is a shoulder-width bar with an open-toe shoe at each end that rotates the feet outwards.

Euphrasie makes good progress in the weekly sessions and even seems to look forward to them. She wants the security of her mother at all times but enjoys having Sonny with her as well. Perhaps because of his limp and his cane, she perceives them to be kindred spirits who need each other to fight a similar battle. Sonny picks up on this and becomes very fond and protective of the child.

Before the eighth and final cast is applied, Euphrasie's Achilles tendons are cut through tiny incisions. By the time the casts are removed three weeks later, her tendons have extended to the proper length. Euphrasie is thrilled that she can finally stand on her feet like everyone else she has ever known.

A few days after the three-week confinement in the post-surgery prosthetic, Juliette and Euphrasie prepare to return to Haiti. Through one of her artist friends, Juliette has found a new apartment and is anxious to get back to work and her art routine. While she appreciates how Sonny has covered the full cost of the baby's medical treatment and her stay in New York, she seems overwhelmed by his generosity and has come to feel that she and Euphrasie were heavy burdens.

Euphrasie is not ready to leave. She wants to stay with Sonny and can't understand why her mother doesn't also want to stay. It is an emotional departure with both Juliette and Euphrasie crying as the two say goodbye and board their flight to Haiti. Sonny promises Euphrasie that he will see her again soon so that they can go out walking together without canes.

Legacy

The day after Juliette and Euphrasie leave for Haiti, Sonny receives a telephone call from Lilly Rodride. The call is in response to a letter he had painstakingly composed and sent to her a few weeks earlier during Euphrasie's treatment.

Louis Montasse
P.O. Box 8089
Morrisania Station
Bronx NY, 10456
212-526-8629

Professor Lilly Rodride,
Hofstra University
Hempstead, New York

Sept 3, 2001

Dear Professor Rodride,

By now, you have heard about the passing of your colleague, Fernand Pierre-Paul, who died suddenly on June 1, 2001. Because he was my oldest and closest friend in life, I would have preferred to contact you sooner so that you wouldn't have to hear such tragic news from Haitian media. Especially since the coverage was so negative. But I was seriously injured in the same incident that took Fernand's life, and I wasn't able to write. I now offer my condolences.

As you have unfortunately come to learn, there were many sides to Fernand. I would like to tell you a bit more about the man I knew so that you won't judge him too harshly. I first met him in 1982 when he was a twelve-year-old orphan living in the streets of Jérémie, our hometown in the southern peninsula of Haiti. I was a few years older and looked after him as best as I could. He became a trusted and loyal companion, and together we battled many hard times. In those days, I knew him as Jacques, and he knew me as Sonny. He later adopted the professional name you knew.

Jacques was an unusual mix of brainpower, optimism, ambition, and street savvy. He was a self-made guy who pushed himself through college with no help from anyone. I was proud of him and amazed by his accomplishment. He was still a young teenager when the Duvalier regime fell, and we got involved in politics. Amid all the anger and the settling of scores, he always maintained a spirit of forgiveness and justice. At least in the beginning.

But he also had a strange attraction to fast money and the streets that did not square with the positive things going on in his life. In his final days, he sensed that you had learned of his street activities. It troubled him that he had disappointed you.

It was always my hope that he would be successful in his struggle with conflicting goals and values. I prayed that, in the end, his better angels would prevail and he would turn all his energies toward a career as an educator. Sadly, that didn't happen, and now he's gone.

In his memory, I would like to do something he might appreciate.

I am not an educated man and don't understand much of what Jacques described to me about your work. But two words stuck with me: 'Machine Learning.' How anyone could get a machine to learn is beyond me. But Jacques believed it could be done, and that you were the person to do it.

Since he and I enjoyed success in business, I would like to put our resources to good use. I want to donate $250,000 to the university to set up a laboratory for you to continue the kind of work that Jacques believed was such a major scientific breakthrough. It would be nice if I could make the donation in his honor so that the lab could be named after him.

But I wouldn't want the unpleasant aspects of Jacques's past to cause embarrassment to you or the university. For that reason, my contribution must be anonymous. There's only one other string attached. The university must put you in charge of the lab.

If my offer and conditions are acceptable, I am ready to proceed immediately.

Sincerely yours,

Louis Montasse

p.s. When I make the offer to the university, I will make no mention of Fernand. What I have said about him in this letter is between you and me.

Lilly read the letter many times, a flood of emotions accompanying each reading—sadness and remorse at the loss of her colleague, and shock and horror at the thought of the violent end he likely suffered. She also felt compassion for Sonny in his effort to make amends for his companion's failures and transgressions. Any satisfaction she may have experienced in receiving such a generous donation, or for the positive way it might boost her career and reputation at Hofstra was muted by the tragedy of Fernand's death and the circumstances surrounding it.

The relief she had begun to feel when she first heard Fernand had taken a leave of absence was now replaced with a sense that somehow she might have failed him. She wished that she had been able to react to the sad event as had Sonny, who grieved at the passing of a deeply flawed loved one for whom he still had affection.

Lilly showed the letter to Gil. Touched by Sonny's words, Gil implored her to not be too hard on herself as she was justified in wanting to put space between herself and a man who had lied to her and hid a criminal double life. But Gil also urged her to be hopeful. Fernand had a dark side and had come to a violent end. But his death inspired an act of kindness and generosity from his closest friend.

After thinking about Sonny's offer for several days and discussing it with Gil, Lilly calls to set up a meeting. She is nervous about meeting Sonny once again. But the big man puts her immediately at ease when he makes it clear he doesn't want to dwell on Jacques's problems or anything about her relationship with him. He wants only to learn about her work and her plans for the future. After a tour of the lab, introductions to her team, and a slide presentation on anonymous author profiling, Sonny feels he now understands the significance, if not the technical details, of Lilly's breakthrough research.

Lilly walks with Sonny across the expansive campus to the president's office. She introduces him to Dr. James Shuart, who is to retire later that year. With Shuart are several administrative staffers from the endowment office who will accept Sonny's gift. The burly administrator, a Hofstra alum from the 1950s and a former player on the school's football team, asks Sonny what college he had attended. When the big man replies that he had never made it to college, the genial president laments that back when he played, they could have used a man like Sonny. Even though he is now beginning to show gray around his temples, Sonny still looks trim and buff.

The introductions done, Shuart tells Sonny how grateful the university is for his offer. He opines that anonymous gifts are the best contributions as they are not made for publicity or to enhance the image of the giver. To the president, this gift is even more significant because Sonny has never been to college but still appreciates the importance of higher education and the need to support it.

After the transaction is completed and the papers signed, Shuart asks Sonny how he happened to pick Hofstra as the recipient of his donation. Sonny replies that he had heard about Lilly's work from a friend affiliated with the institution. If Shuart suspects that because of his Haitian background, Sonny might somehow be trying to repair the sullied image of the recently deceased Haitian professor, he conceals it well.

Shuart and his team promise Sonny a place of honor at all future commencements and special events. His only reference to Haiti is the mention of a young PhD student of aquaculture from Port-au-Prince who is researching the concept of establishing fish-farming operations in Caribbean countries that, through poverty and lax environmental safeguards, had been fished out. He offers to make the necessary introductions as Sonny might be a vehicle to implement the technology in Haiti.

Lilly had been relieved that Sonny had not tried to engage her in any awkward talk about her relationship with Jacques. But, as they leave the president's office and stroll back across the campus to her lab, she now wants to talk. She knows she may very well never see Sonny again and needs to get a few things off her chest that wouldn't have meaning to anyone who hadn't known Jacques. She doesn't ask for any of the details of Jacques's death, and Sonny offers none. But she confides to the big man how troubling it is to discover she had been such a small and insignificant accessory to Jacques's life. She expresses deep regret that in his hour of need, she didn't even know his life was in jeopardy. She asks Sonny if he had any idea why Jacques lived such a life and why he kept her in the dark about so much of it.

Sonny wants to put Lilly's mind at rest. That had been an important part of his motivation to make the donation. But he doesn't have a good answer. "I'll never understand how he thought he could inhabit two such completely different worlds. To achieve success in either one would have been a serious enough challenge, but to try to live in both at the same time was impossible. Somehow he thought he could pull it off.

"I can only say that you are the kind of inspired academic I had always hoped Jacques would become. Maybe in some strange way, he also admired that same aspect of you. Perhaps he believed that by keeping one foot in your world he might someday achieve the same academic commitment and fulfillment.

"There is no way of undoing the harm Jacques did to himself and others. But I hope I've created an academic legacy for him that will help you and other deserving scholars reach your goals. That's all I can do. In some small way, maybe it helps to balance the books on his troubled life."

Seventeen

Mèsi Letènel

Sonny is happy to be back in Jérémie. His hospital stay, recuperation in Monte Carlo, and time in New York for Euphrasie's treatment have kept him away from home for almost six months. He had developed an affinity for New York and loved being with Miranda in her slice of the Riviera. Still, he missed so many things about Jérémie, its lush beauty, the feel of its clay-colored soil under his feet, and the sights, sounds, and ocean smell of its busy waterfront. On his way home from the airport, he stops at the harbor market. He walks along the shore, watching the endless flow of fishing boat traffic: departing crews hopeful for a good catch, returning craft queued up to sell their modest takes to middlemen buyers.

In the years he sold drugs with Jacques, Sonny was usually too busy to visit the area. But today, he had no pressing responsibilities or time demands. As he strolls, he reflects on the simple fishing culture in which he had grown up, one that pit men against nature in a daily struggle to feed themselves. Each morning, fishermen venture out to sea in search of the catch that will end up that night on dinner tables in Jérémie and neighboring towns. It is Haiti's version of the food chain cycle. Sonny misses it.

Even though things looked the same, they weren't. Sonny remembered the days when the sea was allowed to sea rest between January and April. But in recent years, fishing seasons were ignored, and anything that got caught stayed caught. Nothing was ever thrown back. The delicate cycle of harvest and regeneration was out of balance.

For years, Haiti's trees had been aggressively cut down to make charcoal, the country's primary energy source, and a major export. With fewer trees left to hold the earth in place, heavy rainfall at the waterfront caused landslides that brought topsoil and silt down into the sea, killing the nutrients on which aquatic life depended. Fish were pushed farther and farther out from the shore. Soon, they were beyond the reach of the tiny dugouts and small rowboats traditionally used by local fishermen who couldn't afford the bigger boats needed to venture out to sea in search of decent catches.

Increasingly irregular rainfall and continuing soil erosion also made things tough for farmers as the land was producing less and less each season. Many quit farming and took up fishing. But because the fish had been pushed so far out and there were fewer of them to be caught, fishermen began using nets with smaller holes to increase their take. This led to smaller, younger catches and fewer fish left to reproduce. The depressing situation was aggravated by the widespread dumping of all kinds of plastic and petroleum solid waste into the sea.

Sonny couldn't understand why the government hadn't brought in new technologies and enforced reasonable rules to improve the environment and replenish aquatic life. Why wasn't it helping fishermen acquire the bigger boats and other equipment needed to reach the distant locations where fish could still be found? The new crop of Haitian leaders should be addressing these problems, but weren't. Instead, they continued to distract the public by campaigning on the fumes of Haiti's past glory and rattling the bones of its long-gone founders. No help would be coming from these poseurs.

As he strolls and surveys the scene under bright blue skies unblemished by a single cloud, Sonny is more aware than ever that new ideas are needed. Fresh thinking must come from new players who have the knowledge, resources, and the determination to help revive the dying fishing industry. There might even be new business opportunities in lucrative areas such as charter fishing. With the right kind of planning and energy, Haiti could become a destination for Caribbean game-fishing excursions.

Looking forward to sleeping in his own bed once again, Sonny heads for home. But when he pulls up to the recently installed security fence, he doesn't even open the gate. It would be simple enough to disarm the alarm, as did the maintenance man who looked after the house and cut the grass each week. But something tells him to be cautious.

As he sits in the driveway, he realizes the house looks exactly like what it is, a well-cared-for home lived in by no one. In the months since his confrontation with the Cartel about the money they claimed he owed, he had heard nothing further from them. There were no more threatening notes pinned to the door, and the house hadn't been blown up. He had come to feel that his threats and show of force in abducting the niece of a Cartel big shot had gotten them off his back. Either they found out what happened to the missing money, or decided not to pursue the issue any further since Jacques was dead and his organization gone. Maybe Phillipe paid the debt himself.

But now it occurs to him that he may have misread the situation. No one had seen him coming and going from the house recently, and he hadn't been spotted in Haiti for months. That didn't mean the *Medellín* had lost interest in him. They were likely just waiting him out, knowing that sooner or later he would resurface. They would then settle the score.

That has to be it, Sonny concludes. These people don't write off bad debts. If they did so just once and word of it got out, every deadbeat coke buyer in the world would be trying to stiff them.

Without stopping to pick up a change of clothes or even a toothbrush, Sonny pulls away from the house and begins driving. Six hours later, he is in Jacmel, 300 km east on the southern coast. He stops at the first decent looking hotel he sees, the *L'auberge Du Vieux Port*, and checks in under the name Charles Jolebois, his old alias. Exhausted from the flight to Haiti and the long drive to Jacmel with nothing to eat along the way but a gas station sandwich, Sonny eats a quick dinner in the hotel restaurant and crashes as soon as he walks into his room. He sleeps most of the night on top of the covers wearing his street clothes. The rumbling thunder of an all-night storm and the sound of heavy rain pelting the shutters is the perfect sedative.

The following morning, when he steps out of the hotel and opens his car door, he surprises a sleeping boy. The young teenager tries to slip out of the passenger door, but Sonny grabs his shoulder. "What are you doing in my car?" the big man demands, tightening his grip as the youngster stands mute.

"I needed a place to sleep," the kid finally answers.

"Why my car? Where do you usually sleep?"

"Over there," the boy says. He points to a three-story building across the street with a sign over the door that reads: *Sementha Haiti*.

"So, why were you in my car?"

"It was too hot and crowded in there last night," the boy answers. "I usually sleep on the back porch or in the yard. But it was raining so hard last night that everyone was packed inside. I was sleeping on the floor, but two of the bigger guys kept messing with me, poking and pinching me until I just had to get out of there. Your car was the first dry place I could find."

"All right, I get it," Sonny replies, relaxing his grip. "I guess you're pretty hungry by now. Let's get some breakfast."

A few minutes later, they are seated at one of several small eateries near the hotel. When Sonny tells the boy he can have whatever he wants, the kid orders almost half the menu: *ze ak pen*, (egg sandwich), *vèmisèl*, (spaghetti) and *soup joumou* (squash soup). Sonny orders only *chokola peyi ak pen* (cocoa and bread) and *avwàn* (oatmeal).

Young Anel tears into his food as if he hasn't eaten in days. His ravenous appetite reminds Sonny of a young Jacques in the first few days after they joined forces back in Jérémie so many years ago. When the boy appears to be past the panic stage of eating, pausing for a moment to glance at Sonny, the big man asks him how old he is.

"Twelve," Anel answers.

"And what is that place you live at?" Sonny asks, "An orphanage?"

Anel nods.

"What happened to your family?"

"My mother, father, brothers, and sisters live about two km from here," Anel answers, his head dropping. He stops chewing even though there is still food in his mouth.

"So, why are you at *Sementha*?"

"Too many people at home. I guess my father didn't want me there anymore," the boy answers almost in a whisper.

Sonny knew about these orphanages. Often church-supported, they tried their best to help but were usually overcrowded. Many didn't have adequate funds to feed and care for the kids properly. And they not only had to provide shelter for orphans, but also for children from families that couldn't or wouldn't provide for them.

Sometimes it was about a child's education. It could cost a working man a quarter of his salary to send one kid to school. A man with several mouths to feed could never afford that kind of expense. So when an institution like *Sementha Haiti* promised parents that their child could receive a proper education at the home, many decided that there was no better choice for their child no matter how painful the separation.

Children placed in the orphanage by their parents usually felt they were not loved as much as those who got to remain at home. That's probably what happened to Anel, who now resents the father he thinks kicked him out of the house.

To Anel's relief, Sonny changes the topic.

"Some years ago, I spent a season working these docks, going out on fishing boats and repairing nets." Fleshing out new ideas as he talks, Sonny continues: "I've been away for a while, but I'm thinking about coming back. Maybe I'll get a boat and start up a fishing business or a charter boat service for tourists who want to go out on the water for a day, catch a big fish and take pictures to show off back home. If I do, I may need a few guys like you to work on the boat. Would you be interested in doing something like that?"

"A job? On a boat? Yeah, for sure," Anel replies, a big smile flashing across his face.

"Can you work hard?" Sonny continues.

"I work hard all the time at *Sementha*. All the kids have cleaning jobs. But I'm always one of the fastest and best cleaners."

"How are you with your schoolwork? I can't have any dummies working on my boat."

"Sometimes it's hard to concentrate on schoolwork when everything is always so crowded, and there's not enough to eat. But I'm doing ok."

"To work on my boat, you'll have to do better than ok. I need smart people working for me. It's going to take a minute for me to find a boat and get everything organized. When I do, I'm coming back to check with the people who run the orphanage. If I get a good report, you got a job."

"I'll check in on you again soon," he tells Anel as he drops him off at the front door of *Sementha*.

———•◆•———

Sonny found temporary quarters in Jacmel and began his search for a boat. But locally available ships weren't suitable. Most were small, flat-bottomed, and powered by either tiny outboard motors or sails. Sonny needed a seaworthy boat that could venture beyond the coastline out to locations where full-grown grouper, snapper, and tuna could be found. The ship would have to double as a game-fishing charter boat that could go after deep-sea catches of billfish and other large species. It would have to be able to operate in moderate storms, and most importantly, it must have refrigeration or at least ice-cooling capabilities. Because the small boats on which he had always worked had no cooling, close to half the catches were usually lost before reaching the market. The situation was the same for every fishing boat he had ever seen in Haiti.

Sonny's search takes him all the way to Port-au-Prince, but he still doesn't find the right boat. He sees only dugouts, rowboats, and a few luxury ocean-going yachts owned by wealthy tourists, nothing between. He discovers suitable options when he begins scouring boat and fishing trade journals from the US and finally reads about a perfect boat operating out of Cape Hatteras, North Carolina. The forty-foot fiberglass ship was built in 1980 and has twin diesel engines, a wheelhouse, and deep decks that can accommodate large catches. It had been used as both a commercial fisher and a sport-fishing charter boat and is equipped with four aft-mounted, swivel fighting chairs. When the ship is operated as a fisher, all the chairs can be removed and bins installed to hold 12,000 pounds of fish. Based on the advertisement, the boat is just what Sonny wants, and the price is right.

He catches the first available flight into Norfolk International Airport and rents a car for the drive out to Cape Hatteras. With him are his old waterfront companion and mentor, Angel Baptiste, and two other men who had worked with them on fishing boats from time to time over the years. If Sonny buys the rig, Angel will be his insurance that they can navigate their way almost 1,400 nautical miles back to Haiti, much of it in open seas. A top-notch seaman who perfected his piloting skills in the days when seamen navigated only by compass and dead reckoning, Angel knows the waters of Haiti and the surrounding area as well as any man. One of the others, Albert Gracien, had been a mechanic in a boat dealership in the Dominican Republic. Gracien is an expert on all types of marine engines, electrical and mechanical systems. He had often worked on the types of *go-fast,* offshore boats used to smuggle drugs in the waters around Haiti. All four crew members would be needed, not only for their seamanship skills but also to deal with any pirates or smugglers they might encounter on the voyage.

The big boat lives up to its advertisement. Sonny immediately likes the long, lean, and unadorned ship, which has no fringes and is designed only to catch fish efficiently. In addition to a V-berth that sleeps two and a head under the forward deck, it has two long cushioned benches that run along either side of the open deck. It also has a rounded stern. When the boat is used for game-fishing and has to reverse engines toward a big fish, the rounded aft end keeps the anglers in the fighting chairs from drowning in the water kicked up by the maneuver. And with a wide flat apron curving around the stern, commercial fishing will be easier because crew members retrieving nets will have a high, stable platform on which to stand. Since Elijah Rudd, the elderly fisherman selling the craft, is retiring from the fishing business, he includes in the package deal, electronic fish-finding gear, several fish-aggregating devices, and two large Seine fishnets.

Sonny decides he wants the boat. He has Alfred give it a thorough inspection to make sure the engines are in good working order and the hull is tight and dry. When everything checks out, he proceeds with the purchase. As they sign the transfer papers, Rudd asks Sonny whether he will ship the boat via freighter or take it back to Haiti himself. Before Sonny has a chance to speak, Angel answers.

"Ship the boat?" Angel asks, rising in indignation from his chair in Rudd's small office/den. "What kind of seamen would we be if we couldn't take our own boat home?" the grizzled old sailor demands in broken English, his voice charged with a passion that didn't surprise Sonny.

"Haitian sailing masters have run cargo and contraband along this coastline and through every island in the Antilles since the 1600s. We sailed these waters long before the colonies even thought about becoming the United States. We cherish our tradition as the finest sailors in the Caribbean... And you think we would have the boat shipped? No, sir, we will take our boat home ourselves! And with the blessings and protection of eternal and all-mighty God, we will make the voyage safely."

In the spirit of the moment, Sonny pours a toast of the champagne he had brought along in anticipation of the purchase. He stands and raises his glass as his crew and Elijah Rudd join the toast. He announces: "Gentlemen, let us celebrate this great occasion by calling on the blessings of the Almighty. In His honor, I rename our ship: *Mèsi Letènel* (Thanks to the Eternal)"

For the next few days, Sonny and his crew prepare the boat. They gather the maps, charts, supplies, and equipment that will carry them through the first leg of their journey. The GPS units and VHF radios they install will take the guesswork out of Angel's navigating.

The entire voyage will take five days and involve fuel stops in Jacksonville and Miami before moving out to open seas. There will be additional stops in Nassau and Turks & Caicos Islands. The final and most dangerous leg will follow the *Windward Passage* to Haiti. Two days before their scheduled departure, Sonny calls the Jacksonville marina, where the boat will make its first stop, and arranges for refueling and overnight docking. He also calls ahead to the Miami facility where they will refuel and dock the following night.

Hoping for a peaceful and uneventful trip, Sonny's plan is to cruise in daylight hours as often as possible. In the final two legs, he will avoid areas where pirates are known to operate. But to be prepared for the worst, he calls a weapons dealer in Miami. He arranges for the purchase of four AR-15 automatic rifles and an ample supply of ammunition in large magazines. He also orders four bulletproof vests and helmets. Finally, he asks the dealer to try to find him a few special items: two grenade launchers and three dozen grenades.

Sonny believes the weaponry and protective gear will be needed if pirates or smugglers confront them in the waters around Haiti. Outlaws in the region are always on the lookout for boats they can commandeer to transport refugees to the US. Sonny knows he'd never be able to out-run the powerful offshore vessels favored by the pirates, so he'll have to match their firepower. But he knows he has one advantage. Because the pirates want to capture boats undamaged so that they can be used immediately to transport human cargo, they will fire on their prey only as a last resort. Sonny and his crew, however, will have no such restrictions. If they believe they are in jeopardy of a hijacking, they will respond with maximum force as they have no reservations about killing their attackers or sinking their boat.

The *Mèsi Letènel* sets out from Cape Hatteras before daybreak on Wednesday, March 6, 2002. Cruising calm waters at a comfortable twenty-four knots under bright and sunny skies, they encounter no traffic other than an occasional pod of dolphins that might swim along-side the boat for a short period. They dock in Jacksonville nineteen hours later. They have completed the longest of the voyage's five legs, the only one in which their destination couldn't be reached in daylight hours. Their after-dark arrival is not a concern in the safe waters of Jacksonville.

The second leg, also in good weather and calm waters, takes the ship to Miami. After refueling, Sonny accepts delivery of the firearms he ordered. The weapons are hidden inside a waterproof container built to resemble an auxiliary fuel tank. They will be kept out of sight until the final legs of the trip.

The real voyage begins the following morning before dawn. Sonny and his crew leave the security of the US coastline and head out into Atlantic waters that are not as calm as those along the shoreline. On this leg to Nassau, the *Mèsi Letènel* is frequently observed by US Coast Guard helicopters. With their orange bodies, white striped tails, and black nose cones full of radar and thermal sensors that can track ships from long distances, HH-60 *Jayhawks* approach from the horizon and circle above. Their orange-helmeted crew stares down at the boat through wide-open side doors. Once satisfied that it is not a refugee craft, the choppers peel off and disappear into the distance. Sonny welcomes the visits and hopes they continue throughout the voyage. The attention will help keep away undesirables. Since the papers of both the crew and the boat are in order, it will not be a problem if the ship is stopped and inspected by the authorities.

The good weather continues on the next leg to Turks & Caicos. But storm activity predicted for the Windward Passage prompts Sonny to take a two-day layover before setting out on the final leg. Skies are once again bright and sunny, and the waters calm and azure blue when the *Mèsi Letènel* resumes its voyage. For the remainder of the trip, Sonny directs his crew to wear their armored vests and keep their AR-15s slung over their shoulders. He tells them to be ready to don their helmets at his command. When the ship is clear of T & C territorial waters and well out to sea, Sonny instructs each of the crew to test their weapons by firing several bursts of automatic fire. He and Albert also fire several grenades from the launchers and watch them explode in the distance off the ship's stern.

Whenever he spots a Coast Guard chopper, Sonny has everyone stow their weapons in the wheelhouse. While there is no prohibition against firearms in international waters, he doesn't want the *Mèsi Letènel* to be mistaken for an outlaw ship. Since their boat is outfitted as a fishing vessel headed toward Haiti, not away from it, and since it is not crowded with what could be refugees fleeing Haiti, the coast guard doesn't pay it much attention.

It is not until the halfway point of the final leg that another boat is sighted. An offshore powerboat, the kind often referred to as a *cigarette boat,* appears on the horizon and approaches. At a distance of one kilometer, it turns onto a parallel course and begins tracking the *Mèsi Letènel* at its same speed, always maintaining the one km separation. Sonny's crew keeps their weapons cocked and visible as they move about the deck in their vests and helmets. Sonny and Albert station themselves in fish-fighting chairs at opposite ends of the deck. Propped upright next to their chairs in devices that normally hold fishing gear are the two loaded grenade launchers.

The cat and mouse game continues for almost an hour, with the two boats maintaining their parallel courses. Sonny and his crew closely watch the unwelcome visitor through binoculars, looking for any sign that it might be preparing to move in on them or open fire. The stand-off ends without a signal of any kind when the visitor throttles up, turns and speeds off into the distance. Facing a well-armed adversary that appeared ready to fight had probably convinced the cigarette-boat crew that the prospect of capturing a new prize was not worth the battle damage and injury they were likely to sustain in a confrontation.

A few hours later, still in good daylight, the *Mèsi Letènel* works its way through the Windward Passage that links the Atlantic Ocean to the Caribbean Sea and pulls into the docks of Jacmel. Elated that they have made it to Haiti without serious event, Sonny and his crew break out a bottle of rum they had purchased in Miami and toast the occasion. Sonny is pleased to have brought the *Mèsi Letènel* safely back to Haiti. But he knows the hard work of building a fishing enterprise in the ruins of Haiti's devastated marine environment is just beginning.

⬩◆⬩

After a few days of rest, the *Mèsi Letènel* sets out on its first fishing outing. Using its fish-finding equipment, it combs a five-mile stretch of the coastal waters around Jacmel. While they search for the kinds of fish they had always gone after in the past, mackerel, snapper, pompano, and grouper, the crew will settle for any catch as they are not familiar with the waters of this region. All day long, they traverse back and forth, not only using the fish-finder but also watching for other signals and queues like seagulls and other birds flying over a school of small fish near the water's surface. The presence of the little fish means that larger predator fish are likely soon to appear.

With each new sweep, Sonny takes the ship farther out from the shore. By afternoon, they are two miles out to sea and have not yet spotted any potential catches. With the shoreline no longer visible, Sonny and the crew sling their weapons since there is always the chance they will run into pirates before they find a decent catch.

The crew continues the same routine for several more days. The *Mèsi Letènel* ventures farther and farther off shore in each successive outing. On the third day, they place two fish aggregators into the water. These are brightly colored floating devices, each tethered by rope to a stone dropped to the ocean floor. Knowing that fish are fascinated by floating objects and use the visual stimulation to mark the spots for mating and refuge from predators, the crew returns two days later. They are pleased to find a large school of Yellowfin tuna in the top 100 meters of the water column in the area surrounding the devices.

Sonny and the crew immediately begin setting a net, a Purse Seiner 200 m long, and 20 m deep. Floats support the top part of the net, and weights hold down the bottom edge. Along the bottom of the net are a series of rings through which a line passed. The crew circles about the fish continually dropping net until the entire school is encircled. The line is pulled, and like the drawstring of a purse, it closes the bottom of the net, preventing the fish from sounding and escaping down into the depths of the ocean. Once the purse is closed, the crew begins the back-breaking job of hauling the net and the fish into the boat. Although aided by winches, hard manual labor is required to muscle more than a ton of fish into the ship's bins.

When they return to shore later that afternoon, Sonny has the crew round up Anel and some of his Sementha buddies to help clean the catch so that it can be sold to a local wholesaler. A bit of a delicacy in Haiti, some of the tuna will be consumed locally, but a good portion will be exported. Although this maiden take is far below the maximum capacity of the *Mèsi Letènel*, it is a respectable catch. It is proof to Sonny that with the right equipment, technology, and know-how, there is still hope for fishing in Haiti.

Eighteen

Enemy of the Good

The once-bustling mansion where Jacques used to party, carouse, and hold court is now ghostly quiet. Catheline and her sons had moved back after his death, but there were too many bad memories and negative vibes for them to consider it home. Two months later, they moved out and put the place up for sale. Although she kept a few family photos and personal items, Catheline disposed of most of the expensive art, furniture, and automobiles Jacques had accumulated. The house is now empty. All that remains in the cavernous garage is the Cadillac in which Jacques was traveling the day he was killed.

Ironically, the expensive armor plating and bulletproof glass that had always given Jacques a sense of comfort and security had done him no good in his moment of need. He had already fled the car when his attackers killed him. Although there wasn't a drop of blood or a scratch on it when it was brought to the mansion by the *Fah'D*, the vehicle had been left in the garage unused ever since Jacques's death.

Catheline was a smart businesswoman who personally supervised the sale and disposal of everything in the mansion except for the Cadillac. She couldn't bear to even look at the big SUV. It symbolized Jacques's tragic end and all the pain she had suffered in their brief and unhappy marriage. When she decided to get rid of the house, she called Sonny and asked him to dispose of the vehicle. She didn't care what he did with it; she just wanted it gone.

A few days later, Sonny gets a ride into ViVi Michel. After a battery charge and a carwash, he drives the Cadillac back to Jacmel. To him, there is no sentiment involved; the Caddy is just another piece of transportation. With all the supplies and equipment he is hauling to outfit the *Mèsi Letènel* as a proper fishing and charter boat, he is glad to have the use of the huge SUV since it is much larger than his Jeep.

The Cadillac would also come in handy for a new project he is spearheading, the establishment of a tilapia fish-farming plant in Jacmel. His first few fishing runs aboard the *Mèsi Letènel* had brought into full focus the devastation that had been wrought in Haiti's coastal waters by years of overfishing and pollution. Although he had the equipment to get to places where fish could still be found, the prospects for most of the country's poor fishermen were grim. Something had to be done to help these men and the families they supplied. The new plant would help relieve the shortage of fish.

On the recommendation of Lilly Rodride and James Shuart, Sonny met with Felix Paulin, the young Haitian Aquaculture PhD student from Hofstra who was researching processes for farming fish in Caribbean communities that had damaged or destroyed their marine environment. He and Paulin agreed to set up an experimental farm in Jacmel. If the idea proved successful, they would expand into other cities.

Sonny was well-set to invest in the experiment as he had saved most of the money he made in his drug-dealing days. Although he was happy to have been able to donate money to Hofstra in Jacques's memory and to contribute to Euphrasie's medical treatment, he had looked forward to the opportunity to put his money to work back in Haiti. He funded the experimental farming operation with startup capital of $300,000. Paulin leveraged these seed funds to secure matching grants and donations from US sources.

The two set up a company they named: *Haiti Marine Recovery.* They purchased a one-acre plot of land outside Jacmel and installed three circular 12,000-gallon tanks where they began breeding fish: 10,000 each month. Six weeks after the birth of the first batch, they transferred the fry to growing cages in three nearby lakes. The cages were divided among local fishermen who tended and fed the fish for a six month maturation period. The fish were then sold in local markets with the fishermen splitting the profits 50/50 with the company.

The operation was a success from the start. The fishermen made good money, more than they had ever earned from their previous anemic catches. The public got affordable, fresh fish, and the company more than covered its costs. The environment also benefited as there was less pressure to continue overfishing the coastal waters.

Sonny never wanted or expected publicity from his new activities and took pains to keep a low profile. But a stir was created when a member of parliament ventured out on one of his deep-sea fishing excursions and pulled in a 220 kg Yellowfin tuna, a record catch for the region. Photos were taken, and in one of them, the beaming MP stood next to Sonny. Between them hung the record-size fish which was bigger than both men.

A few days later, Sonny was surprised to see the picture on the front page of a local newspaper, the *Haïti Progrès.* Although the photo caption identified him by his current alias and a fishing hat and dark glasses partially hid his face, anyone who knew him would be able to recognize him in the picture. Sonny cursed his carelessness in allowing himself to be caught in a photo that got news media exposure. He could only hope that interest in the coverage would be local and short-lived.

In the following weeks, Sonny's concerns eased as it appeared that the newspaper story had been quickly forgotten. But he'd misread the situation. The article had attracted unwanted attention, some from outside Haiti and as far away as Colombia. The *Medellín* had pieced together his new identity and whereabouts.

The night before he is to take a charter group out for a deep-sea tuna fishing excursion, Sonny stops at a Jacmel market to pick up several cases of bottled water and a few other items needed for the outing. As he sits in the big Cadillac soaking up a bit more air-conditioning before stepping into the stifling heat of the market, he doesn't notice the two cars pulling up parallel to him across the street, the front and rear passenger windows open on both vehicles. As he checks his shopping list, the Escalade is rocked by an eruption of ferocious gunfire from the two idling autos. The surprise attack throws the quiet neighborhood into a panic and sends terrified passersby scurrying for cover. With the muzzles of their weapons flashing in the darkness and shell casings flying into the street, four gunmen pour non-stop fire into the Cadillac until their large ammunition magazines are empty.

The deadly fusillade doesn't last more than a minute and ends as abruptly as it began, with the assassins speeding off into the night in a noisy, tire-spinning spray of gravel. Their target is riddled with more than 500 rounds of automatic weapon fire. The driver's window has been shot out, and the vehicle tilts awkwardly on two flat tires. Sonny is nowhere to be seen.

The *Police Nationale d'Haiti* arrive at the scene and find Sonny's body sprawled motionless across the front seat of the shot-up vehicle, his head and shoulders on the floor under the dashboard. They are sure he will have to be taken straight to the morgue. But the window that had been blown off its tracks now lays across his face, shattered but still in one piece. Seeing no bullet–entry wounds on his body, the police conclude that the vehicle's armor plate and bulletproof glass had shielded Sonny from the gunfire. He had been knocked unconscious when the thick glass hit the side of his head. The big man is rushed to *Saint Michel de Jacmel* hospital, where it is determined that he has suffered only a concussion.

Word of the attempted assassination spreads throughout Haiti, and Juliette hears the news on the radio in Jérémie. The next morning she and Euphrasie take a bus into Jacmel. Sonny is resting but conscious when the two walk into his room. Euphrasie tears up when she sees 'Suniman,' her baby-talk nickname for Sonny, tethered to the many devices monitoring his vital signs. The bond she had formed with him during her months in New York remains as strong as ever.

After Juliette's first few words about what she had heard on the news, it begins to register with the still groggy big man that he had been the target of a hit. Realizing that the killers will still be after him to complete their botched attempt, he demands that Juliette and Euphrasie leave and return to Jérémie. When they refuse, he snatches off his monitoring gear and jumps out of bed. On shaky legs, he stumbles into the bathroom and pulls off his hospital gown. He puts on the street clothes that had been stuffed into a plastic bag and thrown under the sink by the crew that had transported him to the hospital the previous night.

With Juliette and Euphrasie in tow, he pushes his way past the surprised duty nurse and out onto the street where he hails the first tap-tap he sees. He has the driver take them to the nearest car rental, and shortly afterward, they are on the road back to Jérémie. As he struggles at the wheel, Sonny explains to Juliette why she and the baby must never see him again. The usually stoic and unemotional Juliette pushes back.

"How can you do this, Sonny? Not just to Euphrasie and me but to yourself? Except for my little sisters, Euphrasie and I have no family, and neither do you. You're all we have, and you're the only father figure Euphrasie has ever known.

"Doesn't that count for anything? Don't you ever want to have lasting ties to anybody? Or do you want to continue living on the run in your macho world of violence? And if you should happen to survive all this, are you ready to drift into old age with no one around you to care about you and look after you?

"And what about Miranda? It's supposed to be a surprise, but she's flying in and will arrive in Port-au-Prince tomorrow morning. She had planned to be in your hospital room early in the afternoon. It'll be quite a disappointment for her to find you're not there and that you don't want to see her.

Sonny tries to explain why he is attempting to cut all ties to his past life. Until those ties are completely severed, he believes, she, Euphrasie, and Miranda are in danger. But Juliette isn't having it.

"So you're going to run and hide? You're going to let the only friendship and love in your life die while you try to work out your problems all by yourself? Don't you even care how your actions are affecting others? You're not the only one with issues!" she persists.

"When Jacques got me pregnant and then turned on me after finding the baby was deformed, I was at the end of my rope. I had reached the lowest point of my life. It was only because of the baby that I didn't end it.

"Then you stepped in and became part big brother and part father. You looked after Euphrasie like she was your own. I know you did it because you felt some responsibility for Jacques's awful behavior. But I came to know you as a friend and a nurturer. Your strength and support helped restore my hope and make me want to live again."

"One of the main reasons I wanted to see you in Jacmel is to ask your advice about something very important that is going on in my life. I've gotten close to a guy in Port-au-Prince who wants to marry me. Before I make a decision, I want you to meet him and give me your advice. If everything works out, I'd like to get married in a church ceremony. And if you're willing, I'd like you to give me away.

"So how do we do all this if I'm never to see you again? What do I tell Euphrasie when she tells me how much she misses her Suniman? Exactly how do I tell her you'll no longer be in our lives?"

With no response from Sonny, Juliette stops talking and soon drifts off into a restless sleep.

Troubled at the prospect of abandoning those he cares for and walking away from his new ventures, Sonny drives the last few hours in the silence of his thoughts. When he finally drops his passengers at their apartment, he says his goodbyes with a hopeful comment about the future. But both Juliette and Euphrasie sense this is a final farewell.

Sonny knows he will have to face Miranda in the morning, but he can drive no further. He needs rest and crashes at the first motel he can find. He is too tired to even think about how he will make the break with Miranda. He only knows that he can never allow her to leave the airport and venture into Haiti with him.

Somehow, after a few hours of fitful sleep, a long, therapeutic hot shower, and several cups of strong coffee, Sonny finds his way to Louverture Airport and stands at the gate where the daily flight from France is taxiing in. When Miranda spots him, a surprised and confused smile flashes across her face as she rushes toward him.

"I'm so happy to see you standing here before me all in one piece," she says after dropping her bags and throwing her arms around his neck. "But aren't you supposed to be recovering in a hospital somewhere? I know you're the big, strong man, but in your condition, this can't be good. Please explain to me what the hell is going on?"

"Let's go get a bite to eat," Sonny responds, "then I'll tell you everything. I'm too hungry to talk right now. I can't even remember when I had my last meal."

Over American-style bacon, eggs, biscuits, and more coffee at one of the airport restaurants, Sonny tells Miranda the whole story about how, despite his best efforts to cover his tracks and start fresh, the Cartel had tracked him down and put a hit on him.

"For sure, they'll be coming after me again. While I may have a few tricks up my sleeve for them, I can't take chances on any harm coming to you. I had this same talk last night with Juliette and Euphrasie. They had come all the way to Jacmel to be with me yesterday. But I turned them away and told them they could no longer be in my life.

"Even though I came here this morning intending to say the same thing to you, I can't seem to get the words out. The truth is, I could search for the rest of my life and never again find the happiness you've brought me. But my life is way too complicated and dangerous to have you in it right now. There's no way I'll drag you through all the trouble I'm facing."

"Hold on, Sonny," Miranda interrupts. "Slow down a minute, and let's try to make some sense out of this. We both know you're a marked man here in Haiti. There's no disputing that. But that's nothing new. You started digging that hole when you and Jacques made your first drug sale. Things only got worse when you got tied up with the Cartel. You knew they were snakes when you first threw in with them, so you can't be surprised that they've now turned on you.

"But did it ever occur to you that they might have a legitimate claim about the money they say they're owed? Maybe Jacques had never bought anything from them on credit before that last buy, or at least had never told you about it if he did. But how do you know he didn't try it that one time? And how do you know that, in his arrogance, he really didn't try to stiff them?

"There was a lot he kept from you. Like the shabby way he used and misused Juliette. Who knows why he would do something like that and then keep you in the dark about it. I'm guessing there was a lot of shame. You were the one person in his life to whom he could never reveal the full extent of his evilness. For all his shortcomings, he held you in that kind of reverence."

Unable to continue eating, Miranda focuses her full attention on the big man. "Sonny, I've thought long and hard about whether I could ever find happiness with a man that has a past like yours. Sometimes I think I must be crazy even to consider it. But I'm guided by my belief in redemption. My take is that you're a good man who's now trying to live a decent life.

"But there's this complication—Karma. The revenge killing and attempted assassinations you've faced and will continue to face in Haiti are rooted in the justice of the universe. Even though you're now living a righteous life, I believe the troubles you're going through are the price you're paying for your past sins and misdeeds.

"Whatever the case, there's no peace for you in Haiti. And there never will be unless you're willing to become some non-descript fisherman hiding in poverty, surviving by catching a few undersized fish in a worn-out dugout. But that said, there are still many positives in your life, as long as you understand that you'll never be able to enjoy them in Haiti. You've got the love and admiration of the mother and daughter you rescued when life was the bleakest for both of them."

"And you've got me," she adds, smiling and reaching out with both hands to touch his cheeks. "True, you didn't have to rescue me, but you're not going to hold that against me, are you? You've shown yourself to be a positive father figure for little Euphrasie, so why not share some more of that kind of love. You and I can have some little ones of our own, pals for Euphrasie to play with when she and Juliette come to visit us. If we're lucky, we can even have a son to fill that void in your life."

Sonny stares across the table at Miranda for a long moment before he answers. Miranda was right about Karma, he thinks. But, for him, the Karma ran far deeper than payback for sins and breaking laws. It was the shame he lived with for the way he and Jacques had hurt people and devastated lives during their drug rampage.

Things might not have been so bad if they had sold their poison only to hardened addicts who were determined to get a fix no matter who supplied them. But how many innocent people, even kids, had they hooked on drugs? How many lives had they ruined? How many babies came into the world addicted to the drugs he and Jacques sold to their junkie mothers? The devastation they wrought couldn't be undone with all the good deeds in the world.

That was the Karma he was grappling with, a burden he would carry for the rest of his life. Maybe Miranda had also thought it through to this level but didn't want to bring it up and add to his pain. Whether or not she had, he didn't want to drag her into his personal suffering. It was his burden, not hers. But with her compassion and understanding, maybe he could get over it in time.

"I was a lucky man to have crossed paths with you back on the *Invictus*," Sonny finally responds. "Much luckier than I deserved. How did you once put it?" he asks, trying to recall her earlier movie-inspired quip about how they met. "'With all the ships in all the ports in all the world, how is it you happened to run into me on one of them?' I never saw the movie that motivated those lines, but I felt the same way about my good fortune. The *Invictus* was the most unlikely place in the world for me to meet *fanm rèv mwen* (the woman of my dreams).

"Although I was crazy about you by the end of our voyage, I never thought it would come to this. I even fought the idea. Because I never had blood family of my own, all I ever knew about family is what I had seen from the outside. And that hadn't been pretty. With parents often thrown together in chaos because of unexpected births and all other kinds of trouble, most of the families I've known suffer in poverty and desperation. When I once tried to create family of my own with a son not of blood, I failed and ended up more alone than ever.

"I've known of a few relationships that began in happiness and hope. But even those always seemed to crumble under life's relentless barrage of trials and tribulations. The early affection between most married people I've known always disappears or fades into little more than grudging obligation.

"Because of these kinds of experiences, I've always stood alone and depended on my willpower and strength to make it through tough times. But I wouldn't want to take the chance of losing you by continuing to be the loner who doesn't depend on anyone or anything. Just because I've seen so many relationships fail doesn't mean I have to go down that same path. In fact, being aware of the risks and knowing what I don't want may give me an edge and make me work harder to keep our good thing going.

"So baby, I'm ready to roll the dice with you and take the chance that we can find happiness together. And having children of our own would be icing on the cake."

"Maybe our only problem is figuring out where we can live," Miranda answers, once again smiling. "I would have considered coming to Haiti, but that's not in the cards. I know it's a disappointment for you," she continues, "but it's not like you're deserting your roots without ever having contributed anything. Your fish-farming experiment will benefit Haitians for generations to come. And with the start you've given them, I'm sure Angel and the crew will build a successful fishing venture. Just keep in mind that you were the energy and driving force behind all these efforts. There's nothing you've done in Haiti that can't be repeated elsewhere. It doesn't have to be in Monte Carlo or any other place in particular. But it has to be somewhere we can live in peace.

"It would have been perfect if we could live out our dreams in Haiti," she sighs. "But life is rarely perfect. And we can't let the perfect be the enemy of the good. So let's grab what good we can while we have the opportunity."

"You've said it all," Sonny answers as he reaches across the table to take Miranda's hands in his own. "I couldn't possibly add a thing to all that wisdom. Now, let's find us a room where I can get some real sleep before our next step in this crazy adventure of ours. And by the way, I'm ok with it if that next step is in Monte Carlo for either a short stay or for the rest of our lives."

"Wonderful," Miranda answers. "But no sleep until you get Juliette and Euphrasie on the phone and tell them you've recovered from your recent attack of madness."

A short while later, in an airport motel room, Sonny kicks off the clothes in which he had almost been killed two days earlier. He relaxes in bed as Miranda makes reservations for their flight to Monaco. When she passes the bed to make him a cup of tea, with one last burst of energy before falling asleep, he pulls her onto his lap.

"Godmother, you know everything," he says, attempting to lighten the moment with a parody of words from one of his own favorite movies. The two share a laugh as he takes her in his arms and pulls her close. "I'm up for whatever good we can find together. But somewhere in this great big world, there's got to be at least one lucky couple that will somehow find perfection. Who says it can't be us?"

Papa Legba

Papa Legba is a powerful loa who serves as the intermediary between all loa and humanity. He speaks all languages and stands at a spiritual crossroads, granting or denying access to spirits. He is invoked at all vodou ceremonies.

BARON SAMEDI

Baron Samedi is the judge of the dead and a guardian of the past, history and heritage. He is usually portrayed spewing obscenities and dressed in a black suit and top hat. He wears dark glasses with one lens broken out, demonstrating that he can see in light and dark worlds. His veve contains skulls and/or crosses.

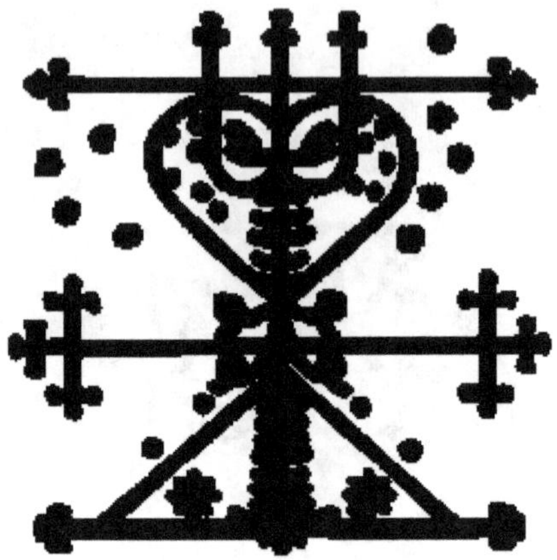

Maman Brigitte

Maman Brigitte is a death loa and the consort of Baron Samedi. She is also the loa of justice, motherhood, fertility, cemeteries, crosses, gravestones, and deceased relatives. She drinks rum infused with hot peppers and is often depicted as a black rooster. Like Samedi, she is foulmouthed.

Ayida-Weddo

Ayida-Weddo is a loa of fertility, rainbows, wind, water, and fire. She gives rain to the earth and restores its beauty. She is often depicted with a placid smile, rainbow-colored rays of light streaming from her hands, and a green snake encircling her feet. She shares a veve with the loa Danbala.

Erzulie-Freda

Erzulie is the spirit of love, jewelry, dancing, luxury and flowers. She wears three wedding rings, one for each of her husbands. Coquettish and fond of beauty and finery, she is femininity and compassion embodied. But she also has a dark side and is seen as jealous, spoiled, and even lazy. She enjoys the game of flirtation and seduces people without distinguishing between sexes.

Danbala

Danbala is one of the most important of all loa. He is referred to as the Sky Father and believed to be the creator of all life. He is depicted as a great white serpent. By shedding his serpent skin, he created all the waters on the earth. He is one of the three husbands of Erzulie Freda (Agué and Ogue are the other two).

Agwé

Agwé is the loa that rules over the sea. He is the patron loa of fishermen and sailors and one of the husbands of Erzulie.

Papa Loco

Papa Loco is the patron of healers. He is considered the first houngan (priest). He is a powerful guardian of the correct form of vodou and is often said to hold up the roof of vodou.

William G Herbert was born in Harlem to a Trinidadian Father and an African American mother. Raised in Brooklyn and South Jamaica, he attended New York City public schools. After military service as an army paratrooper, he earned degrees in engineering and began working as a computer scientist in the aerospace and automotive industries.

A lover of the oral story-telling tradition passed to him by his family, he began a side career in travel-writing. In 2017, he published his first historical fiction novel: A PLACE NEAR THE FRONT.

Herbert resides in the Detroit area. Information about him and his writing can be found at: http://williamgherbert.com. Interested readers can sign up there to receive his newsletter.